SHOCKERS
IN
LURKHAM

Solntse Burrows

ISBN: 979-8-6437-3758-2

CONTENTS

page

FRIDAY 3 OCTOBER 380

Careering around the bend of the single track; screaming, hollering even, at the languid tractor ahead to make way for them.

Yes, in a rush they were, that autumn yesterday ...

The farmer began to gesticulate as the fat skinhead in the driver's seat threatened him with a repeat performance.

He gave the tractor some more gas - but the shiny, red Turbo Convertible still came slamming into the back of its large tyres, knocking temporarily both vehicles out of kilter.

Next, the blond passenger leant out of his window, with the gun trained on the faltering farmer. 'OFF!' he bawled, with a dark look in his eyes. 'Off this funkin' road NOW!'

Farmer Robson was taking no further chances. It was clear to him these were not just a couple of boisterous, local lads out on a ride. No, the degree of derangement there informed him that this pair were concerned with darker deeds. Many shades darker.

He turned the tractor sharp right, cutting straight into the boundary hedge of Farmer Jarvis' field. There, he sat dazed in the cab for a while, furrowing his brow long after the lunatics had swept past in the direction of the village, blaring their horn.

'Can't you get us some proper speed out of this contraption?' shouted Dobermann, banging noisily his plastic gun to the rhythm of the stereo.

'Uh?' shouted across his driver.

'To show us some urgency!' And with that said, Dobermann attempted to wrest control of the gearstick.

'Oy, oy, oy, oy, oyyy! Look! A road sign!' called out Schofield the driver, more to distract him. 'What's it tellin' us?'

Dobermann caught enough sight of it in the glare of the early morning sun. 'Lurk … ham,' he said slowly. 'Lurk 'em. Hmmm.'

The single track started to widen. Hedgerow receded to grassy verge. Their vehicle passed by the first residential roads of posh houses. Along the main street they continued, past the village's two cafés to the oldest part of the High Street, where the antiquated set of traffic lights turned from amber to red.

'Want to run 'em?' asked Schofield.

But he got no immediate response.

Dobermann seemed distant: entranced by the faces of the assembling stallholders on this,

9

Lurkham's market day. His head flitted to both sides of the High Street, allowing the ambience and general bonhomie of the scene to infiltrate him.

'Ugly lot, don't you think?' mumbled Schofield, bringing the car safely to rest without incident or collision.

'Not so,' said Dobermann, in awe. 'Simply different to our folk. Can't you feel it? They're so naïve and ... uncorrupted.'

The only thing Schofield could feel was that the Securitat patrol was surely closing in on them: probably storming down all those narrow lanes which they had just traversed. This stolen Convertible certainly had the potential to outrun plenty. And such a pity it would be if their jaunt from Swarbrigge was going to be ended so prematurely.

The amber light appeared, then the green. He started to rev away.

Dobermann leered back at him triumphantly, almost distracting him. Tipping back his head, he roared: 'Ha! These people!' He trawled an arm out of the window and encompassed the crowd of villagers in his sweeping gesture. 'This community is ... *beautiful*. They'll definitely do for us.'

Schofield was by now slipping it into fourth. 'Do for what?'

'STOP THE CAR!' shouted Dobermann suddenly.

But Schofield was going too fast for that, already at the village outskirts, heading along the Eastern Track. 'Uh?' he grunted, as though mishearing.

'STOP THIS THING IMMEDIATELY!' ordered Dobermann, grabbing for the wheel. 'WE ARE HOME!'

The girl, who would later come to be known as Prima, stretched her arms expansively and regarded the view from her box room window, right along Church Lane to the village centre.

Despite the fine morning and the fact that this was the start of her half-term college break, she sighed. Her quiver of exhalation was, however, one not borne of contentment.

Her eyes drifted from following the erratic acceleration of a bright red car, as it pulled away from the traffic lights, to the foreground, where Giles the milkman was collecting the empties from Marge and Brian's doorstep.

Starting to dress, she regressed in time again, to Tuesday night. To images of Jess, of course: in particular to those looks he'd been giving the other girls at that wretched Swarbrigge dive bar. That practised look of innate sophistication and animal cunning - the very one he used to transmit to her on their earlier encounters.

What could be the cause of his reduced focus on me? she mused. Am I starting to bore him, or is his interest in me commencing a natural, hormonal decline?

She roughly brushed at her blonde hair. And why no contact over the past few days? she fumed. We always *used* to communicate following a date …

The girl stepped down for breakfast. She only half-read her mother's shopping list, propped up against her cereal plate.

Well, really! If Mother thought she was going to spend her time shopping for all those items, she had another thing coming. For this dutiful daughter still had Gran's to do - her priority - which she'd planned for this morning.

She crunched slowly on her first mouthfuls of bran, deep in thought.

There *is* a way, she told herself. A definite way to get his attention firmly back on me. The definitive, biological way. To be viewed by outsiders, perhaps, as an act of desperation: a last resort.

Not by her.

She mulled it over for a little longer, then gave a curt nod. 'Let's try it.'

She looked at the clock and realised she was losing track of her time. Soon she would have to be off, to avoid Mother's return from work.

How irritating she seemed to have been lately! Needlessly intrusive and clucking round her daughter like a fussing hen.

She wondered if Mother had been detecting any signals of this growing unease. Sincerely, she hoped not. Like Sasha before him, Jess was a secret - and had to remain so ... for a while longer. She knew Mother and Dad viewed such types as being clearly unsuitable for her, in terms of class and upbringing. And she knew that if their romance

13

were to be discovered, Dad would react and display his ready temper to herself and her illicit lover. It would not be a calm occasion if that day came.

The girl took a last look in the mirror, grabbed hold of a couple of shopping bags and made for the door.

Walking down Church Lane towards Gran's, the girl could at last feel some optimism coursing through her system.

She had the power to turn this around, to Her Way. Yes. She would jolt him back on course with a little shock therapy; to refocus his roving eyes.

She picked up her pace, beginning to hum something melodic; breaking off, now and then, to smile to any passing neighbours.

Schofield grappled for control of the wheel, trying his damnedest to prevent the Convertible from veering into the kerb on t'other side of the street.

'But I thought you wanted us to keep our speed *up*?!' he protested, exasperatedly.

'Yeah. Well, I've changed my mind!' breezed Dobermann.

Schofield decelerated, then reversed a bit with a screech to take the preceding right - whose sign was reading something like Wilbur Avenue.

'That's my boy,' said Dobermann, patting his shoulder. 'Heyyyy, look!' he cooed, pointing at the corner building, maybe to placate. 'Nice pub - The Dashin' Rodent! That is to be our local.'

His fingers were squeezing the shaft of his trusty bat of willow. 'There's likely to be some decent space here also for a knockabout smash of cricket.'

'I guess so, yus.'

They turned into a residential road of bungalows with long front gardens.

'Continue onward,' he said.

The road was lined by avenues of saplings, at the onset of their fiery flourish to abscission. Not many cars there; but parked on the other side, half on the kerb and half off it, was a white van with some lettering on the back doors.

'Go right up to it,' instructed Dobermann. 'Right up to its bumper.'

As they approached, a callow youth appeared from one of the driveways. Wearing a brown overall and carrying an empty crate, he was returning to the van - a van which they could now see was a greengrocer's. The youth seemed to be whistling a tune.

'Isn't it amazing,' smiled Dobermann to Schofield, 'how things sometimes fit into place? Sometimes one doesn't even have to try.'

'Yus,' said Schofield, none the wiser, bringing the car to a clunking halt on the van's bumper, rocking it slightly.

'C'mon!' hissed Dobermann. He flung open his door, with the fake gun handle protruding from his trouser pocket. 'Let's get our man!'

The young chap was just lifting out the next batch of vegetables from the side doors when Dobermann pounced.

'Inside! Quickly!' With gun raised, he hustled the boy into the van's dim interior. Schofield brought up the rear, slamming shut the doors.

The boy's mouth twitched as he tried registering a protest of indignation - but no words would come out.

Dobermann had the weapon pointed at the boy's chest area. 'Tell us, young man, the nature of your employment and the full details of your personal background.'

'My ... my name's John ... John Pelham. I'm workin' for Jimmy the greengrocer,' he stammered. 'I'm nearly twenty an' I live in the lower class bit of Ankovi.'

'Where in hell's that?! You mean as in Anchovy, the fish?!' spat Dobermann, raising the gun to the lad's throat. 'Tell us some more about the place!'

'Ankovi! 'Tis the 'amlet to the south of 'ere.'

'You live there with your Mummy and Daddy?'

'No! Just me mum. Dad's dead.'

'Ah, thass a shame,' chortled Schofield, scratching an ear.

Dobermann viewed their charge more searchingly in the meagre light, the only illumination coming from the van's central skylight. 'Tell me this. I've a question for you! Do you prefer football to cricket? Or cricket to football ..?'

Pelham looked wary and answered: 'I'm not really into stupid ball games, but ... if I had to choose -'

'Assume you have to choose,' said Dobermann, with rising intensity.

'T-then I would have to say ... prefer cricket to football.'

A slight nod from Dobermann, possibly of approval.

Pelham slowly shook his head and folded his arms. 'Look, I dunno what it is you want wiv me ... the reason you've got me kidnapped in here. But, pretty soon, Mister Jimmy is gonna be gettin' concerned 'bout me and the disappearance of this van. Blimey, he only sent me out on a ten minutes' errand!'

It was at this point Dobermann discarded the replica gun, thrust his hand into a back pocket and flicked out the glinting blade; drawing up the flick-knife to Pelham's unprotected throat.

'There's conditions,' he said.

'Eh?'

'Conditions you must follow, in order to maintain your existence.'

'God! I don't believe this. Don't believe this is happening.'

'Oh, but it is,' said Dobermann reassuringly. 'This is the reality. And the reality is, that my good friend and I need some means of temporary accommodation.' He looked aside to Schofield. 'How's this place grab you for starters?'

'Grabs me, jus' fine,' grinned his pal.

'See, me and he, we can't return home for a bit. Not until the flames have been properly extinguished, the casualties counted and the furore's died down.'

Pelham's frown lessened. 'You mean the fire? The fire in Swarbrigge?!'

'Yus.'

'We do. How did you learn of it?' asked Dobermann.

'The radio. This morning's broadcasts are full of it.'

Dobermann looked solemn. 'Tragic,' he tutted. 'Such a waste of property and of resources.' He tipped an inquisitive eye to their captive. 'Any news of the casualties, is there? Not much loss of life, I hope.'

'Twelve, at least.'

Dobermann and Schofield exchanged some overly horrified glances. 'That's tragic!' they said in unison, sounding definitely more cheered than chilled.

Pelham cleared his throat. 'Now, if you don't mind, I've got my job to do. Mister Jim-'

'FUNK YOUR MISTER JIMMY!' roared Dobermann, thumping Pelham in the solar plexus with his free hand.

Pelham buckled in the tight corner of the van, as Schofield kicked over the nearest crate, sending the apples and pears rolling about the floor.

'YOUR CONTRACT WITH THAT MISERABLE EMPLOYER IS NOW TERMINATED! YOU'RE NOW A CITIZEN OF SHOCKERS REPUBLIC!' And he thumped Pelham again, higher in the ribs. 'Your operational name is … Pelius. Your first requirement will be to -'

There was a sudden 'rat-a-tat-tat' on the side of the van, breaking Dobermann's flow.

' … hello? Everything alright in there?' called out the compassionate voice of a well-spoken, elderly man.

Dobermann pressed the knife tip to Pelius' throat again. 'Shhhhhh!'

Silence for a few more seconds, then the passer-by said: 'Come on, Larry. Let's go home.' The sound of his pooch's claws was heard, receding along the pavement.

'Good boy,' said Dobermann, when all was quiet.

He helped up Pelius - who was almost knocked down again by Schofield, following a couple of his friendly pats to the shoulder.

Pelius was becoming withdrawn. Even in the gloom, he was looking pallid.

Dobermann tried one of his charming smiles to coax him back. 'I am Comrade Doobie. This tub of lard is Comrade Scolex. Here is your first requirement ...'

And he began to reel off his list of additional items for procurement to the cowering, ex-greengrocer's boy.

FRIDAY 10 OCTOBER 380

The seniors did their best in navigating the anomalies of the sloping, cobbled path up to the opened doors of St. Bertrand's, and into the church's cool vestibule.

Facilitated by their walking sticks, aluminium frames and built-up shoes, they were perhaps hoping that these valiant efforts would be sufficient to find them some later reward.

After some moments to catch their breaths following this determined advance, the villagers of retirement age and beyond made it through the nave, sidling along those same pews from this time last year; whilst at the front, the Reverend Okumbwe looked to be fussing over his remaining preparations.

Those assembling were by no means exclusive to Lurkham. There, for instance, in the second row were Randolph McTurgess and his wife, Mary. Both stalwarts of the steam age they were; from when Swarbrigge had existed as a peaceful hamlet and not as today's incinerated, sprawling incarnation.

In the row behind them: Joan and Jake Liddicoat - those well-respected members of the Ankovi Conservation Society and of the regional Floral Association. Even at the delicate age of ninety-five, Jake could still offer some robust opposition to the octogenarian upstarts of Lurkham's bowls club.

Reverend Able Okumbwe clasped his hands and smiled warmly at the congregation. 'Firstly, we must pray for the recovery of all those afflicted by the devastating fire of Swarbrigge, and for the blessing of the souls of those departed.

'Secondly, let us raise our arms affirmatively in the air and rejoice at the great benevolence shown to us by our Good Lord, in sustaining us with the riches of this land. It, who exists around us as a colourless, respiratory gas, must receive our unbridled appreciation. Come on, brethren! Give to It some praise!'

He began to loudly clap his hands,

attempting to summon a degree of religious fervour from his decidedly pasty audience. He gestured to his organist to literally pull out all the stops in this regard. And so the ruddy-faced man duly obliged him, starting to improvise a jazz-infused riff.

Some of those gathered exchanged a crusty look or two, before effecting their vague hand waving and their half-hearted applause to the Good Lord around them.

It was left to the traditionalist sisters, Molly Ringworm and her equally motile sibling, Midge, to shuffle along their pew and to vote about this with their feet. A resounding NO! it was to the clergyman's *Festival Of Thanks For All The Fruits And The Vegetables*. In their eyes, standards had most certainly *not* been maintained since the retirement of the revered Father Hugh, some five months previously.

'O, that is heartwarmin'!' smiled Reverend Okumbwe, trying not to notice their egress. 'Our Good Lord will be most gratified by your response.

'And now,' he said, picking up the hymn book, 'we need to sing a song called "All Things Bright An' Beautiful".'

The ruddy-faced organist played a cheeky run to its intro, while the congregation shakily leafed through the pages.

'Hey, stop it! Who's that throwing stones?!' exclaimed Midge, at the top of the cobbled path.

'What did you say?' asked sister Molly, watching Midge scan the surroundings.

She was peering up at the church tower for some reason; then at the porch's tiled roof.

Nothing up there that Molly could see - save for the progress of the cotton wool clouds, scudding across the canvas of bright blue.

'Stones!' repeated Midge indignantly. 'I swear they are a-coming down at me!'

'Ah, stones. I'm sure that's so,' smiled Molly sceptically, escorting her by the arm. 'I think that a nice, milky coffee indoors will put things right.'

They continued down the path, as another handful of stone chippings showered the ground at Midge's last position. And, as a surplus handful rained down, there was a suggestion of someone's stifled giggle.

' … for this be Its Kingdom, for ever and always, Ahh-men.'

Reverend Okumbwe's face was beaming, upon successful recital of his remixed Lord's Prayer. 'And now be the time for us to distribute our Good Lord's gifts of benevolence. Now be the time to enjoy Its effortless handiwork.'

He turned to the table behind him and raised the first two baskets, passing them to the white-haired widows of the first pew. 'Here you are, ladies,' he said. 'Enjoy Its pleasure.'

From aubergines to tomatoes, from pears to pomegranates, the spectral selection of produce seemed gloriously enhanced by the light streaming through the stained glass windows. Fruit and vegetables: received, as always, by kind donation from the local traders and parishioners; then lovingly arranged and prepped by Reverend

Okumbwe and his tireless church helpers.

'There we go, sir,' smiled the reverend to Vice-Admiral 'Randy' Dick Radford: he with the handlebar moustache, who clutched the final basket's handle with a doggedness he had seldom exhibited since his days of naval service.

With all gifts now gratefully received, the congregation began its ungainly procession from St. Bertrand's, down the path again to the waiting cars.

However, those parishioners requiring a right turn at the end of it found that their pavement access was significantly restricted. For, jutting across it, was a dirty white van in the tenuous stages of a respray to blue - which hadn't been there earlier.

'A bloody disgrace this!' fumed Mr McTurgess, rapping his stick along its flank a few times.

'Yes, and an eyesore, to boot!' agreed his Mary with a frown.

But it mattered less today, since the McTurgess homestead had obtained its fruit basket of goodies. Instead of further concern and fretting, Randolph simply resolved to inform Thomas Turby about the presence of this offending, dodgy vehicle in the morning.

They crossed over to the other pavement without further complaint, keen to get back home.

If only they and the rest of the congregation had known the specifics of what they were transporting homeward in their baskets of plenty.

Almost too minute to be espied by naked eye - let alone by failing eye: a tiny, weeping hole within the integument of every fruit. The tell-tale entry point of injecting needle.

Another handful of roof chippings pattered down just behind the cassock of Reverend Okumbwe, who was assisting the last stragglers over the cobbles. The sound caused him to peer up at the roof and for his brow to furrow somewhat, before returning to the task in hand.

Unobserved, the bonce of a skinhead popped up from the church tower's parapet. To its left appeared the head of a larger, more globular skinhead.

Doobie and Scolex then hauled up Pelius by the ears, so that he was kneeling between them.

'See?' said Doobie, thumbing at the rump of geriatrics. 'See what a good turn you'll shortly be doing for these remarkable veterans?'

'They will be surely grateful,' smiled Scolex.

'Yes, undoubtedly. Ahh-men to them all!'

Pelius tipped his head to them, displaying doubt. 'You're both lying,' he said in the chill breeze of their loftiness. 'You've both tampered with Mister Jimmy's produce, 'aven't you?'

Doobie and Scolex exchanged some surprised glances.

'Would *we* do such a thing?' spluttered Doobie in camp outrage. ''Tis a wicked slur on our good characters.'

'You 'ave, 'aven't you?' repeated Pelius.

Doobie scrunched him painfully about the ear, beginning to twist it. 'As you well know,' he snarled, 'you are becoming a vital cog of the magnificent Shockers Republic - and soon you'll be entitled to a percentage of our profit-share scheme.'

'Oh, right! Yeah, sure!' sneered Pelius. 'So when can I expect to receive such a pay cheque - next week, or on every fourth Friday?'

'Cut the sarcasm!' This time Doobie yanked on his ear. 'You tell him, Scolex!' he said, biting his lip to prevent himself from inflicting some actual damage on their guest.

Scolex slapped down Pelius with another hefty pat to the shoulder. 'Chief speaks the truth, John. Show us some zeal, some dedication, some impressive teamwork; then all our long-term aims will be realised ... and you will receive your bonus.'

'Which long-term aims?'

Doobie spun back to him. 'Why, pain and misery for the general populace I should think. Power and control fully ceded to ourselves of Shockers Republic infamy.'

'From regional to national to ... global would be the icin' upon our yummy cake,' smiled

Scolex cheerily.

'And your help in sourcing us those additional substances keeps us bang on course,' said Doobie, in rising tone.

'Welcome to our future, Pelius!' wheezed Scolex to their first recruit - who seemed to be growing paler again.

MONDAY 20 OCTOBER 380

The fully blue van slunk its way into Lurkham the night after the last fatality's occurrence; in a parallel road to where the Turbo Convertible had been dumped some two weeks earlier.

The white street lamps were unhelpfully highlighting all, so the passenger instructed his corpulent driver to proceed further along it until they reached an overhanging tree, parking it nicely in its mottled shadow.

'I wonder what's the recent news with Lurkham,' mused Doobie brightly.

'It's quieter than quiet,' muttered Scolex, his arms resting over the wheel. 'Do only the dead folk sleep in these 'omes?'

The smaller passenger, who was squeezed up between them, creased up his forehead and began to look agitated.

Indeed Lurkham *was* silenter on that night; and lighter in terms of life force and of those collective years of accumulated wisdom and experience.

Around half of the village's elderly population was gone with the fruits of harvest. Stored at the Swarbrigge mortuary they were, while the pathologists began their unexpected surge in investigative work.

Already there seemed to be a pattern emerging. Extremely high blood levels of ethylene glycol and methylene chloride were being encountered. The Liddicoat corpse [male / age 95 / Caucasian] and the Radford one [male / age 88 / Caucasian] both exhibited traces of metaldehyde and phenoxyacetic acids in their tissue samples.

The pathologists frowned at each other over

their masks. What on earth was going on here? Oh, surely not. Not antifreeze and paint stripper; slug pellets and weedkiller.

'I'm tired,' said Doobie to the others in the cramped cab. 'I'm going for some shuteye.'

He pulled open the improvised curtain and started to climb through the recently constructed hole in the bulkhead, to the dark interior of the van. 'And I'll wager you're feeling knackered, too!' he said, grabbing Pelius by the ear. 'Come back 'ere so's I can keep an eye on you.'

Pelius began to object - but soon went quiet when Scolex lent assistance in the manhandling of him inside.

'You are to be up there, in the top bunk opposite me. And I want you sleeping soundly without a problem, right?'

Scolex poked through the curtain, looking a little concerned. 'Mind where you're steppin',' he said. 'Forgot to tell ya! I've started work on a small incendiary device for later. Some of the components are very delicate an' wouldn't appreciate being stepped on.

'Any'ow, sleep well, you two. I won't be long out of bed myself. I'll jus' stretch me legs awhile an' maybe check the tyre pressures or somefin'.'

He tumbled out of the cab, gave the front tyre a lusty kick, then leant back on the van's side and surveyed the nocturnal scene before him.

Belching at the cool night air, he watched the resultant mist rising towards the diffuse pattern of the constellations. He rubbed his bare arms for warmth, looking across at the detached bungalows with their long and rambling gardens, pondering just how many of their occupants were now extinct and would never be coming home again.

Suddenly he turned his head: certain that he could hear some furtive whispering. He tucked in his belly as best he could and ceased his slouching - focusing on the more distant houses of Walford Grove for signs of activity.

He was right!

Two figures were slipping past the fences

and the border shrubs, merging into the dappled shadows of the trees. Darkly clad and sinister, they paused at the gate of a well-maintained bungalow and whispered some more. Then they advanced down its path, both unfolding the sports bags they carried in their jackets. One tried the side gate on the left, the other tried the right - both of which were locked - so they scrambled their way over into the back garden.

Scolex swallowed excitedly as he yanked open the door to the cab. 'Chief! Chief!' he puffed, ripping at the curtain. 'Some breaking news for ya!'

The keen eyes of Pelius looked down. There was the violent thrashing of sheets from the opposite bunk, then Doobie was staring out, too.

'What?' he glared. 'What's so important at this late hour to rouse me?'

'It's good news for us. A pair of tea-leaves working not far from here - right now!'

Doobie leapt down, withdrawing the flick-knife from his back pocket.

'You come and watch this,' he said, ordering Pelius to follow. 'Observe Shockers Republic on its recruitment drive.'

The trio stepped from the cab as some house

dogs started to bark.

Doobie signalled for the pair to keep tight and low to him, as they ran towards the trespassed garden. He peeked round the side of the rhododendron and whispered with a leery grin: 'Here comes the action!'

The sound of those angry, confined dogs was growing louder now.

There followed the sound of trainers striking and scaling gate, then the thump of feet onto garden path. Racing along the path came the two figures with their hastily filled sports bags; their legs really starting to pump.

The Shockers stepped out from behind the bush and gave them both a big surprise.

Doobie barred their egress, his flick-knife in stabbing position; while Scolex lumbered across the rear, to prevent either of the burglars from squeezing through. Pelius was still crouched by the shrubs with arms folded, neither able to condone nor to participate in their actions.

'We are the police,' said Doobie airily, waving the knife at their faces. 'We have reason to believe you have just carried out a burglary at this property. Tell me which of you is the ringleader.'

The burglars looked stunned. The smaller, curly-haired one began to stammer and retreat, accidentally backing onto his friend's trainers. Then he legged it over the neighbour's low wall, pushed his way through the straggly claws of rose bush and made it to the pavement.

Scolex started to shuffle off in nominal pursuit, quickly returning to position once Doobie had hissed the command: 'Let him go!'

The dogs were still yapping when Doobie addressed the shaved head youth standing motionlessly before them.

He saw that his brow was deep; his features handsome in a rugged sort of way. And he didn't appear fazed by the Shockers' attention to him. He simply stood his ground - and Doobie could only respect this attitude coming from an outsider.

'So *you* must be the ringleader!' he said.

The burglar sneered a little but said nothing.

'You must join us in the police van for a spot of questioning.'

'Says who?'

'Says Shockers Republic, that is who.'

When he showed no sign of complying with this, Scolex began to march him, flanked by Doobie on the outside.

'In!' said Doobie, jabbing the lad's jacket arm with the blade.

Scowling, the burglar trudged inside, followed by the silent Pelius.

'Shift this vehicle a couple of roads down the block,' muttered Doobie to Scolex. 'We don't want to encourage a face-to-face meeting with Securitat just yet.'

He scratched at the growing stubble on his cheek and fished out a gnarled note from his pocket, handing it to his driver. 'That's the very last one, and then we're on our own. We need a cash injection ruddy soon. Anyhow, see what you can scrounge with it from that Dashin' Rat place, around brunch-time. Ten minutes of good, persuasive chat and great take-away cuisine is all it will take to get this boy on our side. A boy whom we shall term as … hmmm … let's try as Frenchie.'

'You think that's all it will take?' murmured his large associate.

'Yeah, I do!' he glared, loudly enough for any neighbours to hear. 'Following that, it will be through either freewill or mind-bending injection cocktails, that this pair of delightful fellows *will* be incorporated into Shockers Republic.'

Following a couple of false starts, the great blue van trundled lumpily out of view, as a bedroom light came on here and a net curtain twitched there.

It was a few minutes past the hour of three.

FRIDAY 31 OCTOBER 380

The pair of young teens were dashing towards their neighbouring homes down Wilbur Avenue, clutching their newly purchased Hallowed Eve masks.

Relieved they'd been, to discover that Mrs Perks' newsagents had been still open at this late hour of afternoon, and for them to have acquired their ghoulish masks of latex.

Naturally, they had no idea that their every move had been under observation in the darkening gloom.

'Back to my folks',' said the shorter boy, 'for a spot of tea. Then we'd better be on our way to the old crumblies of Sweet Drive, before the dearies go to bed.'

They both had to squeeze past an unnatural bottleneck of pavement, caused by the irresponsibly clumsy parking of a van; its battered front panel sharp with twisted metal.

'Yeah,' the other agreed, 'It's the old'uns who give the most generously. 'They're much more trusting and easy to get around.'

'Stupider, in a word, yes.'

They were within closing distance of their homes, when an agile silhouette reared suddenly before them: seeming to appear from the concealed driveway of Old Mr Trevor, the widower.

Both boys jumped, and the overcoated figure with scarf wrapped about his lower face advanced upon them, stating in a muffled, yet menacing way: 'I am the police. I have reason to believe you are intending to use those face masks for malicious purposes. I order you to hand them over immediately. If you refuse, they'll be forcibly confiscated and you will both be punished.'

'How come?' remonstrated the shorter one. 'For what malicious purposes?'

'You know what I mean. To terrify the older population here. We see it happening every year.'

'No!' said the taller one. 'Never to terrify.

These are for domestic use only!'

The muscular silhouette advanced a step. 'Hand over your purchases now.'

'No!' said Taller again. 'We've only just bought them!'

'You need to know that I possess knowledge of both your addresses,' hissed the silhouette. 'Be under no illusions that my force will start to make both your lives hellish.

'And there's always … this,' he said with a probable grin under his scarf. Next, he produced from the overcoat's inside pocket a carving knife, which he proceeded to swish in diagonal slashes through the air. 'With this instrument, it won't be difficult to return your deepening voices to a register that's higher!'

The figure with the glaring eyes advanced another step … and that seemed to do the trick, in terms of securing the desired effect.

The pair tossed their unopened masks before his boots, and their brief defiance was broken.

'Instead, why not try spending some quality time with your families on Hallowed Eve ..?' he cackled in the direction of the scampering teens. 'Treat every day as a precious one from now on!'

Solntse Burrows

SATURDAY 1 NOVEMBER 380

A little earlier, the girl who would be known as Prima, had watched from her box room window with Jess, the latest funeral cortege snaking its way into Church Lane.

'How awful this poisoning thing has been,' she had said.

Jess had made a disrespectful, flippant remark about there being an over-abundance of the elderly. She had signalled some mock outrage at it ... so he had enveloped her in his arms, said that he of course hadn't meant it, and they had tumbled back on her duvet, full of giggles.

A little later, the girl raised her legs higher, allowing Jess even greater access. 'Come on, Lover,' she whispered; her head arched back over the side of the bed, glimpsing his athletic form jerking above her. 'Give me all the love you've got.'

The sensation was good for her; hard and tight. The external situation was ideal, too. Alone in the house they were today, as Mum and Dad were out a-visiting, so the girl knew she had the freedom to shout things out and express herself.

'Ah, Baby,' mumbled Jess through a sheen of perspiration, as his thrusts started to intensify. 'I'll give you plenty.'

This is more like it, she thought to herself, as a deeper feeling began to spread throughout her. Good boy. You've been bad … been away. Now you're back … to find something in me that you've been missing …

'Come along!' she cried.

These words seemed to drive him on and, as his face contorted and he buckled over her, the girl sensed this time a significant connection would soon be occurring. How she relished this lingering, fluid donation: retaining it for as long as she could.

'My Jess,' she smiled at him alongside her, stroking his warm cheek. 'You are my best boy.'

SUNDAY 9 NOVEMBER 380

Reverend Okumbwe was just leading in the choir of St. Bertrand's to the second verse of "Hark, What Have We?! Some Angels Do Sing!", when the stained glass window of the chapel came shattering in.

A few of the young choristers wailed in fear as the first coloured flash shot towards them, along the carpeted nave.

The ruddy-faced organist allowed his powerful sound to swirl away, and Reverend Okumbwe's lower lip twitched a little at this most unwelcome intrusion of the Good Lord's house.

Next, a shower of primary colours was ejected, which nearly reached the altar. This was followed up by a loud bang, and then the whole process started to repeat itself.

Reverend Okumbwe dashed the last few steps and extinguished the firework, smothering it with his trusty cassock.

While the organist checked that it was well and truly out, Reverend Okumbwe hurried to the main doors, hoping to round up those alarmed choristers who were now exiting.

'Boys and girls! I assure you that the excitement is now over, so please do come back!'

There were no takers, however.

He stepped back inside, his shoulders slumping at a more downcast angle. 'You may as well all go,' he sighed to the choral remnant. 'We'll have to try for a longer session next week. But we're getting uncomfortably close to Christmastyde.'

The boys and the girls filed out, and the cool air came draughting in through the smashed stained glass.

Reverend Okumbwe fingered the warm casing of the Firebomb Repeater and said, more to himself: 'Who in all the village would do such a thing? Who would contemplate tossing this inside the home of the Good Lord?'

'Well, Reverend, there is always young Troy, I suppose,' said the organist, folding up his sheet music. 'Then again, it might be someone from beyond Lurkham. An outsider.'

'Troy?' Reverend Okumbwe creased his brow. 'Remind me of him, would you? I'm still putting names to faces here.'

'You know,' he replied, tapping his temple a couple of times. 'The slow one. The one who holds conversations with himself.'

'Ah-ha! No, I think it is not him. I do not believe Troy functions on such a malicious level.'

'So what exactly was the point of that?!' said Pelius, with eyebrows raised to the wheezing hulk beside him.

'Simply because,' explained Scolex, propping himself up on the other side of the graveyard wall, 'we were under orders to. And orders are to be obeyed, are they not?'

'But why a lit firework? What quarrel 'ave you got with the church?'

'We - not me! Quite a bit, actually. They fully deserve a broken window for makin' such a bleedin' cacophony as we just 'eard.'

'Yeah, but not Okonkwe, or whatever. "E's alright,' said Pelius shirtily. 'A good customer of Mister Jimmy's is he!'

'Is that right?' Scolex was grinning. 'Well, the last thing I 'eard about yer wonderful Mister Jimmy was that 'e'd been arrested for the murder of eighteen of this village's finest wrinklies - and denied bail, to cap it all!'

He jabbed a fat finger beyond the stone wall to some of the fresher graves, which were marked by temporary, wooden crosses. 'They were somebody's grannies an' grandpas, of course. It's a cruel and rotten thing he did,' winked Scolex with a hearty laugh.

'Now come on, young Pelius,' he said, suddenly extracting the flick-knife from the bulging sports bag at his feet, and throwing to his charge what looked like a green rubber mask with narrow eye slits.

For himself, he brought out a larger, white

50

rubber mask in the shape of a skull. 'Let's proceed wiv our next task, then back to base. Our General Secretary is timin' both these operations, most probably.'

'You mean Doobie is,' said Pelius tonelessly. "E ain't no general secretary or president. 'E's just a psycho who ain't yet met 'is match.'

At this, opted Scolex to sling the whole bag at him, whumping his shin with a metallic clang, and causing Pelius to wince in pain.

'Don't you ever speak again about the President of Shockers Republic in that tone of voice,' he warned. 'Or this matter will 'ave to be taken 'igher … and you won't want that.'

Scolex picked up his bag of tools and began marching his rebellious comrade, via the privacy of the allotments, towards the other side of the village.

'Where are we off to now?!'

'To call on someone. A bit of easy cash we need, in order to 'elp finance our campaign.'

Pelius sneered as they trampled over the carefully tended plots. '*Campaign ..!*'

'Indeed. An' if for some reason they won't cough up the necessary finances, then we'll be givin' 'em a scare wiv these - and to bring on their 'eart palpitations and erratic beats.'

'That would be a really mean thing to do.'

'Yus,' smiled the big man. 'You *really* are goin' to enjoy the new world order.'

MONDAY 8 DECEMBER 380

In an aura of festive cheer, the Winter Tree was prepared for erection in Lurkham's village square. The High Street had been closed to traffic to allow the transportation of the twenty foot spruce.

Uprooted yesterday morning from its birthplace on the higher slopes of Winter Tree Field, it arrived on the trailer of Farmer Robson's rusting tractor.

The pillars of the community were already there assembled, as they were at this time each year, to welcome in the season's opening gift.

Standing beside Mrs Perks, the veteran newsagent lady, was a solemn faced Dr Burns. Understandably, he was looking somewhat preoccupied by other things: troubled, no doubt, by the enormity of the Mister Jimmy poisonings, and more recently by the repercussions surrounding Molly Ringworm's untimely passing.

Next to him stood Reverend Okumbwe, turning to smile proudly at the choir flanked behind him. Once the decorative lights had been switched on, the choir of St. Bertrand's would be performing their medley of Christmastyde carols, which they had just about perfected.

To his right stood the diminutive figure of Mrs Turby in her trouser suit; who seemed rather eclipsed by the presence of her husband, and by his bleak stare towards the partially adorned spruce - which was now being hoisted off the tractor to its final resting place.

'Is that really the best he can do?' said Mr Turby harshly in her ear. 'Yet again, it seems Robson creams off the best of his conifers for quick sale, leaving us lot with the pleasure of dressing his smallest runt. Don't think for a minute I won't be raising this with him when we next meet - I surely will! He takes the biscuit, he does.'

'Oh, for goodness sake,' said Mrs Turby to her hulking husband. 'Do calm down! It's the same size as last year's.'

'Do not start telling me that things are the

same around here as they were last year!' he snapped. 'Clearly they are not - in fact nearly all aspects about this place are declining. And rapidly! Any fool can see this.'

'Ah, but do take a look at those lovely lights,' she implored, as the switch was flicked, and the myriad of multicoloured lanterns illuminated the faces of the villagers in the advancing half-light.

TUESDAY 9 DECEMBER 380

Eleven hours later, the tree was lying flat on the pavement; its lanterns ruptured and its ornaments shattered.

Neither poor mounting nor a freak wind of nature had been responsible: its jagged stump and deposited sawdust was proof enough of that.

A sole villager had witnessed the scene which took place in the light of the waning moon.

The supposedly retarded boy, known as Troy, had watched the display of extreme tree surgery from within the steamy confines of Lurkham's public telephone box, further down the High Street.

It was Troy who had caught sight of the fat

shape in bulging summer t-shirt trundling round the corner of the side street.

The bald man had seemed to be shunting someone along, his meaty hand upon their shoulder. In his other hand he'd carried a holdall or a sports bag.

Troy recalled how he'd begun to drool a little, misting up the glass panes with his quickening breaths of anticipation.

He studiously monitored the two shapes approaching the pretty tree.

The fat one put down his bag and produced from it a thing with a flat blade, its edge glittering in the moonlight.

The fat one pointed it near the base of the pretty tree, as though instructing the far smaller man about technique and how to do it.

Next, fatty man pulled a cord and his flat bladed thing roared into life. Its glittering teeth became a shiny blur.

Troy started to imitate its wondrous sound. 'Nhheeaaarrrrr.' Already, he wanted a go with it - or with one of his own.

It was himself who noted the spray of

sawdust and the quivering of the pretty tree and its rocking, jangling lights.

Fat man was still imparting advice to his young novice - who looked to be shuffling his feet uneasily now, and checking for any bleary, puzzled faces at the first floor windows.

Then, with a final lunge of the chainsaw to the heart of its trunk, the Winter Tree was felled, hitting the pavement with a whoosh and a tinkle of broken fairy lights.

Troy alone it was who studied the villains' rapid egress from the crime scene, up Church Lane towards St. Bertrand's.

He was in half a mind to follow them, to see whatever violent excitement it was the pair might get up to next ... and then to happily report all his observations to anyone who would listen - if they would believe him!

But then his other half spoke and urged caution and good counsel.

He must instead prepare to spend the rest of the night in this secure telephone box, and to keep to himself the images of this rare event.

Troy had learnt it wasn't wise to be too open and carefree in the village.

For a recent, troubling feeling had taken root: a feeling that people here weren't taking him seriously enough; that he was not commanding enough of that thing they called Respect.

WEDNESDAY 10 DECEMBER 380

'Firstly, I want to convey my respect to you all for agreeing to convene with me at such short notice.'

Mr Turby looked squarely at the three villagers seated round the polished oak table of his kitchen diner.

He reserved his longest, most appreciative smile for Dr Burns. 'I know this is taking away precious time from your morning surgery, Doctor, and I thank you for it.

'Now, permit me to inform you of the reasons for my summoning yourselves to this Extraordinary Meeting of the Residents' Association.'

Mr Turby took the final swig of his lukewarm coffee, then curtly indicated to his wife, who appeared to be resting *casually against the dishwasher*, to wake up and get on with the next round of drinks and chocolate biscuits.

'In my decade-long role as Chairman of the LRA, I feel duty bound to now propose that Lurkham village should enjoy for itself an enhanced level of security and protection: by our requesting a significant increase in the frequency of Securitat foot patrols - and from the commencement of other crime prevention measures.

'It is obvious to many of our residents that this village is becoming woefully crime-ridden, lawless and disordered. Such a crackdown on ill behaviour is the only solution.'

Dr Burns sat there stony faced, deep in thought as always.

Mrs Perks' brown eyes sparkled above the frame of her horn-rimmed glasses. 'Well that's an interesting suggestion, Thomas,' she said. 'I am sure we are all aware of the recent spate of crime - but how, might I ask, would you be able to sufficiently interest Securitat in diverting its resources from the major towns to the needs of Lurkham?'

'Quite effortlessly!' spluttered Mr Turby

against the kettle's rising scream. 'I do have my contacts, you know. I can pull the necessary levers if we agree upon it!' And he afforded himself a rather smug look.

'Mmm,' she said, a little taken aback by the punchiness of his response. 'I was only making polite enquiry as to whether we yet have enough of a case here to get Securitat to take notice - and to get off their shiny backsides.'

Dr Burns was wearing that slightly amused smirk as Mrs Turby passed him his black coffee.

'Oh, we most definitely do have,' nodded Mr Turby, feeling the wet nose of Larry, his needy spaniel, beneath the table. He regarded them both and started to recite: 'Four outbreaks of criminality committed here in the past two months - not including the wave of muggings. Some of this criminality being hugely serious.'

'Four?' repeated the previously silent Mr Rogers, raising the same number of fingers.

'Indeed. Let me refresh some apparently hazy memories. Firstly, those agonising deaths of *eighteen* of our beloved elders in what must be the darkest days of Lurkham's existence: October tenth to October twentieth, in the year three eighty. *Eighteen!* Think about it! That's eighteen of our most respected neighbours, wiped out in a single, monstrous act: namely the deliberate poisoning of the fruit in their harvest festival baskets. It defies comprehension that such *wickedness* could take place in such a peaceful village as this.'

'Yes, Thomas,' said Mrs Perks, whilst Dr Burns and Mr Rogers nodded.

'One thing that *I'd* really like to know,' said Mr Rogers, as he stirred the sugar in his tea, 'is why our new clergyman hasn't been interviewed yet by Securitat in regards to this. Am I the only one here who seems to think he looks very shifty beneath that mop of frizzy hair? All I can see are the whites of his tricky eyes.'

'Mr Rogers!' cried Mrs Perks, quite appalled by his line of questioning.

Mr Turby seemed to be nodding in apparent agreement with the man on his left - but ceased this when he saw Dr Burns was about to speak.

'Michael,' said the doctor with measured deliberation, 'I know I speak for the vast majority of the LRA, when I tell you I believe there is - and can be - no place here for the inclusion of such crass and racist statements as that.'

'Hear, hear,' spoke Mrs Perks.

'Through my dealings with Reverend Okumbwe, I know him to be a man of completely upright character, with not an antisocial bone in his body. I believe he has acquitted himself very well in his new surroundings,' continued the doctor. 'And I believe Lurkham should be thankful that it is his hand which is guiding our spiritual keel during this troubled time.'

'Well said,' muttered Mrs Perks.

'That being the case,' sniffed Mr Rogers haughtily, 'Jane and I know we were fully correct in withdrawing our daughter from his choir. We do not want her supping with the diabolical Okumbwe and his cocktail of antifreeze and weedkiller, that's for sure.'

'Mr Rogers!' the doctor snapped. 'Simmer down with these objectionable insinuations!'

Mr Turby cleared his throat. 'Incidentally, Doctor. Do you know, via your contacts, how the murder inquiries are proceeding? To be concluded shortly, aren't they?'

'Yes, Mr Turby,' he replied, somewhat reluctantly. 'The panel will soon be arriving at the first verdicts, I understand. Most likely they shall be called as … verdicts of Misadventure, I am reliably informed. But please keep this snippet confidential.'

Mr Turby's mouth was agape. 'Am-azing,' he said, exasperated. 'Quite unbelievable, isn't it, Ladies and Gentlemen? Misadventure - ha! To me, this shows that the whole process is screaming Incompetence, Indifference, Cover-Up.'

He tilted his head to Dr Burns again. 'And whilst we're on the subject, what's the news on poor Molly Ringworm's inquiry? When's that one "booked in" for?'

Once more, Dr Burns gave the impression he would rather not be divulging such information to those assembled.

'All I can tell you is that Miss Ringworm's heart condition was, in all probability, fatally exacerbated by the presence of the pair of burglars who were in her midst.'

'Yes, Doc, I think we've already worked out that one for ourselves,' said Mr Rogers, not looking up. 'Talk of the bleedin' obvious ...'

'And do we know yet the identities of those criminals?' glared Mr Turby. 'Of course we do not! It would appear that the crime scene of Molly's bedroom yielded *no* clues to those masterful sleuths at Securitat. None at all.'

He looked across at Dr Burns and teased for

further details. 'I understand you were the first to arrive there, following up on her emergency call. Did you *really* not get any sight - a glimpse, even - of that bastard pair?!'

Dr Burns put down his biscuit and stopped chewing.

For he *had* been growing increasingly sure about something he'd spotted that afternoon.

A blur of green face kept flitting across his memory nowadays: yes, a figure with a green face; transiting the landing past the smashed window - as he'd himself gained access through the front bay window.

Yet his protracted Securitat interview had been and gone - and he'd not been able to recall it then. So, there seemed no point in mentioning it now. Not to this little grouping, chaired by this most bumptious of little men.

'No, Thomas,' he said, resuming on his biscuit. 'Not even a glimpse.'

Mr Turby pushed back his chair and took his cup over to the sink, handing it at the last moment for his wife to deal with.

He spun back round, wiping a hand across his hot forehead. 'So there we have it, folks,' he told them. 'Now we're up to the magic number of nineteen. *Nineteen* unsolved murders of our village elders!

'The death of Molly Ringworm - frightened to death in her own home. The spate of muggings for cash. The lit firework, put through the stained glass of St. Bertrand's. And now, to cap it all, last night's destruction of the Winter Tree! Can somebody tell me what the *PHUCK* is going on around here?! Any takers?!'

His ironic smile vanished just as quickly as it had appeared. His tone deepened. 'Ladies and Gentlemen. In my role as Chairman of the LRA, I must now request each of you to cast your vote: to show it by the raising of your right hand.'

His next words were spoken with greater resonance. 'Fellow villagers, do you wish to join with me in unanimous vote: to rid Lurkham of this spiralling crime wave - by demanding *total* Securitat enforcement here, and to enjoy the crackdown on *all* outbreaks of antisocial behaviour?'

His raised hand was quickly joined by that of Mr Rogers, who murmured, 'Okumbwe out,' upon doing so.

Mr Turby looked challengingly towards Mrs

Perks, who was tracing round the wood rings of the kitchen table. 'Do we have any more takers, Angela?' he smiled fulsomely. 'You wish to vote with us for the guarantee of a return to peaceful village life? And you, Doctor? For the same? Surely you both do!'

Dr Burns shook his head. 'We can't agree on that, Tom. Sorry, but we do not envisage Lurkham existing in a state of martial law, what with the restrictive curfew and the adverse publicity it would bring. Not in today's age - we'd become the absolute laughing stock of the Westernlands. We need to be moving beyond the medieval.'

'Medieval?!' spluttered the chairman in a numb and hurt manner. 'And that is how you see it, is it ..? That's all my efforts count for!'

And it did not take much longer for Mr Turby's rage to finally break surface, thus instantly terminating the ill-fated Extraordinary Meeting of the LRA.

It was when the vitriol and the verbal abuse - directed particularly towards Mrs Perks - started to become downright offensive, did Dr Burns grip her arm and swiftly escort her from the Turby residence on the south side of Sweet Drive.

'It is a great pity that Thomas' temper is

anything but sweet,' he sighed to Mrs Perks, driving her the short distance home in his saloon.

'If further murder is what that dumb, bearded prick and Mrs Head-In-The-Sand vote for and want,' spat Mr Turby, 'then that is what they will get! Fate must take its course, so it would seem, without the intervention of Securitat.'

'Never mind, Thomas,' said Mr Rogers, laying a consoling hand upon his shoulder. 'I guess it's best to sit back now and to allow the mayhem to continue over the winter festivities; then to put it to another vote come the new year. Burnsy and Crabby should be jolted to their senses by then.'

' ... surely,' said Thomas distantly.

A few moments later, he turned to his firmest ally. 'Oh, Michael, I know what it is I meant to say to you.'

'Yes?'

'I meant to ask if you could keep an eye

open for a van of dark colouration which might be mucking about in your vicinity.'

'Oh. Some of your Securitat colleagues already on a stakeout, perhaps?'

'No, without such luck - yet,' he grimaced. 'No, I've had a couple of reports from some folk down Walford Grove. Mention of a tall, dark van that's been parked up overnight from time to time.'

'Will do,' smiled his friend.

'Thanks. And be on the lookout for up to three or four male malevolents wearing little hair - I've had reports about such, too.'

'Right-o.'

'I shall be busily monitoring again tonight with Larry. I'm convinced that even he senses the change here. He can't even cock his leg now for fear of disturbing a mugger villain round the other side of the tree!'

'Chin up, Thomas,' said Mr Rogers. 'We'll see a better day here. We have to.'

'Well … I suppose they do say that "Bad Comes Before Better",' muttered Mr Turby, looking out of the window again.

SATURDAY 27 DECEMBER 380

By a unanimous vote of two, Shockers Republic had elected to spend its evening in a dingy seating booth in the smokiest, dankest and foulest quarter of The Dashin' Rodent.

Doobie was still glaring at Scolex by the time he'd lumbered back to their table with the slopped out refills.

He watched him negotiating his way past the nearest festoons of tinsel and paper decorations and said: 'Where is my Christiemastyde present from you? Still you keep me waiting.'

Scolex looked quite blank as he dished out the pints of ale. 'Ah, … gift. Yus, I was keepin' that one as a surprise for a bit longer.'

'Nice!' grinned Doobie. 'So, it will be in the next few days then, that I can look forward to receiving my nice, new vehicle in which to conduct our administrative and strategic operations, yes?'

'Uh?' mustered his associate.

'And after all the efforts of that blue spray paint,' smirked Frenchie. 'It seems you've been working Mr Scolex here for no reason!'

'Untrue!' spoke Doobie, taking a swig of the stuff, then allowing some to trickle down his chin to the carpet. 'We need to keep ahead in this game,' he said, tipping a nod to the chatting villagers at the bar. 'Lots of eyes around here. So Comrade Scolex will be seeing to such necessary things in a timely manner if he's enough worthy.'

The big man nodded and downed a hearty gulp of ale.

Pelius cleared his throat and looked as though about to speak - then remained silent.

Observing a few more villagers through the arse of his glass, Doobie slowly half turned to him. 'Air your curiously withdrawn comment.'

Pelius cleared his throat again and puffed out his chest.

'Right. Well, as it's now the Winter Season,' he said, a little tremulously, 'is it alright, I wonder, if I spend, say, tomorrow with me mum ..? She'll be gettin' lonely, 'specially at this time of year, and wantin' to see her son back 'ome again.'

Doobie placed down his empty and gestured to Scolex by the snapping of his fingers to commence the fetching of the next round, before he issued the following, sober announcement: 'I regret to tell you that there's some rather bad news concerning your mater.'

Pelius sat up in his chair, his eyes starting to widen. 'Bad news, you tell? Why? What's 'appened, mate?'

Doobie looked mournfully down to the drink-splattered table. 'It distresses me to inform you that your dear mother … *died* … about a fortnight ago. Yes, a tough thing. Me an' Scolex heard about it as we passed down Ankovi way early one morning whilst you two were sleeping.'

'*Dead ..?*' said Pelius, as though mishearing. 'Ma?'

'Yus,' nodded Scolex. 'Ma … gone-y.'

'Afraid so,' replied Doobie, not looking up. 'It would seem from first reports that your good mother must have had some sort of an altercation with someone in her entrance hall.'

'She's dead?' mumbled Pelius. 'O, I can't believe it. Can't believe it's true ...'

'Oh, but it is! They say she got coshed round the back of the head - all for the prize of her fake gold necklace. Painless, so they said ... all quite painless.'

'Enough,' said Pelius, leaning forward and starting to sob.

Some of the villagers were watching the developing scene from the corners of their eyes.

Scolex shielded him, donating a couple of heavy pats to his shoulder blade. 'Do not cry, little fella,' he said in his throaty way. 'It was all over in a flash. And she struggled 'eroically.'

'So said the news report, comrade!' hissed his friend above Pelius' rising wails. 'We don't know that bit for sure, do we?!'

'Yus, that's right. It's what they allege *might* have 'appened.'

Doobie tapped on his forearm a couple of times and mouthed to Scolex: 'Is it not Time?'

With that, the big fellow helped up the reddened, bleary-faced one from the table and escorted him, slowly yet firmly, towards the exit doors of The Dashin' Rodent.

Frenchie, who had remained the remote bystander for the past quarter of an hour, turned his head to Doobie and said with a half-amused smirk: 'Quite a performance all that, I must say. Some classy acting in there.'

'Yeah,' responded Doobie, observing the villagers again. 'It's the ideal time for Pelius to partake of his final Mindbender - to ensure his loyalty to our burgeonin' Shockers Republic.'

'Oh, right,' smiled Frenchie. 'And how about mine?'

'Your what?'

'Loyalty. Sure you can count on it?'

Doobie started to spin his glass round on the table. 'Yep,' he said. 'Surer by the minute.'

'Oh, really?' sneered Frenchie, drawing up his chair. 'Tell me more. You sound so certain about me; so confident.'

'We are, we are,' he said, with slight irritation. 'Ever since this mornin', when your booster was administered.'

Frenchie laughed. 'Booster? You never did! No one would jab me without my knowing of it - you can be sure of that.'

Doobie looked him briefly in the eye. 'Who says we jabbed?'

'What?'

'Well, obviously, the rate of absorption's slower when via … that way, but …'

'Uh? You didn't!' Frenchie was beginning to lose some of his colour. 'You wouldn't!'

'Surer by the minute!' grinned Doobie, closer up now. 'Your Mindbender will fully bend you within the next couple of hours. All malleable you will become, as squidgy as putty in the paw.'

He moved in even closer. 'Can not you feel yourself - your old self, I mean - slipping away? As every minute passes … O, BLIMEY! THAT REMINDS ME!'

His head spun to the face of the grandfather clock, presiding there against the far wall between the pair of cloakroom doors.

'Ten minutes past eight it be. Quickly! Get

up!' he said, ushering him off his chair. 'We've got an appointment with someone.'

Frenchie started to protest but, somehow, there *was* something lethargic about his action.

Why, just ten minutes earlier, he would have thrown at least a warning punch at Doobie - and have told him to leave things well alone with Pelius. Now it felt quite easy to be led out of this boring pub session and into the exciting possibilities beyond.

It was nippy outside, but Doobie kept him running.

Down Walford Grove he urged him, on past the first of the detached bungalows with their long gardens, until they reached one with a decorative brick wall at its front.

Doobie crouched and advised Frenchie to do likewise. 'Get low, mate,' he whispered in the dark, his misty breaths rising in the street lamp's glow.

At his side was a coil of wire. Now he brought out his flick-knife.

Frenchie watched as Doobie set to work, running the wire from one wall pillar, across the driveway, to the one opposite, keeping it taut the whole time.

'For what's that?' pointed Frenchie. 'Whose appointment at this late hour?'

Doobie gestured for him to keep quiet. 'Soon to meet,' he smiled.

There had been not a sound in Walford Grove until a dog started to bark, several houses away to the right. It continued to and, shortly after, a second dog began to yap.

Over the wall peeped Doobie, turning back triumphantly to Frenchie. 'Our appointment is almost upon us!'

All of a sudden, there was the thump of feet onto someone's path.

The sound of hitching breath - and then a fast moving shadow appeared to vault over the neighbour's fence.

Onwards down this very driveway it was intending to sprint ... instead, promptly tripping over the wire snare, and landing with a clatter to the pavement.

Doobie was all over the tousle-haired character in a flash, pinning down the arms and kicking away the scuffed sports bag from its flailing fingers.

He turned its head to Frenchie, to reveal its identity. He was grinning, rather insanely. 'Remember 'im? Remember your good old partner in crime?'

Frenchie looked down at the pale, struggling youth. Something like recognition passed through: but it was the dimming memory of a past which meant little to him.

'Recall 'im?' repeated Doobie, above the din of those dogs. 'I do. He's the bastard who got away. Champion at wall jumping, who can doubtless walk on water also.'

The burglar was starting to panic; moving his head from side to side and trying to buck off Doobie from him.

'No one successfully runs from Shockers Republic and lives to see another day,' explained Doobie, quickly raising the flick-knife. 'Your gamble of tonight has been an … unsuccessful one!'

He jabbed at all that was necessary, until reaching that point when he could see the fear draining from the eyes of the tousle-haired one.

'Come on!' said Doobie, snatching up the sports bag which contained their spoils for later.

Together they scarpered, their footfalls

almost in synchrony; as Frenchie's once had been - prior to his conversion - with the unfortunate burglar's.

He never considered a final look back at the still form; as it wept its remaining, vital fluids onto the pavement of Walford Grove.

NEW YEAR'S DAY 381

And so, in the first afternoon of the shining new year, did Shockers Republic find itself temporarily the worse for wear; having safely imbibed way beyond its limits on a right old bender in The Runnin' Rat or Scamperin' Hamster - or whatever Stupid Animal Name that drinking den had been given.

A foolish thing, yes, not to be in full control of one's faculties and bladder, Doobie reminded himself, as they staggered across the deserted High Street towards St. Bertrand's. Well, to stagger to anywhere but Walford Grove for a bit. But ... this day was worth a celebration or two - oh yes, oh yes!

For the Republic was now up and running. Undeniable. Obvious. Its two converts were toeing the party line: without doubt appreciating this unique, fraternal opportunity on offer to them here. For only a limited time, gents!

Doobie turned his fuzzy head to his lurching comrades and communicated to them, in the most basic of terms, to reconvene at the vehicle - once, that is, they had cleared their heads in the churchyard's solitude and had obtained satisfying relief over the gravestones of the extinct.

'How lovely and quiet it is around here,' he smiled, zipping up behind the quadricentennial yew's trunk. 'Where on earth *are* all the villagers? One would surely expect to see a few of 'em wandering about, taking a leisurely post-lunch stroll or something. Let us hope that all last year's ... unpleasantries ... haven't soured the people's collective, good spirits? That would be an awful shame.'

Doobie was the last of the quartet to return to the shabby estate car with the darkened glass.

Once inside, he turned to his comrades. 'The first thing I want to say is: well done Scolex, my friend, for acquiring this replacement vehicle. It's tighter than our previous accommodation, for sure, but we needed a change. That van was gaining us too much of a visual presence and ill reputation.' He stretched out fully in the passenger's seat and commented: 'The legroom here is actually quite good. Tell me, my comrade, from where and from whom did you obtain this motor? You didn't overreach yourself financially, I hope?'

'No, no,' replied Scolex. 'Was gratis from a friend of a friend, down south of 'ere.'

'I see. Would that location happen to be … down Ankovi way?' he enquired, with a crafty peek back at Pelius - who appeared blissfully unaware of the name-drop. In fact, it seemed that he and Frenchie were both too soused to register much today - maybe watching all of this through glazed eyes … there being a genial smile planted on Frenchie's lips nearly all the time.

'Ankovi way, yus,' replied his colleague.

'The second thing I want to say is: this is the year of our Great Culmination here. Though Lurk 'em is in denial, we have it in our firm grasp. This year it shall yield itself to us. But … we must all be aware that the further we go in our project, the greater is the inherent danger of us getting caught. Understand that the possibility of the magnificent Shockers Republic becoming cornered and outfought by the forces of law and order is not to be realised, okay?'

'Yus,' said Scolex quickly, followed by the dreamy pair, who nodded with eyes closed.

Doobie prodded Pelius awake. 'So tell me, young man,' he smiled, handing him a pristine tube of power-glue. 'Tell me what type of weather it is you see out there.'

Pelius fingered the glue tube in bemusement, blinking at the pale sunshine which was slanting in. 'I'd say it's an alright kind of day, s'far as January goes.'

'Oh yes,' agreed Doobie, scanning the hazy blue sky. 'Nice it is *now* … but I sense a colder front advances - exclusively for Lurk 'em. Only for here!' And the raucous sound of his laughter began to impinge a little on the others' inebriated states.

MONDAY 12 JANUARY 381

His forecast had been a pretty accurate one.

The cold front from the east had swept across the Westernlands, ferrying with it bruised cloudbursts of stinging sleet and deep frosts by night.

The villagers braced themselves for the onslaught, glad to remain indoors; only stepping outside if they had to, with faces pinched.

All, that is, save for one.

The boy called Troy …

There was he, in the forbidding silence of evening; venturing across the frozen surface of Sebus lake, to the west of Lurkham. Boldly he made it to the centre, feeling like an early polar explorer, about to plant the flag.

Then he cut loose, starting to accelerate on the virgin ice, nearly falling arse over tip.

'If we keep this up,' he told himself, 'we can skate ourselves all the way to the village!'

So far, so good.

He managed to build up some more speed, keeping low-slung and pumping his legs in the fashion of a speed-skater. He enjoyed the cold airflow over the reddening blooms of his cheeks.

Pushing down further, Troy overdid it and slipped, hitting the deck like a felled ice-puck player. He lay there, winded; nearly regurgitating the scant meal of an hour ago - those morsels that Reverend Okumbwe regularly left outside the vestry door, probably intended for the foxes.

Recovered again, Troy's mind touched upon his favourite obsession of late. He felt the stiffening sensation in his groin and put his hand to it. He started to rub at the surface of his trouser, increasingly oblivious to the depth of cold around him.

Of course, the youth was unaware of the four pairs of eyes focused upon him: watching in its entirety his pleasure exploits from their elevated vantage point.

'What ... a ... prat ..,' said the one with the most intense stare. 'Yet, might not even that divot down there be of some use to us, in the wider scheme of things?'

Troy skated off - looking good for brief moments - before another miscalculation took his feet from under him and he clattered to the unyielding sheen.

SATURDAY 7 FEBRUARY 381

Even worse conditions followed during the next month.

Over Thursday and Friday, strong blizzards from the northeast buffeted the area, driving in snow to a depth of four feet. The villagers hunkered down and paused for a respite from such polar activity.

Sadly, the life of one Lurkhamite was claimed over this period: Old Mr Trevor, the widower, of Wilbur Avenue.

Hypothermia. Yet ... it hadn't been due to the usual reasons, such as the non-functioning of the heating system in his large, detached house, or due to him carelessly not wearing enough thermal layers, or through going hungry by underfeeding.

No. The hypothermia had occurred as a result of Old Mr Trevor being bound and gagged to the metal clothes-line pole, halfway along the snowy expanse of garden.

When his neighbours found him, as stiff as a board, his skin gone the colour of his frosted, grey hair, they had also discovered the ruination of his home's contents. Mirrors had been shattered, carpets soiled, keepsakes stolen.

This awful news spread through the village in the wake of the thaw.

With trembling hand, Mr Turby replaced his blue and white paperweight on the window ledge and marched over to the cabinet on the other side of the living room. He turned the key of the glass doors and opened them.

His hand made straight for the leather bound book of the top corner. He ran his index finger down its ribbed spine and felt comfort in its age. Some silver lettering ran down it in hieroglyphic style, but it was only partial now.

But Mr Turby knew well its title.

A trace of perspiration started to form on his top lip and he felt that curious, crawling sensation in his abdomen. With tingly fingertips, he extracted the book.

Yet before he could open it, came the insistent sound of telephone in the hallway.

He allowed the tome to rock back to its original position. A sigh, perhaps of both relief and of scuppered schemes, issued from him as he attended the call.

Of course, it was likely to be his Securitat contact returning his earlier, forthright messages.

One more chance, he told himself, as he prepared to receive. One more chance for them to get their act together round here, to issue the blessed curfew … or else it will be down to my assuming proper control round here.

Indeed it *was* that certain someone at the other end of the connection. Mr Turby listened calmly as the familiar, metronomic voice began to speak.

SATURDAY 14 FEBRUARY 381

She had been lingering by the lounge door for a good while. Proximal to the hallway, she was in prime position to intercept anything that Pietr, their regular postie, might deliver.

For the girl, who would shortly be known as Prima, was hoping that Pietr might well deliver her something special on this day.

She had awoken with queasiness. Whether or not this was a symptom of the general anxiety and uneasiness which seemed to be stalking her, or the first signs of a chill from the past weeks' inhospitable weather, it was hard to tell. But she was in no doubt that the sight of a coloured envelope arriving on the mat, bearing a trace of His aftershave, could only be of benefit to her body and soul.

'Morning,' said Dad, coming down the stairs already dressed - unusually early for the weekend. 'Hanging around for anything in particular?' he asked, tipping out the dregs of his tea cup. 'I don't expect you to be hanging around here whilst Thomas is visiting. We have plenty on our agenda to discuss, you understand.'

The girl mumbled some desultory response to her father and sloped off, taking a cursory glance at the window in case Pietr Postie was on his final approach. She knew also that the relevant item would have to be quickly plucked from the usual mail before Dad got a sniff of it. Otherwise, a barrage of questions would follow, demanding answers to more and more of her private life. And private should all Jess matters remain.

She sighed and went to the fridge for some milk, her ears primed for the sound of that opening letter box flap.

But her efforts of the morning went unrewarded. The postman shoved in all of Saturday's post a few minutes after four o' clock.

She quickly sifted through them.

What looked like an invoice or something

for Dad; a fat, gossipy letter from Mum's friend in the Southern Heartlands; an updated newsletter from Dad's LRA concerning Mr Trevor's awful demise; an offer of a free set of bloody cookware - but that was it! No coloured envelope infused with the hint of His aftershave.

Nothing for her here bearing the promise of romantic bonhomie, from the guy she loved so much. No cards, no flowers, no promise of anything from her Jess.

The girl flung today's post back to the mat and stormed up to her room.

This display of stroppiness caused her father to break off briefly from the rather intense conversation he was having with Mr Turby and to regard her, noting that here was the latest of her strange reactions.

Hormones it may be, perhaps, but he might need to have a word or two about her with Jane later.

Then, it was back to facing Thomas' flushed visage and to listen to his next grandiose proposal: this time it was only for the establishment of an *armed*, voluntary Citizens' Patrol to protect his embattled village ..!

The content of the postal delivery certainly caused a chasm of despair for someone within the Rogers household. But the girl, shortly to be known as Prima, should have counted her blessings on this St. Valentinian's Day. It could have been worse. Much worse.

Several of the other village girls received postal communications which generated the emotions of fears and tears; neither hope nor joy remotely. One after the other, their clumsy, error-prone handwriting expressed the same, crude aspirations in foul explicitness.

Never before had a day of such tantalising, amorous prospects been so brutally dashed to the rocks of such a lachrymal destination as this.

MONDAY 16 FEBRUARY 381

He finally came across them along the path with the loose chippings, which led towards the village surgery.

Troy had heard some raucous voices whilst pacing up and down the High Street, and had grown curious as to their origin. They weren't local voices - especially not the dominant one he'd been hearing. Too coarse and rough for these parts.

And now, here were those voices' owners: that sinister quartet all in a line, facing him. He wasn't sure whether to scarper and to put some distance between himself and their tangible malevolence - or to try and sate his curiosity. He'd witnessed the largest and the smallest of this lot felling the Winter Tree. He'd seen their determination to get the job done, admiring their team spirit; wanting to feel part of such a cohesive structure, too.

This gang of outsiders, slowly advancing on him. Troy had internally elected not to run.

The hardest one advanced closer. A kind of cracked smile widened across his face.

'Howdy!' he said. 'You must be the one they call Troy.'

He was a little taken aback by this, his mouth giving an involuntary twitch.

The main skinhead held Troy in his stare. 'We know of you. And you need not fear us.'

He dipped some fingers in his trouser pocket slit and plucked out a wrapped, coloured object. Opening his palm to Troy, he handed him the boiled sweet. 'Take it, my friend,' he said. 'Take it from Comrade Doobie and trust us.'

Troy twitched briefly and snatched at the strawberry flavoured delicacy. He was always partial to those.

'Go on!' smiled the skinhead as Troy unwrapped it, still a little warily. 'Enjoy. Definitely no harm will come to you from it.'

Troy wanted to trust and, ignoring the accrued experience of his lifetime, he popped it in his mouth and began to chew.

'Good boy!' said the skinhead, and his other mates started to break out in smiles and to regard him with some warmth.

The big, fat, chainsaw chappie put down his sports bag and came over to give Troy a gentle slap on his shoulder. 'A bit of trus' don't cost nothin',' he chuckled.

Several boiled sweets later, following a relaxing stroll with them to the allotments at the rear of the big church, Troy was feeling most at ease in their company. He couldn't remember the last time he had so enjoyed holding such intelligent and civilised conversation as this. It provided him great satisfaction to demonstrate to others that there was much, much more to Troy than the occasional, facial twitch and oft-drooling lip.

Their main man, Doobie, stepped over the damp earth and placed a caring arm about his waist. 'So, young Troy,' he smiled. 'Just how good's your life here? You get everything you want and need?'

Troy rolled the sweet wrapper into a ball between thumb and forefinger. 'Well ..,' he said, somewhat hesitantly. 'Well, yes! I've got some brilliant new friends now,' he grinned. 'I really have!'

'You have.'

'Yus, you know you can rely on us,' added Scolex.

Doobie drew in closer, looking concerned. 'Tell me this though. Do you prefer football to cricket? Or cricket to football ..?'

Troy pondered this for a bit, then announced: 'Tennis only, really. Ladies' tennis.'

Doobie appeared somewhat disappointed - but not overly. 'That's fair enough. Are you sure you have everything you need? Is not there some kind of a void in your life?'

Troy sensed the other three drawing in on him. He narrowed his eyes in the manner of cool Doobie ... and tried to consider about what on earth his enquirer was alluding to.

'You *are* missing out on something,' Doobie informed him.

'A-Am I?' he said, with slight stutter. The sheer excellence of today seemed to have blinded him from all life's cares and disappointments, albeit temporarily.

'Yes,' answered Doobie. 'Women.'

'O, you do not have girlfriends?' added Scolex.

Again, Troy sensed the others drawing in on him. 'Y-You are right, friends,' he said. 'Troy's knowledge of a good woman is what's missing. I'd like one.

'Hey! Recently, I've been trying ever so hard to impress them by writing 'em things.'

'By writing to some? Gosh!'

'Yep. Our best effort was probably this one: "*Roses are red / Violence black and blue / Your face be a mess / Your cunnie I could screw*." You like it, too?'

'Well ..!' laughed Doobie amid the Shockers' general, rising titter. 'What can I say ..? What's there to dislike about it?! Only to remark that I feel it consists of some excellent poetry!'

'A tad unsubtle though, is it not ..?' proposed Frenchie. ' … cunnie I could screw. Hmmm …'

'Yus. It mightn't pass muster with a real female,' added Scolex.

'Oh, right.' Troy was looking a little

crestfallen by now. 'Useful comments for us, yes.'

Doobie patted his shoulder a couple of times. 'But cheer up,' he said. 'I don't believe a girlfriend will be difficult for us to source for you.'

Troy shot him a sudden, hopeful look. 'You mean you really could get me one?' he smiled.

'Yes, but why to stop … at one?' said Doobie, and the others started to giggle. 'Why don't we start to prepare for you a collection of them - plus lots more besides? Are you game?'

'A collection, you say?!' Troy internally elected not to dither for a moment longer. 'I am game, friends. Definitely game. Count us in.'

Scolex and the skinny one both tenderly bashed him on the back, as Main Man guided him along the path with the loose chippings.

'Then let us waste no time,' said Doobie, with a winning smile. 'Listen up, pal, here's what needs to be done in order to obtain all your romantic success.'

Back to their cramped estate car they led him, to further brief him in the ways of wooing … and in other things besides.

SHOCKERS IN LURKHAM

SUNDAY 22 FEBRUARY 381

Thankfully, the caller was persistent.

Mrs Rogers was just placing the last items of clothing into her walk-in wardrobe as the phone started to ring. Down the stairs she bounded, two at a time; almost slipping on the last stair, but reaching it before it rang off.

'Hello,' she said breathlessly. 'Jane Rogers speaking.'

'Jane,' said the voice of Dr Burns, in his clipped, succinct tone. 'Hope you are keeping well. I've some confidential news to relate. Are you sitting comfortably?'

Mrs Rogers began to fear the worst. Her heart started to thump at the vision of her mother having just passed away in her High Street cottage. 'It's not Mum, is it?' she gasped. 'She's alright?'

'Yes, yes, Jane,' soothed the doctor. 'Nothing such as that.'

'Thank goodness!'

'In fact, my news is quite at the opposite end of the scale.'

Mrs Rogers' brow creased. 'How do you mean, Doctor? Some good news?'

He laughed a little hollowly. 'I guess it depends the way you look at it.'

'Oh, do tell, Doctor,' she begged. 'I'm not good with suspense.'

'Well, I think you should know that your daughter made a visit to the surgery on Friday and requested a pregnancy test.'

Jane Rogers gasped again. '*Pregnancy* test?' she stammered. 'But that can't be right - she's only fifteen! She would have -'

'Oh, but she has visited me,' he interrupted. 'I'm holding her sample as we speak.'

'No. Oh, no. Can't be so,' she spoke, more to herself. She was starting to nibble on the flexed joint of her forefinger. Her eyes widened. 'And what have you found? What are you ringing to say?'

Dr Burns cleared his throat and imparted the news in the calmest way possible. 'Jane, I have to tell you that, from provisional analysis, I have no doubt that your daughter is in her second month of gestation. There is no doubt about it at all.'

She had grown noticeably paler. 'Right. Thank you, Doctor. I have to go.'

On the hall carpet she crouched for the next five minutes; confronting her waves of nausea, with tears lining the rings of her eyes.

Recovering, she looked back at the telephone. She would need to share this burden; wouldn't be able to keep it to herself for long. Too damaging. Michael would have to know.

Then her eyes squeezed shut and the tears flowed. She sobbed, fearful of her husband's reaction to both his women of the household.

She was waiting at the open door for her daughter's return from a day out with friends. Or ... had that little minx actually been cavorting around with the one who'd taken her virginity and ruined her young life?

This fleeting, animalistic image caused Mrs Rogers to shield her eyes. She was starting to sob again.

'Everything alright, Jane?' called out the concerned voice of Brian, their neighbour from the corner house. He had stopped the weeding of his garden bed and was looking across at her.

'Oh, yes - I'm fine, thanks. Feeling a little heady today.'

'A-ha!' he nodded. 'That'll be the pollen from the alder and the yew trees, I expect. Drifting all the way down from St. Bertie's.'

'Perhaps,' she said, summoning a smile. She waved, then retreated further inside, closer to the bulky travel case.

'Oh ... do get a move on!' she whispered, peeking through the crack of the door, right to the top of Church Lane. 'Please make it home, you silly girl, before your father does!'

Her daughter *did* return home in time, with around forty minutes to spare.

A shiny car dropped her off in the lane's blind end. She seemed to spend a longer time than usual in leaning in, saying her (fond?) goodbyes to the driver. Then she made her sprightly way towards the garden gate. And next she caught sight of her mother inside the doorway ... and of that look she was giving her.

'Mum?' said the girl, who would be known as Prima. 'To where are you going?'

Her mother raised the weighty suitcase by her side and placed it on the threshold step. Another tear breached its rim as she said: 'It's you. It's for you to go.'

'Sorry?' said the girl, seeking clarification.

'You can't stay here,' cried Mrs Rogers, turning Brian's head from his gardening. 'Take these belongings and stay over at Gran's,' she implored her. 'You'll be safer there. He'll harm us for this.' And she held up the case for her to take.

'Harm us for what, Mum?' said the girl, looking quite alarmed.

Her mother pointed an accusing finger towards her, then downwards, it seemed; to indicate her tummy area. 'For that!' she groaned in searing tone. 'Take your baby away from here!'

Neighbour Brian had ceased his gardening and was staring across at them both.

WEDNESDAY 25 FEBRUARY 381

He had been observing her for the past three minutes and fifty-five seconds from across the High Street.

Searching through her handbag for some change, the girl with the short blonde hair in the blue coat seemed quite keen to make that payphone call, and to summon the services of a Swarbrigge taxi cab to take her home again.

To his knowledge, the girl appeared to have spent most of her day helping someone move into the furthest cottage along the High Street - the cottage where the old lady lived.

There she was, having mustered enough change to make that call.

He watched her open the door of his telephone box home, noting her slender fingers and the shape of her appealing behind as she stepped inside. Right now she was probably being assailed by his musk of urine, which he traditionally deposited in the left corner. And these thoughts pleased him; pleased him greatly.

'Go!' said his inner voice. 'Get your girl!'

So Troy crossed the street and, in his excitement, nearly tripped over the leading edge of the vast overcoat he'd been lent from Main Man Doobie. He recovered his poise and continued the nonchalant approach.

Her back was to him, and he saw she was running one of those sexy fingers through her dyed strands.

Troy stepped on to the pavement and stopped right outside the door.

His breaths were becoming tight gasps by the time she replaced the phone.

He uttered a short, sharp cough to settle himself before the show.

The girl turned, glancing at him momentarily as she pushed open the door. Upon realising that the dishevelled fellow was rooted to his spot and focused entirely on her, she deftly sidestepped, heading eastwards along the High Street.

'Excuse me, young lady,' he called out.

The girl half turned to him, raising a wary eyebrow.

That's when Troy allowed his grotty trousers to drop and his overcoat to part, gabbling huskily to her: 'Let me be your special one! Look at what I can offer!'

The girl recoiled in horrified exasperation, almost losing her footing. She started to run past the closed shops as Troy shambled after: parting his overcoat with one hand and stimulating himself with the other. He was grinning now.

She changed her plan, crossing over the street. Starting to shout and to holler, she made for the residential homes of The Chase.

It was only when the first couple of front doors were opened by their mystified owners, at the sound of the girl's pleas for help, did the car with the tinted windows draw up beside Troy.

At first he didn't appear to notice it: his dark eyes totally focused on his quarry - who was by now being comforted by the second of those residents and taken indoors. His cheeks were apple red and his breaths rasping excessively.

'In here! Now!' hissed the familiar voice from the gloom of the back seats.

Troy's fixation was now over and his intensity instantly switched off.

'Oh, hello,' he smiled, as they dragged him inside. His thumb was raised aloft as the door was closed. 'Was a good debut, yes?' came his voice. 'Have we got potential?'

SATURDAY 28 FEBRUARY 381

Some elements of good, sporting banter were developing in The Dashin' Rodent when the identically-clad figures of Doobie, Scolex and Pelius sauntered in at half-past six.

The football crowd there were in fine spirits - and song - having just made it back to this watering hole from the away leg of the annual charity match. In Swarbrigge they had witnessed the surprise, injury-time equaliser by Dougie Sparks - son of Brian, the landlord. Dougie was now back home, too, pulling the pints with his old man. First orders were certainly 'on the house' tonight.

'Jus' wait til the Briggers are brought down to earth here next week!' laughed one. 'We'll bag three against them after this, I'll wager.'

'Four!' shouted another.

'Down to earth with a bump!' chuckled another.

'Yeah. Their goalie was visibly quaking when the ball left my foot,' grinned Dougie. 'Come next weekend at the Commoners, I swear I'll reduce him to a quivering blob of jelly!'

Brian piped up: 'It just shows that eleven part-timers with enough guts and determination can beat anyone on their day - even the league's posh toffs - *and* provide our selected charity with a bonanza.'

'Way-heyyyy!' went up the cheer, as the doors were pushed open by a second wave of supporters, happily bundling inside.

Doobie tilted his head to Scolex and Pelius, who were seated opposite him. Both were looking bored and fidgety. 'This type of social behaviour is pathetic,' he said, indicating to the Lurkham fans in their replica yellow shirts. 'This herd mentality.'

Scolex and Pelius shuffled on their clammy, leather seats. 'Yus,' agreed Scolex, looking slightly nonplussed.

Doobie cleared his throat, spat out a little something extra, then mumbled that he was going up to the bar to claim his complimentary drinkie.

He stepped silently over the hideous carpet and ambled up there, pushing past the select, inner circle of supporters.

The conversation level dropped a notch as he looked Brian Sparks square in the eye for the first time, and requested a pint of his costliest ale.

Brian did the honours - but Dougie stood beside him, watching warily this mysterious, t-shirted skinhead.

He'd noticed him and his similarly attired mates in here a few times. Something was not quite right about them. Something not quite right about their demeanour - other villagers had remarked on it, too. Surely Tom Turby and his LRA were also aware of this grouping by now?

Brian raised the foaming glass and Doobie impudently snatched it off him, slopping some of the drink onto the shoulders and laps of those whom he'd just pushed past.

'Oy! Careful what you're doing!' yelled the nearest, giving him a quick elbow in the midriff.

Doobie registered no effect - but this action unfortunately seemed to cause his wrist to be tilted ... and to cause some further spillage onto the saloon's lovely carpet.

He strode off, gulping down great mouthfuls of the stuff, as the protestations mounted of both patron and proprietor.

'Hey, hey, hey!' cried Brian in the intensifying atmosphere. 'Where's my recompense for the pint you've just thrown about the place?!'

Doobie leisurely cleared his throat, belched, then said: 'You an' your dippy son just announced the message of free drinks. Have you pair of inbreds got a memory problem or something?'

That was enough for Dougie's ears - more than enough! He had raised the bar hatch and was marching out to confront his dad's abuser.

At this juncture, Scolex hauled up the smaller of his quiescent trainees by the t-shirt and led him straight into the arena of hostilities, himself flanking Doobie - who had by now raised his glass in a most threatening manner.

'You lot get the hell out of here!' shouted Dougie, stopping short of any physical intervention for the moment. 'You are all lawless outsiders and you are banned from here forthwith!'

Doobie saw that Daddy Sparks was busily dialling the phone at the back counter; most likely to Securitat. Some of the more nervy patrons were getting to their feet on the far side.

The remaining time for the mSR in this location was strictly limited, he considered.

'You are all a sad, sad bunch of frass,' he said gruffly, waving the empty glass to his audience. 'You lot adhere to the sport of association football - that game with the overblown leather bladder and the poncey shirts, shorts and socks. Well ... someone needs to tell y'all that you're chasing the wrong goals in life!'

The braver patrons made to apprehend this antisocial ringleader - but Pelius was ready with the bar stool: swishing it in front of them, back and forth, as he peppered the air with foul obscenities.

'Cricket is the game of true men!' continued Doobie, clamping his muscular arms upon the charity box which was affixed to the bar's corner pillar ... and trying to wrench it off. Yet it was too well attached for that.

Instead, he chose to spend the remaining seconds exchanging punches with the closest available yellow-shirted poofters - who admittedly seemed up for the scuffle.

Football plus a trace of alcohol seemed to

alter the blood chemicals - make people so aggressive, he reckoned, thumping one upon their greasy head.

Scolex, meanwhile, had a grander scheme in progress. The robust combatants were buffeted by the onrushing Shocker, as he charged towards the venerable timepiece at the far wall.

Landlord Brian extended a flailing arm but it was going to make little difference: that driven look in Scolex's face told all about the certainty of outcome.

In the last instant, he shimmied sideways and delivered a crunching blow to the face of the grandfather clock.

Its casing shuddered at this extraordinary disruption and its rasping rhythm stuttered.

Rebounding from the wall, it began to topple forwards … and it was given more encouragement to do so by a high tackle from Scolex, which dispatched it to the ground. A clatter of disarranged, internal mechanisms followed, then all was silenced.

Frenchie busied himself in maintaining the exit route and keeping it clear: upturning the closest table in front of the enraged patrons, and hurling at them all manner of glasses, utensils, cruet and beermats.

He was the last of the Shockers to exit the doors of The Dashin' Rodent.

Chased for a while they were down Wilbur Avenue, by the assorted angry publicans and football fans.

Then Doobie chose to take the wetter option: splashing into the Sebus brook; heading for the lake. Once there, he planned that they would conceal themselves and bide their time: waiting for any Securitat presence to diminish.

Checking over his shoulder, he wasn't surprised to find that their pursuers were easing off the pace already. There seemed a general disinclination to chase through these shin-deep waters. A growing homesickness, perhaps, for the cosy interior of The Runnin' Rat - and its novel, horizontal clock feature.

'Football's definitely for wimps!' he shouted to his comrades, above the splashing, sploshing sounds of their boots. "Tis one nil already to Shockers Republic in this 'ere village!'

SATURDAY 7 MARCH 381

It was about an hour to sunrise when the first, subtle movements appeared in the border vegetation of Commoners Common. A steady rustle gave way to a brazen, stick-snapping crescendo, once it had been established that the open expanse beyond them was free of a Securitat presence. All was serene and secured here.

Following that 'mayday' call from The Dashin' Rodent's landlord, it seemed that a cohort of Securitat officers had indeed taken a genuine interest in discovering the whereabouts of this quartet of skinhead troublemakers.

They *had* to be hiding somewhere in this sleepy village, they reasoned. Lurking in Lurkham. Waiting for that next opportunity to cause yet more trouble.

Upon liaising with the overly pushy representative of the residents' association, the Securitat Field Officer had deemed it appropriate to permit the dispatch of a second detachment to the village, in order to root out this growing menace.

So, during this past week, Shockers Republic had lain low.

Doobie had decided that the time was right to relocate themselves to the sinuous streets and anonymous avenues of Swarbrigge. There, they'd prowled around in the estate car until they had found what they were in need of.

Now they were back: carrying in their clenched hands some of the spoils of their sojourn.

Doobie led out his team onto the pitch and reminded them, in harsh whispers, to spread themselves evenly along its length, so that the goalmouths and the midfield areas could be intensively worked.

He raised the pickaxe above his head, a little theatrically, and said: 'I dedicate these blows to the pursuit of a football-free life for the confused souls of this place. May they all soon comprehend that Shockers Republic is the only viable team around -

and cricket the only sport.'

"Ear, 'ear!' cheered Scolex, as his comrade's implement chewed into the damp turf of Commoners Common. 'They won't be playin' their return leg 'ere for weeks, once we've finished wiv our little dig!' he chortled, making for his designated sector of the pitch.

SUNDAY 8 MARCH 381

The evening light was closing in by the time the four of them called on Troy.

Doobie was impressed to see their new ally had listened to their sound advice, and was nowhere to be found around his old stomping ground of the stinky telephone box. This was a very necessary piece of advice to be followed, after Troy's first attempted exposure of himself and this currently heightened Securitat presence around here. It would not have been the cleverest of ideas to be out in the open.

Ah, there he was, waiting in the agreed location. Good. His gaunt, unshaven face poked out from behind the yew tree in St. Bertrand's, the one nearest to the path.

He was wearing a slightly fearful look as Doobie approached, though he relaxed once his friend had clasped his shoulder and given him the Shockers' Salute - the one that Troy had been trying to master earlier on.

'Hello, Mister Doobie,' he smiled. 'What are we going to do today?'

Doobie beckoned him to the gates, where a car was just rolling into view. 'We've got some entertainment lined up for you,' he said.

The clouds lifted from Troy's countenance. 'For us? How marvellous. How kind of you!'

Doobie winked as he ushered him to the passenger's door of their jalopy. 'No problem at all, Troy,' he said. 'Sit back and relax. Prepare for your visual feast. That's all there is to it.'

In Troy stepped. Scolex was behind the wheel, like last time. Pelius and Frenchie greeted him warmly from the back - with Pelius handing him a freshly opened can of lager to be getting on with.

'I'm glad to be with you all again,' he laughed.

Scolex drove them, in an unusually calm and responsible manner, around the roads of Lurkham.

Passing by a couple of parked up Securitat vehicles, they observed the residences of Wilbur Avenue and of the lengthy Sweet Drive to the south. To their right were the more compact, semi-detached houses of smaller frontage.

'Now looking over to the left,' said Doobie, like some experienced tour guide, 'we can observe the contrast. Notice the obscene areas of front garden and the palatial splendour of each dwelling. This, my friends, is a prime location for the average housebreaker.'

Scolex tittered, and Frenchie remarked: 'But we are not average housebreakers. We are -'

Just then, the door opened of the next house they were trundling past.

Silhouetted against the light from the kitchen was a short, broad man with a small, flappy-eared dog beside him that was starting to yap. The man inclined his head, and the dog appeared to be equally intrigued by the car's languid cruise; its barks taking on more urgency.

Then the man launched himself from the doorstep ... and started to bound up his gravel drive with pooch tearing alongside him!

Doobie broke the stare, spun around to

Scolex and calmly instructed him to, 'Give us some throttle. Take us down the single track towards Ankovi. Once there, cut the lights and land us in the second passing place.'

Pelius' ears seemed to prick up at the mention of his previous stomping ground. 'Oh, Ma,' he sighed. 'If only I could see you now.'

Doobie heard him, coldly responding: 'I don't think you would like to, comrade. Her flesh would be crawling now. Spoiling. No, I don't think you would relish the sight, young man.'

Pelius winced, then had no option but to settle again into his subdued state.

Back to the rear window peered Doobie.

Although the man and his doggy were, by now, distant figurines, he could still make out their eager strides: could still sense the man's determination to discern the malign intentions of this car's occupants.

'Do not utilise the brakes here!' he ordered as they came to the sharp turning for Ankovi.

Scolex gripped the wheel more tightly. 'Then … brace yourselfs!' he grunted, spinning it hard left down the narrow, unlit trackway.

The tyres squealed a bit - but that was all. Then, it was steadily along to the aforementioned, second passing place, before Scolex cut the engine.

It was very dark around them. The moonlight was mostly obscured by low cloud, and the tall, spindly branches of the surrounding copse further shrouded them in gloom.

'Where to now?' piped up Frenchie. 'This doesn't look like much of that "visual feast" you've been promising our friend here.'

'That comes later!' snapped Doobie. 'Right now, we wait.'

'For what - the floodlights to appear?'

'No, comrade! We wait to discover if one man and his canine pet will be foolish enough to continue their pursuance of us - and to lose both their lives as a result.' Doobie was pointing his flick-knife at Frenchie, indicating his favoured throat slash.

Their guest in the front seat started to grow animated. He spoke a few, indecipherable words to himself, adjusted his crotch, then announced to all those assembled: 'That be Mister Turby and his doggy, name of Larry, what you're talking of.'

'Who? *Turby*, you say?' growled Doobie,

grabbing Troy's shoulder. 'You know more details about him? Tell me why he's so obsessed with us!'

Troy stammered a little at all the sudden attention. 'H-he's the village watchman round here,' he said, spittling the dashboard. 'He finds out things - all kinds of things - and tells the information to the Doctor, Mr Rogers and the newsagent lady.'

'Does he now?' whispered Doobie, running the knife up and down his forearm. 'Hmmm.'

'Yes, yes. I seen him from inside the phone box the last time I was there. Speakin' to these Securitat men in their unmarked car, he was.'

'Securitat, you say? How are you so sure?'

'Cos of the way they just sat in their cars. Their lack of mobility. They just stare, straight ahead. It looked like he was beggin' with them in there! They were just listening ... tilting their heads occasionally like machines. I hardly saw a word come out. Weird phuckers be they.'

In the distance behind them a dog barked.

'Everyone! Shut the funk up!' hissed Doobie, turning to the rear window and waiting for any new signs of movement.

His eyes were now accustomed to the dark.

The length of the single track to its narrowed neck could be made out. Approaching figures would be quickly discerned and the suitable response prepared.

There they waited for a sighting. Ten minutes passed. Quite long enough for the Neighbourhood Snoop Man and Detective Dog to have passed by their way.

Or perhaps they *were* close by, observing them in this vehicle right now from a convenient vantage point ..?

Doobie began to scan the verge on the far side. No vegetation appeared to rustle or to twitch in the still, night air.

The watchful silence was finally punctuated by the sound of corduroy trouser being rubbed, and by Troy's distressed cry of: 'Our bladder's bursting! I need to relieve it!'

Doobie elected to pronounce that the alert was over.

'Snoop has seen sense tonight,' he concluded. 'He and his doggy can still enjoy each other's company for a while longer.' He indicated with a sweeping motion for them to exit the vehicle. 'Out!'

When all were relieved and with legs stretched, Doobie led them through the tussocky grass of the other verge. In orderly file they pushed past the young saplings and trampled underfoot a rusted boundary fence.

The five of them were now standing on the back lawn of the corner property of Sweet Drive. Doobie turned briefly and smirked at Scolex and the vacant Pelius.

He was looking at the side of the next house. The house in which the pair had been inside about four months previously. In materialistic terms, apart from the useful cash stash they'd found under the mattress, their visit had proven to be something of a disappointment: only some nick-nacks and some uninspiring jewellery gleaned from the old biddy.

Scolex placed his sports bag on the patio and started to get busy with his implements, working on the sliding glass doors.

Pelius pointed up at the light coming from its landing window. 'Excuse me, but isn't there someone in?' he mouthed.

Frenchie shook his head. 'Not so. It's one of those cunning timer devices.'

'Been like this for the past week has it not,

Scolex?' checked Doobie. 'Six pm till eight twenty pm, is that not right?'

His friend grunted in concentration, levered his implement inside the frame and waited for the click. When it came, he uttered a grunt of satisfaction and slid open the door.

'Shoes!' said Doobie to all, indicating their immediate removal. 'Although these stinking, kulak residents are undoubtedly whooping it up somewhere on the other side of the world, it is not advisable to display our footprints. We don't want to make things too easy for the forces of law and order. Not just yet.'

The internal layout was similar to that of the late Molly Ringworm's abode next door. Yet there were more home comforts, everyday luxuries and possessions here. A family clearly lived in this one. Two nice bathrooms plus four toilets - one for each Shocker, if one included the gold tapped bidets.

Doobie noticed that Frenchie, Scolex and even Troy were getting quite light-fingered with some of the ornaments. 'Yesss, there's a lot of temptation here, comrades,' he remarked, upon checking for himself just how well stocked was the fridge, and how full was the wine rack.

Fine. There was more than enough food,

drink, tea and coffee to see them through here. What a nice home!

'And, a quick reminder for you all: we haven't forgotten the reason we've come here, no ..?' he enquired.

'We haven't,' smiled Frenchie.

'We are 'ere for Troy,' remembered Scolex, regarding benignly their overcoated friend, who had sunk into one of the leather armchairs with his eyes closed.

'That is right. For Troy's visual feast. Let us prepare the resident hardware for our software.'

Scolex cocked him a wink and lumbered over to his bag.

'Pelius, to the kitchen, please, and prepare for each comrade sufficient coffee and ginger cake to last for the next two hours.'

Doobie turned to the others. 'We'll work it as a rota. Troy's visual feast *must* run continuously. That way, there will be a greater impact upon our great friend.'

Troy seemed to sense their burning eyes upon him, waking with a start.

Briefly, he looked fearful and unsure of such sumptuous surroundings. Then his eyes focused on the flickering television screen which Scolex was retuning. 'Aha,' he smiled. 'It is time for our feast?'

Scolex forced the first disc into the player. 'O, yus,' he smiled.

The white noise subsided to an image of people in a room. The quality was not that good to start with and Troy had to squint.

He hadn't watched television for a couple of years now, not since his enforced spell in Quietwaters Secure Home, so he was curious to see people moving about within the confines of the screen.

He laughed, a little embarrassed. Doobie and Scolex joined in, too.

Why, these miniature people in the television weren't wearing any clothes!

Three muscular men on a double bed - and their ... tubes ... were on show. Openly so! They were busily elongating them.

Troy's concentration was broken by Pelius, who handed him his coffee and his broken slice of ginger cake. ' ... ta,' he said, absently.

Then the image broke up ... and when it returned, it seemed that another person had joined the restless men. They started to touch, to grope this other person. Now they were surrounding it and laying their tubes on it.

'Advance it to the next bit,' said Doobie, getting up from the sofa and fully drawing the front curtains. 'You'll find this gets way more interesting.'

Scolex dutifully obliged, before returning to the other leather armchair.

A new image was confronting Troy.

A different person was with the men: of different shape, age and inclination. Its clothes were being torn off in a rough fashion. This different person was doing all it was told to, even when unwilling.

'Pause the screening,' said Doobie, turning to Troy in the electric glow.

His eyes burned into Troy's. 'You've done yourself proud so far, my friend,' he said. 'That girl of a fortnight ago. The blonde in your telephone box.'

A smile flickered in the corner of Troy's mouth. His brown eyes began to possess a dreamy look about them.

'You showed her what you've got and what you could provide. And she was afraid to take the risk of enjoying your asset.'

'Yeah,' agreed Troy. 'Afraid.'

'She's simply a cautious one. Plenty of braver ones existing out there, comrade.'

'Yes. To enjoy my asset.'

'That's quite right.'

Doobie regarded his tubby technician. 'Recommence the visuals for our most worthy friend.'

The strange film continued - but down a stranger path.

People and other life forms were being forcibly confined and infilled. The trio of men seemed to be losing their humanity: communicating their demands in bestial grunts, all muscular jerking, swathed in their glaze of perspiration.

Troy sensed Doobie's eyes upon him, as though he was studying his responses to these shocking stimuli. Certainly he was reacting - in several ways.

'You see, girls aren't everything,' said Main

KHAM

Man from the sofa. 'Other life treasures are there for the plunder if you want.'

Troy attempted some of the ginger cake but couldn't seem to taste it. His appetite seemed to have quickly diminished.

The room went totally quiet as the onscreen obscenities moved towards their culmination.

'It never ceases to amaze,' remarked Doobie with folded arms, 'how they manage to stuff quite so much into such confined spaces. Incredible achievements!'

Troy jumped as Pelius tapped him on the shoulder, to remind him about the coffee. It was going cold now.

The footage concluded, in the most abominable and fluidic way.

The next round of coffee and ginger cake was provided as the first disc was extracted from the player, and the second one forced in.

Similar themes, it must be said. Different, elongated tubes exploring all possibilities available and open to them.

The new day was waiting to greet them behind the drawn lounge curtains. Once all was

over, the warm television was snapped off by
Scolex.

It was Doobie who began it, before the
rising chant was taken up by the others.

*'Show them the delights / of your elongating
tube.*

For Troy's tube / is neither rude / nor crude.'

Something was different about him by the
time they started the fire in the downstairs cupboard
- to burn to the ground the corner house of Sweet
Drive.

Not just the grey bags under his eyes from
the lack of sleep, no. A remote, wide-eyed look, as
though his mind was in pursuance of a tangible
future: somewhere else, where Troy could obtain
greater spiritual and physical satisfaction than he
had currently known. He could effect the change all
by himself. And it was his right to.

He and the Shockers exited the doomed

house by way of their ingression.

The flame licked expansively at the walls, its crackling red tongue not far in their wake.

MONDAY 9 MARCH 381

The boy was looking up at him with real fear on his face, as they passed into the shadows beyond the church gates. Troy pulled the boy by his reddening ear, almost knocking off his school cap, urging him along faster.

'Oh, where are you taking us?' pleaded the sister with creased brow, racing to keep up. 'Let us go home now.'

Troy paid no attention to her, save to glance at her rosy cheeks and the swellings of her precocious cleavage, as he briefly checked for any sign of the Reverend Okumbwe or his organist loitering around the church doors.

'Keep quiet!' he urged, raising the flick-knife. 'Voice down - or Little Bro goes. I mean it!

You're both coming with me to the allotments.
There I have something interesting to show you.'

Then it was up the church path, which was
neatly concealed by the yews.

TUESDAY 10 MARCH 381

The news of Andrew and Ciara Coughlan's disappearance spread rapidly.

Their distraught parents had contacted Securitat a couple of hours after the elapsing of their children's usual home arrival time. Within twenty minutes a crack squad of officers from the Missing Persons Unit were knocking on village doors, and being shown in by Mr Coughlan to the family cottage at the High Street's eastern end.

Concurrent investigations were taking place in Swarbrigge, at the school gates from where the siblings had boarded the bus. The driver was traced and Securitat were now trying to locate those passengers who had been on that fateful journey.

Even the regional, outside broadcast unit of

Westernlands Telecommunications had made an hour long visit to Lurkham this morning. Not since the consecration of Reverend O'Toole to Bishopric Supreme of All Westernlands some twenty years before, had the floodlights and the furry microphone booms of the film crew deigned to pay a visit to this somnolent area.

The young, rising star of Westernlands Today news programme had spent all of thirty, excruciating seconds grilling Mr Turby in his capacity as Chairman of the LRA.

But the aggressive tone assumed by the greasy little whippersnapper, standing deliberately taller on his wooden crate, had upset and angered his interviewee.

'And now *two* disappearances occur in Lurkham! Mr Turby, what is the general public supposed to infer from the latest crime statistics, which place this oh-so-quaint village of yours at the top of Westernlands' most violent habitations?'

'Well, the general public should realise that such a distressing abduction could have taken place absolutely anywhere. I find it most unfair that you choose to -'

'So what is your response to the growing accusations that, as Chair of Lurkham Residents'

Association, you are playing too quiescent a role in the process? Don't you feel the need to sharpen up your act?'

It was at this point, with eyebrows bristling and with cheeks the shade of medium-rare steak, did Mr Turby rip off the lapel microphone, openly curse the slimy upstart afore him and storm off back home.

Drowning in the depths of his ire and frustration, he almost neglected to give Mrs Turby the cursory peck on her cheek.

Larry pushed his wet snout into the crotch of his khaki trousers, with a look of expectancy in his eyes - but his owner declined.

'Not today,' he said, preparing his cup of strong coffee. 'There's a good fellow. We'll do our walk tomorrow morning, I promise.'

Larry whined for some time longer, then sloped off to his bed.

'Any updates for me?' enquired Mr Turby, skimming through the paper which he hadn't had time for.

'No,' his wife replied. 'Nothing more's come to light than we already know.'

Mr Turby sighed. 'Those poor children. That poor family. The situation makes me feel so powerless to act.'

'I know. I'm just praying that the two dears are safe and unharmed.'

Mr Turby took a passing look out of the back garden window, collected his coffee and paper, and turned to go upstairs. 'Won't be long, Dear,' he said with a quirky, lopsided smile.

Once on the landing, he made more purposefully for the bathroom.

Opening the cabinet, he brought out the nail scissors plus the small specimen bottle which had been concealed behind his shaving effects.

The bottle's screw cap was rather difficult to undo. This was not altogether surprising: six and a half years ago had it last been unscrewed.

Mr Turby's heart fluttered slightly as the flashback came and went.

'Catullevenali mirabilis erebus,' he murmured to his careworn reflection in the mirror. That quirky smile reappeared. So ... the first line from the relevant chapter he could still recite ...

Next, he felt amongst the remaining tufts of

hair on the side of his head. Selecting a fingerful, he snipped them near the base, before dropping them into the specimen bottle. Re-screwing the top, he concealed it behind the shaving effects.

'Soon,' he told his reflection.

Yet, he realised … more ... would be needed this time. More things from life.

Six and a half years before - beset by the problem of the neighbours' pesky kids making regular incursions into the garden - a lock of his fuller hair had been the sole ingredient to add.

Those kids, however, had been small fry in comparison with today's perpetrators of atrocity.

Although he had not yet come across them personally, nor been able to identify them, Mr Turby readily sensed their unit's high degree of cohesion and organisation.

A quartet, in all probability - or maybe more of the foe.

And when they hadn't been spotted cruising through the village in assorted, *stolen* cars and vans with darkened glass, they had been spotted brazenly occupying the snugs of The Dashin' Rodent and exhibiting obnoxious behaviour. Brian had shown him the havoc they'd wreaked there last Saturday week.

On Sunday, the very day before the Coughlan children had disappeared, he'd caught sight of their car again with the blacked out windows.

He had just about made out their pale heads inside, and had noted the predatory way in which the vehicle was passing by. That was not the manner in which a normal group of young people might drive - not in his experience, at least. No, he could feel the intensity of the occupants' information gathering process. And he'd almost caught up with them! He might well have succeeded in discovering more about their intended destination and dark activities, had Larry not become distracted by that wandering black and white moggie, losing their direction.

Mr Turby also discovered that the quartet / quintet's tangible malevolence was making it much, much easier to attribute each and every recent catastrophe from the time of the Harvest Festival murders to them ...

The appalling death of Mr Trevor last month. The vandalism of the pitch at the Commoners over the weekend. The ruinous fire at the Maybank family's property on Sunday, which had rendered it uninhabitable.

And was it under that gang's pernicious influence, he mused, that the normally affable young simpleton, Troy, had exhibited such disturbing behaviour: in performing that awful, full-frontal exposure to that poor Woolf girl of Swarbrigge.

Now he was gone, too, just like the Coughlan siblings - seemingly vanished into thin air, the lot of them! Securitat and the posse of top villagers had been unable to locate any of these missing souls.

Could their disappearance be somehow linked? he wondered. Oh, you bet it could! he told himself. His remaining question remained only this: what despicable things had those marauding outsiders done to them? It didn't bear thinking about.

'You boys will pay!' he said, almost loudly enough for Jill to hear him from downstairs.

He was looking out over the back garden, to the field beyond. Bathed in warm sunshine, its unkempt grass was being rippled by a gentle breeze from the west.

'Spring is nearly upon us. And I shall be the one to consign you lot back to your wintry abyss.'

And before leaving the bathroom, Mr Turby cast back his mind to that previous time.

Six and a half years ago ...

Whatever it was that had unearthed itself from the vegetable patch where his beans were growing, and had pushed aside the intervening conifers, snapping them at their bases ...

Whatever it was that had broken all the toys of the neighbours' pesky kids, and had cleanly bisected their pet rabbits, shelled the tortoise, and malformed their bicycles to works of twisted, unrideable art ...

Whatever it had been ... the thing unseen had done the trick.

Two of the problem families had moved out within eight weeks. The third had simply scarpered shortly after, never to return. And the final lot of bad apples - the Claybyns - didn't even get that far.

It seemed they'd been trying to act up tough: trying to tough it out, yes, and to wait until their easy times reappeared.

But, alas, they were waiting in vain!

For exactly eleven weeks on from Mr Turby's plea of desperation to an unknown, watchful audience, the ground had swallowed up the Claybyns in their entirety: house, garden, inhabitants.

Devoured by the earth.

In awed silence, Mr Turby had regarded their smouldering hellhole from his landing window, hoping fervently that the Claybyns' demise would be the end of it: deeply, sincerely wishing that all things unseen could silently and swiftly return whence they had come; that the land could be at peace again.

And, thankfully, it became so.

It also became apparent that no further incursions ever took place in the Turby's garden by *any* pesky kids of his neighbours, since ... there were none.

SATURDAY 21 MARCH 381

'This one looks to be for you, ducky,' said Gran, placing the envelope on the chair arm. 'Do you feel like any breakfast yet?' she asked, briefly taking the young wrist in her arthritic fingers to check the pulse.

The girl, soon to be known as Prima, shook her head. She rubbed at the blotchy patches of skin around her neck and replied: 'Maybe I'll just have some toast for lunch.'

She picked up the envelope, adjusted her position at the table and opened it. The script she recognised right away, of course: it being of Anita's gracefully curvaceous style.

Her eyes widened a little as she lifted out the navy blue card. Tastefully embellished with gothic typeface, it read:

Dr. and Mrs William Woolf request the pleasure of your company at the forthcoming marriage of their daughter, Anita Jane, to Mr. Wesley Bright at the Church of St. Bertrand's, Lurkham on Saturday, 25th April 381 at 12:30 O' Clock, and afterwards at The Priory House, Swarbrigge. RSVP.

At the lower right appeared Anita's script. 'Please do come along,' it read. 'I've arranged it so you'll only have to cross the street to be there! Who knows, you might meet the man of your dreams - there's quite a few eligible bachelors on the 'invites' list. Hope you've settled in okay. See you soon! Luv, Anita x.'

She lowered it slowly to her lap. 'Wow,' she said in a still-coming-to-terms-with-it voice. 'She and Wesley have suddenly decided to commit ...'

'Who's that?' asked Gran. 'Would I know her?'

'Yes, it's Anita. You know - the one who helped me move my stuff in here. The one who got ... flashed at on the way home.'

'Oh, her, the poor dear,' said Gran with a frown, as she levered in the fresh millet spray for

Daffodil.

Her opaline green budgie inclined his head and proceeded to eagerly husk the seeds.

'I'm feeling there's too much nastiness around here for a village this size,' sniffed Gran as she made her way to the larder. 'It never was so. Now, are you sure about that breakfast, ducky?'

Her granddaughter looked up. 'Sorry?' She had been reading the invitation again. 'No, I'll see to it, thanks.'

She still wasn't hungry though. Slipping her hand inside the dressing gown, she cupped her tummy and tried feeling for the being that was the cause of this morning's sickness. She knew from Dr Burns' information pack that her living cargo of twelve weeks was the one responsible for secreting the high levels of the offending HCG hormone. Just over a couple of inches long and he - or she, if it had to be - was already capable of affecting his mum's appetite! How was that for infant power?!

At the latest monthly visit, Dr Burns had informed her that the feelings of nausea would subside over the next couple of weeks. Hopefully, that would be just in time for her initial appointment at the Maternity Wing of Swarbrigge District hospital on Friday 3rd April, 10am sharp.

The girl would have preferred for some male company to hold her hand at that session, and to present a united front to the world of parenthood's shared responsibilities. To culminate - if all went to plan - in her confinement of mid-October.

Evidently Jess hadn't been man enough to grasp her by the hand and show that kind of devotion and commitment to the cause. Far from it.

A month ago it had been since he'd last shown his face - on that day she'd told him of her pregnancy suspicions; just before Mum had 'greeted' her at the door with a hastily packed case of her belongings. What a traumatic day that had become.

Jess: father of the embryo within. He had *seemed* pleased about the possibility. Yet, in retrospect, wasn't the look on his face really communicating something more like: 'Great news … but count me out of the adventure. This baby thing will seriously cramp my lifestyle.'?

Yes, she indeed thought so.

Thus Jess was now discounted. How then about the other male in her life to support her on that preliminary hospital visit? Dad. Her dear Dad. The girl did not think so, either now or in the foreseeable future.

The latest thing she'd overheard Gran mentioning to her gloomy friend, Iris of Ankovi, was that if Dear Dad ever caught sight of his pregnant daughter near to the family home, he would 'personally ensure that her risen belly would rise no further, with a couple of trusty, well-aimed kicks'.

'I know,' Gran had said to her friend. 'Such an awful lack of respect and tolerance towards his own flesh and blood. I have to say I didn't like him when younger, either. Odd selection that by my Janey.'

This newsflash had, of course, greatly upset the girl. Upon retreating to her poky room, she had sobbed on and off for the next couple of days.

Why, after all, should she have to make that choice between her pregnancy and displaying servile obedience to family and village sensibilities? Those conditions could successfully coexist, she told herself.

Her father's violent hostility to the situation simply meant that, from now on, she would have to become ultra-protective of her babe. Extreme care and caution must be the norm. Down to her alone it would be, to ensure he made it to the world, untroubled.

This was the reason she hadn't set foot out of Gran's door since Wednesday. In an ironic twist, it had been Gran who'd been providing for *her* those groceries of sustenance.

'So, I hope Anita's game,' she said aloud.

Gran looked up briefly from the stirring of her porridge, but saw her granddaughter was talking more to herself.

'I know I can count on Anita's support for that day. She always has mine.'

Yet the fluctuating melancholia of the girl's first trimester began to infiltrate her thoughts for a while.

I may be pregnant, she sighed, but I haven't found the love of *my* life. I may be with child, but I don't have the love and support of my parents either! They are ashamed of me. How terrible that is. Exiled I am, to here.

The girl, soon to be known as Prima, turned aside to Daffodil's quiescent cage.

The euphoria of the millet spray's introduction seemed to have passed. The budgie was looking back at her through the bars; with something akin to recognition in its dark eyes ... perhaps the look of a fellow soul, bound in languorous existence.

FRIDAY 3 APRIL 381

Little did Reverend Okumbwe know he was being watched, as he turned the corner of the gravel path leading to the remoter northern transept of St. Bertrand's. From on high, a pair of narrowed eyes observed the detail of his every move.

It was noted there was a distinctly furtive quality about the holy man today: cautious looks, now and then, to left, to right and aft. He was carrying a tray, covered by a serving cloth.

Approaching the panelled door, he switched the tray to his left hand and adroitly produced a set of bronze keys from inside his cassock.

Another quick turn behind him to check for movement, then he rapped twice on the door and made his hasty entry. 'Are you alright -?' he seemed to enquire, before slipping from view.

From on high, a sneer which seemed to imply: *thought so ...*

Eight minutes and fifteen seconds later, when Okumbwe emerged with the empty tray and the wary looks, today's contingent of Shockers Republic prepared themselves for operations behind the church tower's parapet.

'He thinks he's got away with it,' smiled Frenchie. 'So cool and secret agent-like, that vicar. Oh, I wish I could be more like him.'

'Maybe you will,' Doobie smirked. 'But you'll be needing more of a sun tan first.

'Ah, that reminds me,' he said to the other two. 'We shall need some alter egos very soon. Securitat are not far off our tails, I sense.'

'Altar whats?' asked Pelius with a frown.

'Some new disguises. We need to blend in a

bit more with the locals. That's exactly what Comrade Scolex is researching and sourcing for us right now.'

The main man checked to see that the reverend was safely inside the church's main doors, then ordered them to prepare to 'have some words with that hermit therein'.

Pelius was the first of them to make the descent of the tower - which was not as tricky as it looked. The brick courses down its western edge were weathered and irregular: footholds were a cinch to find.

Frenchie was the next. Once Doobie had lowered Scolex's cumbersome sports bag, by means of the forty foot length of flex, all were on terra firma.

Checking for any unwelcome movement themselves, the trio of white shirted youths followed the reverend's tracks, skulking their way to the panelled door of the northern transept.

Doobie withdrew the hacksaw blade from the sports bag and invited Pelius to commence the initial assault on the mortice lock.

Half a minute into the frenzied rasping came the sound of a familiar voice stirring inside there.

'Hello, Reverend, is that you again?'

'Well ... I doubt that very much, don't you, Troy?!' laughed Doobie, his hands and his forehead pressed against the door's aged grain. 'I'm of the belief that Uganda would be using a key for this process!'

He was satisfied to catch the small gasp of surprise on the other side.

'Mister Doobie!' cried out Troy in probable fulsomeness. 'How's things? Are all the other boys with you?'

'Nearly so,' he replied, as the intense sawing was taken up by Frenchie. 'Three of us today. Uncle Scolex is away on an important project.' Doobie cleared his throat before continuing. 'Anyway, how've you been keeping? We ain't seen you around for ages.'

'Oh alright, thanks.' There was the sound of cutlery on china. 'Reverend Okumbwe has taken me,' said Troy, swallowing his final morsel, 'under his pastoral wing. He's been bringin' us cooked food, twice daily - which I'm very grateful for. He says I'm to stay in his care until we've discussed the best method of changing the path of my life.'

'Oh, does he now?' said Doobie in irritated

tone.

He tapped Frenchie on the shoulder and indicated it was Pelius' turn again. 'Work at a faster rate on it,' he told him.

'Yes!' replied Troy brightly. 'Reverend Okumbwe says my life is unfruitful and is bereft of spirituality, or something. He says I can receive salvation when we are inducted into the Church.'

'Oh, yeah?' laughed Doobie, rather hollowly. 'I think it's all a bit late for that, don't you? Have you told him about your latest adventure? About what you've done to the Coughlan kids? In fact, what *have* you done to the Coughlan kids?'

Pelius spun round with a grin on his face, holding up the warmed hacksaw blade with its blunted teeth. 'Job done!'

'Oh … *them!*' giggled Troy, as Doobie raised the latch and allowed the light of the overcast afternoon to infuse the candlelit depths of Troy's refuge.

The stench of urine and of worse were the first stimuli to assail their senses.

Troy, seated on a wooden bench beside a couple of empty plates, shielded his eyes from the blast of light with a grubby mitt.

'Never you mind what the Reverend Almighty Uganda's been saying,' spat Doobie, with his hand at Troy's throat. 'You need to be following our doctrine - and to get out of this stinkin' stable. You've got some more visual delights to watch, remember?!'

Troy pulled himself clear and dusted down the lapels of his overcoat. There was a look of growing doubt on his face now.

'Come on, pal,' said Doobie, more calmly. He held out a conciliatory hand. 'Let us leave this prison and discuss all our futures in more civilised surroundings, eh? Come on now!'

Troy was flinching, gripping harder on the bench. 'What - you mean in your cramped car with its shady windows?'

'Yes!' said Frenchie, making his first contribution. 'It's sophisticated living, don't you know!'

Doobie, with head inclined, took a mental note of his comrade's latest sardonic comment.

'I think I prefer it here,' said Troy without much confidence.

'You won't feel so when Uganda questions you about the Coughlan kids, that's definite. He's in

league with Securitat - did you know that? He is!
He gets on well with that Turby fellow -
Neighbourhood Snoop Man. Soon you'll be shopped
to Securitat. Best option then, is if you come with
us.'

Troy looked like he might be starting to
consider it. About the consequences he might face.

'You haven't told him yet, have you?' said
Doobie.

Troy shook his head. 'He knows I've got
something big to tell, though. I've just got to pluck
up the last of our courages. Then we shall.'

'Ooooh,' tutted Doobie. 'Silly Troy.'

Frenchie scraped at the dirt under his
fingernails and said: 'So tell us, dear friend, what
exactly did you do with those children? We're dying
to know.'

'I bet you are!' chuckled Troy in throaty
fashion.

'Spit it out!' demanded Mister Doobie,
getting him by the lapels. 'Tell us about the
condition of their health - and tell us it right now!'

'Alright, alright! I will,' he yammered. 'Just
let me do it in me own time. We need time to

compose ourselves.'

Doobie leered right up to him. 'Time is not on your side, fella.'

Troy ceased his slouching and sat up. Placing one hand on each knee, he assumed the pose of some venerated storyteller. He wiped at the remaining crumbs of the reverend's apple pie in his facial stubble and regarded his audience.

'The girl and the boy are not far from us,' he said. 'The girl and the boy are no longer with us. I am afraid I pushed them too far, beyond what they could take.'

'And you have removed them in accordance with our arrangements?'

Troy nodded. 'Yes, Mister Doobie. They lie buried together in a shallow grave, close to the big fir trees.'

'The yews?'

'Mmm. Yes, those.'

'And did you receive some inner joy from your work?'

'We surely did.'

'Tell me how much they struggled. I need to

know it for the purposes of research.'

Troy started to whisper various things in his ear.

At length, Mister Doobie remarked: 'Most interesting facts are they.' Now he pointed to the outside, to the grassy graveyard and to the High Street roofs beyond. 'Why not furnish me with more details out there? For your future life is out there with us. Come!'

Troy began to grow sceptical, as before. 'I don't think so, Mister Doobie. Reverend awaits our confession - and we want to see it through. Reverend Okumbwe says that once I have given it, I can commence the necessary learning to become a Christian - a living, breathing component of the church of Christie, we think he said.'

'That's a load of polwygle frass,' jeered Doobie.

'Ecclesiastical drivel,' sneered Frenchie. 'This situation's a set-up. Securitat will be waiting for you around the corner.'

Troy shook his head and slapped both sides of the bench. 'No, I'm adamant!' he declared. 'This time I am set on improving our lot. I can only hope that, with faith and perseverance, I can tread the reverend's Path Of Righteousness, through which we might be forgiven for all our past transgressions.'

'Pah!' exclaimed Doobie, kicking the bench in vexation. 'This is pathetic!' He turned to his comrades. 'It's impossible to help some people ...'

Pelius nodded and Frenchie stated: 'It's probably too late now for redemption, Friend.'

Doobie knelt down to Troy's level. Tilting his head, he said: 'We're giving you one last chance to reject all this religious claptrap and to follow the True Path Of Righteousness, as defined by the scribes of the Everlasting Shockers Republic. Continue your journey alongside us and study some more visual treats. What say you, pal?'

'Don't throw it all away,' added Frenchie, quite earnestly.

'No - and that's final!' He folded his arms. 'If you don't leave our temporary abode within the next thirty seconds, then we will shout and create merry hell to get Reverend's undivided attention.'

'Undivided attention, eh?' spat Doobie, his irises seeming to darken. 'Then try it our style!'

And before Troy could vocalise a response, Pelius had him by the left arm and leg, and Frenchie pinned down his right side.

From his rear pocket, Doobie had extracted the flick-knife and was pointing its tip upon Troy's chin.

'You know,' he said regretfully, 'I thought you were our man. I thought you could be the one to help transform this hellhole of a village into something of colour and of dynamism. I thought you had the balls … and the spirit to modify Lurkham in perpetuity.

'But I was wrong. Little Troy has fallen for the con-tricksters after all. This funkin' nonsense about *faith and perseverance,* and being *forgiven for past transgressions* - what stomach churnin' bile that is for us!'

He allowed the blade to trace the contour of Troy's chin, towards the tenderer areas. 'You have grown weak and decadent. Now is the time to meet your Maker.'

The edge grazed his Adam's apple.

'Aah … do be careful with that!' protested Troy, prior to Doobie's clamping of his jaw.

'Besides, pal, the thing you've got involved with is downright dark. Paedophilia's a dodgy science. You must pay for your mistake!'

Troy's eyes grew wide in realisation of what was about to follow. He tried to scream out; tried to champ on Doobie's unyielding fingers - but to no effect.

With minimal retraction, Doobie plunged home the weapon, mercilessly.

'No-o-oo,' gasped Troy. His hands were free again, feeling for the ragged tags of his wound; trying to close them over. But it wasn't working. The flow of blood remained constant.

'Yes!' said Doobie with lasting spite. 'Now get the Great Lord Of The Sky to get you out of this one! Where *is* he in your greatest hour of need?!'

He picked up the sports bag and motioned for the others' withdrawal from the ghastly scene. He turned to Troy's fallen figure at the foot of the bench and saw the crimson froth exuding its neck.

'It didn't have to be this way, pal,' he whispered before closing the door. 'Really it didn't.'

WEDNESDAY 15 APRIL 381

About a month on - and they were digging again on Commoners Common.

They'd had to delay activities for a quarter of an hour, following Frenchie's sighting of a pair of Securitat officers over towards the far side of field.

Shockers Republic had kept low in the surrounding vegetation while they tracked the stealthy, silent progress of those stilted figures in black.

'Weird phuckers, indeed,' muttered Doobie as he crouched.

'Yes, they don't move in a natural way at all,' Frenchie whispered. 'Even their heads turn at the same angle and at the same time. Biology not right there.'

When the spooky shapes had slipped from view, presumably returning to the murder scene at St. Bertrand's, Doobie gave the signal for the recommencement of things.

Scolex was just about able to lug the stolen, brown suitcase himself to the centre circle, where the hole was. He plonked it for a moment beside the carefully dug turf, which Frenchie and Pelius would be infilling again quickly afterwards. 'Blimey,' he said, having recovered his breath. 'Either it's got 'eavier, or I'm losin' me muscle tone.'

Doobie propped his elbow on the shovel. 'Yeah, whatever. So *what* did you say that thing is?'

Scolex shielded his eyes from the first rays of the rising sun. Daylight sure was coming earlier these days. 'It's the working parts of a Gammatron I've salvaged from the Radiotherapy Unit of Swarbrigge General,' he replied. 'Obviously, I've disposed of its housin' - cast iron, it was - and the lead protection, too. We need open access for the cobalt-sixty source.'

'We do,' said Doobie, looking at him thoughtfully. 'Yes, of course.' Then, he lifted out a few more clods of earth from the three foot hole. He regarded Scolex again. 'You're absolutely sure it'll do the trick?'

'Yus,' said Scolex firmly. 'The game of football - as we know an' 'ate it - won't be taking place 'ere for a very long period of time.'

'How long's "long"?'

'Well,' said Scolex, brushing away some dust from his imaginary cuffs. 'Eighty to an 'undred years is my conservative estimate, before the level is safe once more.'

Doobie was looking quite impressed. 'That's more like it.'

'Plus,' said Frenchie, pausing to remove a tightly folded piece of newspaper from the chest pocket of his t-shirt, 'there's another benefit which can be gained from pursuing this action.' He unfolded the page of last week's Swarbrigge Herald and started to read aloud.

'It says here that there's a planning proposal in the offing for several of the villages around Swarbrigge - including this one.'

'Is that so?' said Doobie not looking up, putting the final touches to the suitcase's burial chamber. 'That's impudent.'

'Yes. They tell that: *"Due to a forecasted*

housing shortage over the next ten years, the village of Lurkham has been allocated its share of one hundred and eighty new homes".'

'Blimey!' exclaimed Scolex. 'That's too many for the filthy breeders.'

'It says the majority have been earmarked for the field to the west of here - just beyond this hedge. But some will intrude onto this hallowed pitch.'

'No, they won't!' smiled Doobie, stretching his back. 'Firstly they'll have Neighbourhood Snoop Man and Dog Detective to contend with. Then, if the developers are still upstanding and ready for more, Scolex's bastardised Gammatron thing will do the rest.'

'Yus!' wheezed Scolex in amusement. 'It certainly will.'

'So ... what in Hell are you waiting for?' said Doobie, poking the suitcase's flank with his shovel. 'Insert said device in hole and let's kick off the contamination of this centuries old site. This settlement is big enough as it is. We need no more overspill Townies living here and ruinin' this rural idyll.'

With that said, he retreated from the trench,

creating some more space for his comrade.

In went the suitcase. Scolex was glad to let it go. That side of his body bulk which had been more exposed to the cargo already seemed to be losing its 'pins and needles' sensation.

He imagined the paths of those gamma rays being emitted by the radioisotope. He likened them to a million strong army of filamentous worms: burrowing themselves at the speed of light through his skin, tissue, fat and bones - and out again to the other side.

He raised a chuckle at this surreal vision. 'Invisible worms, he told himself. 'Worms are all you is.'

Maybe. And they sure could wriggle ...

FRIDAY 17 APRIL 381

Pelius came to his decision as the Shockers made their furtive return to the shambolic and dilapidated barn in Farmer Robson's field.

The quartet had just partaken of yet another unsatisfactory breakfast, following their hour's long foraging of the border hedges. Berries and spring bulbs it had been for the third consecutive day.

Surely, the time was ripe for some further sampling of the domestic environment? he'd been hoping. Another unprotected house, somewhere in this locality: simply advertising itself ... crying out for a Shockers' style intervention. Yet another orgy of housebreaking, parasitism and destruction soon to follow.

Yet they were still stuck in the barn ...

Pelius was nearly a Shocker; so very nearly.

Over the past four or so months, his resistance to their revolutionary psychology had been weakening. The assorted cocktail of chemicals they had been administering him was hastening this decline.

He was becoming as a moth, replete with the merest of vestigial minds: quite unable to countervail its gravitational attraction to the Shockers' corrupting shade of light. Pelius had found himself locked into this inexorable spiral.

Until … today.

Miraculously, the last part of ex-greengrocer boy John Pelham's functioning brain had somehow latched itself onto an attachment unseen. Against all the odds, it had broken his fall.

Before the occurrence of his permanent blanching by the variant of light illuminating *their* world, that biochemical impulse had made it: saltating his congealing synaptic gaps; journeying a neural pathway that was still sympathetic to the cause of the original John Pelham.

It was the welfare of his mother which broke surface and came to the fore.

Was she really gone ..? Had the leader of

this murderous little ... sect ... been speaking the truth - or was she still alive and vital in Ankovi, full of want and longing for her son?

Coshed around the head, all for the price of her gold necklace. Really so? Pelius had himself some grave doubts about this. He would have to find out the real state of things for himself.

The four of them were just filing along the narrow track of the hollow betwixt the fields, nearly at the barn's weather-beaten door, when Pelius decided to go for it, announcing: 'Comrades, I think I just need to go and open my bowels.' He clutched his belly and grew a pained look. 'It's them berries again.'

Doobie looked a trifle irritated and ushered him away. 'Well, if you must. Just ensure that you close the aforementioned things afterwards. You have yourself two minutes!'

'Cheers,' he said, turning back along the diffuse track.

He wanted to run, of course, but couldn't until he was past the striplings of the copse.

Once there, he did, starting to accelerate. The two minutes' head start would have to be sufficient.

He knew the route back home: to continue along here, then to wade across the knee-deep water of the Sebus; to cut straight through to the similar water channel of the opposite field, which, before long, joined the trackway to Ankovi - and then about another five minutes dash to Mum's.

A minute or so later he was at the Sebus. A couple of local anglers were sitting on the bank before him. Pelius thought about swerving around them - then thought the better of it.

At about the same time that Pelius surprised them both by cutting between them with a passing grab of their rods and a cry of: 'Out of my way, you pair of boring social outcasts!', the leader of the self-proclaimed Shockers Republic was beginning to wonder about his comrade's sense of timekeeping.

As Pelius sploshed into the chill waters, damaging one of the stolen rods amidst the anglers' howls of outrage ... Doobie gave a frown and mused: 'Where on earth's he got to? Doesn't take this long to evacuate such things.'

Then his narrowed eyes widened as a ... possibility ... passed fleetingly into view.

'Comrade Frenchie, come with me!' he ordered. 'Where's the car, Scolex? You have the keys at hand for it?'

Scolex looked up from cleaning his boots. 'Yus, they is 'ere. But … it will be risky. I left it parked midway down the road they call The Chase.'

'That's good,' said Doobie, catching the keys first time. 'Not so far away.'

'But Chief! Securitat could be swarmin' all over it - even assumin' that it's still there.'

Doobie held open the ramshackle door for Frenchie to exit. 'On this occasion, Shockers Republic must take that risk.'

Pelius was in his stride now, running up the gentle gradient of the channel, carefully stepping over the awkward rocks and boulders in his way.

He tried recalling the last time he had enjoyed such a bolt as this one. It didn't matter that he couldn't recall it - adrenaline was in the way of those types of thought. This would be his most significant bolt yet: his jog to freedom, and to hopefully enjoy his Ma's lasting hugs this time and beyond.

He made it to the next landmark of significance - to the road - carefully checking for excess traces of humanity.

Of which there were none.

The single track was rutted and uneven, it being the original surface of some thirty to forty years before, so he had to look where his feet were pounding. He was working up quite some steam now.

Ma's smiling, disbelieving face as he collapsed into her arms: she being so glad to see him, half a year on from his disappearance. Now he would be back - and staying ...

Within the small matter of five minutes, Pelius told himself, this wonderful scenario can be playing out for real. It all depends on me.

Above the sound of his footfalls came the first squeal of some skidding tyres.

He shot a quick look over his shoulder and sprinted on, with acceleration. 'No way!' he puffed at the onrushing breeze. 'No funkin' way, Doobie!'

The estate car was tearing down the track a

few hundred yards behind him, bouncing over the potholes and kicking up the dust.

Pelius knew that his options were starting to slide. The disturbing intimacy was quickly growing between himself and that wheezing, honking vehicle.

He could hear the hiss and spurt of its misfiring cylinders; could almost inhale the fumes of its churning oil; could nearly feel the gnarled projections of its radiator grille trying to snag him.

'I'll make it for you,' he chanted, among his hot exhalations. 'I'll make it there for you, Ma.'

He looked to the verges for emergency alternatives - but the hedgerows were too high.

Down to the last twenty feet and closing.

'Good,' said Doobie to his driver. 'Good … steady … steady …'

Frenchie had the hang of the car's handling

by now. 'Soft or hard? Ill or dead?'

'Oh,' he replied with an odd smile, 'I have some later plans for him. So you'd better do the soft option.

'Steady ... steady ... *Now!* Tip him off the track!'

And so Frenchie did just that: brushing Pelius into the tall thicket, then clunking him in the midriff with the side mirror; sending him to earth.

Since the driver's side was blocked, the pair had to spill out from the kerbside door, round to the torn hedgerow, the swathe of mangled nettle stems ... then onto Pelius.

Dazed and a little bloodied he was as they hauled him up.

'How you doing, me old mate?' spat Doobie in his ear. Not patient enough for the reply, he kneed his fallen comrade in the groin. 'Became a tad lonesome for your dear old Ma, did you? Just how touching is that?!'

Pelius was down to the ground again, clutching his latest injury. Tears were forming at the corners of his screwed-up eyes. 'I'll keep tryin', Ma. I promise you I won't stop.' He started to sob.

At distance there was the sound of an approaching vehicle, coming from Ankovi way.

'Quickly! Behind the car and keep low!' Doobie hollered. 'To the start of this hedge, then left into the field's ditch! Let's be on our rapid way!'

Together, one on each side, they dragged the grim-faced Pelius along the border.

'Back to chez nous?' asked Frenchie, with rising exertion.

'Si, but not for long. I know already the whereabouts of our next residency. And I know also what our next task is to be: it will be to ensure that this dearest chap won't ever be leaving our tribe again.'

THURSDAY 23 APRIL 381

Pelius had lost complete track of time when the door was finally opened and the makeshift curtain was finally parted, allowing him the momentary glimpse of a verdant garden.

Behind the length of sticky tape, his tongue still probed the parched surrounds of his mouth, as might a desiccated lungfish in its burrow; seeking the miracle of rehydration.

In ill-fitting lab coats, Scolex and Frenchie stepped inside the dim compartment. They stomped across the wooden floorboards, over to the floral deckchair where Pelius lay bound and gagged.

All he could do was to assess their intentions through his fear-flooded eyes.

Frenchie looked down at him with that air of superior, half-amused detachment. Scolex, meanwhile, seemed to be regarding him in a more baleful way; but his dull, flat expression betrayed nothing further.

Pelius attempted to articulate some words: to demand the reasons for his imprisonment in someone's garden shed for the past week or so, with not so much as a splash of water to quench his thirst. And without the luxury of even a crumb to comfort the ragged raw linings of his tum. But he couldn't articulate any of this, thanks to the presence of the sticky tape. He began to thrash around, but the rope about his wrists still held him.

Scolex shuffled a half step closer. 'We're instructed to take you to Theatre,' he said quite emotionlessly. 'We shall now untie you.'

Still wearing the gag, Pelius was pulled out of the deckchair. He tottered for support - it having been so long since he had last been standing.

'Come this way,' grunted Scolex, leading them into the searingly bright afternoon.

Along the unevenly paved slabs of someone's garden path, he was frogmarched towards an opened back door of what looked like a detached house.

The shadowy interior revealed itself to be a kitchen. A carpeted hallway lay beyond, with a couple of rooms leading off to the left. To Pelius, its layout seemed pretty bloody identical to that of the house they'd burgled recently, the one where Troy had been entertained.

'Now up the stairs we go,' motioned Scolex.

To the middle bedroom he was led.

Scolex tapped twice on its glossy door and announced: 'The patient is ready, Doctor.'

Inside was a sound like cutlery being quickly rearranged. 'Oh, do please show him in,' said the distinctly muffled voice of Doobie.

Shunted forwards into the brightly lit room, Pelius had to squint before he could see more clearly the Shockers' alterations to the layout of the displaced owners' second bedroom.

Aside from the blinding study lamps which faced in from each corner, a crudely affixed fluorescent strip light now glared down at the stripped double bed. Beyond was a dressing table, topped with the myriad sparkle of, what seemed like, a hundred laboratory instruments: some blunt and rounded; most being saw-toothed and sharp-set - the specialised tools for cutting.

With mounting horror, his heart starting to beat at twice the normal rate, Pelius turned to face the masked figure standing in the angle of the door.

'Hello, my friend,' said Doobie, as though he might be smiling at him behind his muslin face mask. 'Feeling hungry, perhaps?'

At this point, Scolex's puffy hand drew across their captive's face, ripping off the gag of sticky tape in a single action, together with the top layer of his scaly lips.

'Yeeearrgh!' cried Pelius as the pain seared through his already ground down system. 'Of course I'm 'ungry!' he shouted in a slurred, depleted way. 'Wouldn't you be, havin' been left to rot in someone's garden shed for a week?!'

'Well,' conceded Doobie, 'I guess I might feel so, yes.'

'Yeah! So when are you goin' to feed me again and let me see me Ma?!'

Pelius was growing more insistent and stroppy, so in stepped Frenchie to block any possible assault on their leader.

Doobie looked at him with greater intensity; his voice now taking on a more powerful quality. 'You know I am disappointed in you, Comrade

Pelius,' he said. 'Firstly came the rejection of us by that unfortunate, name of Troy. As responsible Shockers we could not tolerate it. And now we face one by you! Neither can *this* wholesale rejection of our ideals be permitted to take root - who knows where it might end?'

'Look, mate,' said Pelius, almost pleadingly, 'all I'm askin' for is some bleedin' nutrition, to put a linin' to my belly!'

Doobie inclined his head. 'Well, surely. In normal circumstances I'd be saying: "Yeah, feed him up. Make him big and strong again." But now is not the right time to be asking this.'

He straightened up. 'Comrade Pelius, are you not aware of the fasting requirements prior to the commencement of an extensive amount of elective surgery?'

'You what?' breathed Pelius, astonished more by the sheer verbosity of the question than by its possible meaning.

'Nil. By. Mouth,' said Doobie, most likely smiling again - as Scolex brought the clipboard containing his medical chart, right up to the tip of Pelius' broad, flat nose to show him something.

Just before his lights were extinguished by

the administration of an effective tap of the mallet's head to the back of his neck, Pelius caught sight of the three words on the chart.

Poorly typed beneath his misspelt name were the words: Gender Reassignment Therapy.

He was hitting the floor by the time his blunted mind cogs began turning for the words' definition; all too late.

Doobie checked the small clock on the dressing table behind the surgical implements.

'Gentlemen,' he said, addressing his junior staff of today. 'Are we ready to begin?'

Both replied affirmatively.

Doobie returned, clutching the largest scalpel. 'Then … let battle commence,' he said.

At a quarter past four, the first incision was made. A little wobbly but the next was better.

Instructing Scolex to hold apart the lips of the great slit he'd created from belly button to left scrotal edge, Doobie spotted the pale worm of vas deferens and started to pull it with the forceps.

'Hold 'im steady,' he said through his sweaty mask. 'With luck the whole testis will come along too.'

By the time he was ready to extract the remaining gland, Doobie felt like a dab hand at general surgery: pretty confident about where to clamp with the forceps and to remember to tug only - so as not to snap the vas bloody deferens.

As Frenchie proceeded with his sewing duties, using some of the black thread he'd found downstairs in a needlework box, the patient began to stir. Scolex, in his role as Chief Anaesthetist, took it upon himself to fetch up his mallet again and to give the aforesaid patient the same treatment, upon the same area of neck.

The dull thwack ceased all unhelpful movement, allowing Doobie to complete his work in peace.

Soon he retreated from the blood splattered mid-section of the bed, turning his attention instead to Pelius' neck region.

Fetching a finer scalpel from the dressing table, he briefly thanked his Chief Anaesthetist for the procurement of this magnificent array of tools, and in such a timely manner.

"S'ok,' said Scolex, groping their patient's wrist for signs of life. 'Borrowed 'em at the same time as I borrowed their Gammatron,' he sniffed. 'Was a physically 'eavy day for me.'

'How accommodating of them,' said Doobie. 'We must repay our debt of gratitude one day to the staff of Swarbrigge General.'

'Yus.'

Doobie advanced on the slightly breathing form of Pelius and got a-cutting, in the second instalment of today's operation. His self-confidence was there for all to see.

Easing the scalpel blade into the Adam's apple in a gentle rocking motion, he was quickly able to expose the inner cartilage. And what a lot there was! Too much by far, if today's objectives were to be achieved.

He started to excise a small cube of it. Then again, explaining to the attentive Frenchie that: 'Without so much of this, our Adam will be sounding more like an Eve.'

With the time on the dressing table clock reading a little past five, Doobie ripped off his stained washing-up gloves and withdrew triumphantly from the field of combat. He gave a yelp of satisfaction and waited for Frenchie to complete the stitching.

'Patient's still alive, eh?' was his remaining enquiry to the big man at the bed's helm.

Scolex nodded, with what seemed a touch of relief. 'Still wiv' us, if that's what you mean.'

'Good. The worst of it is now over for ... her. When she comes round, the oestrogen hormone dosing must commence. Then the electrolysis treatments can start. In that way, we shall see the correct development of the female sexual characteristics - involving the loss of his old body hair ... if that's what *this* can be called,' he said, prodding with contempt the smooth down covering Pelius' chest.

'You want us to take 'im to Recovery?' Scolex asked.

'Yes. Let her sleep it off.'

Frenchie looked up from wiping clean the stainless steel instruments. 'Are we to stay here a while, then? What about the caller who's been ringing here since yesterday? They'll be getting mighty suspicious about their receiving no answer, don't you think?'

'Oh yes, I'm sure they are already,' smiled Doobie. 'And if they come any closer during our stay here, then I trust you'll know what to do: to dispatch them within the bedroom behind us - just like we did to the charming couple who owned this hovel.' And as a sardonic adjunct, he smiled: 'Do please remember to kill them quietly, because as we are all aware, our dear mate, Neighbourhood Snoop Man, his lovely wifey and Detective Doggy only live three doors away to our east - and they apparently see and hear all!'

It was Scolex who carried out the last rites of the day; transporting the unconscious body of their comrade to the post-operative Recovery room.

Gently, he lowered him into the avocado-hued bath. He topped up the chest deep water with some from the hot tap, tossing in a handful of table salt crystals at the same time. They were pretty nifty for the healing process, or so he'd heard.

SATURDAY 25 APRIL 381

The day was set fair, and the bright verdancy of the pastoral scene was ready for the wedding of Miss Anita Jane Woolf to Mr Wesley Bright. Even at around eleven of the morning, there shimmered a warm heat haze in the middle distance, more suitable for the time of June.

The crickets were performing their stridulating rhythms as the first of the guests drew up outside St. Bertrand's in their gleaming cars. It seemed, at least, on this particular morning that the birds from all the nearby fields and hedgerows had congregated especially: to add their melodious voice of endorsement to this occasion of hope and celebration, after such a long and deathly winter.

Within the church, the Reverend Able

Okumbwe was chatting over the final arrangements with the groom and best man. In the choir behind them, the organist readjusted his stool and continued testing his stops, to ensure the smoothest of yanking.

'As I am sure you are aware,' said the reverend with a smile, 'This great institution that yourself and Anita are to shortly enter into is not to be entered into lightly. It represents a giant step in your personal development and in the enrichment of your lives. Of course, part of the Good Lord's design in the concept of marriage is to provide the stable union - the platform, if you like - for the begetting of the heirs and descendants, by the sperm a-visitin' the egg. After all, "The children be the inheritors of the earth; their parents its useful custodians," spake the Good Lord.'

At this theme, the groom smirked a little to his best man.

Now the reverend took on a more jaded countenance, speaking more reflectively to the pair of nervously excited chaps before him.

'The other aspect of marriage concerns the hastening advancement of the participants' maturity and responsibility.' His eyes skirted past the chapel's incongruous, stained glass replacement. 'Maturity and responsibility. Hmmm, it's a crying shame that there is not more of such in this locality. Some elements around here appear to be lacking in even the basics of morality and good brotherliness. Perhaps they are incapable of finding love,' he mused. 'Their souls, as withered and malnourished entities.

'Still, boys,' said the reverend through a smiling sigh, 'you can be rest assured that your special day at St. Bertrand's will pass by with not a hitch. I've been informed there is a low-level Securitat presence in operation, to prevent any unchristian mindlessness from taking place.'

A ripple of disquiet transferred between the pair, before Reverend Okumbwe continued on about the ceremony's specifics.

At around a quarter past twelve, the pale yellow bridal car entered the High Street; passing by The Chase as it made its majestic approach to the gates of St. Bertrand's.

Through the net curtains of the main

bedroom's window, Frenchie had been observing the steady procession of cars past the top of their road. 'Looks like there's a wedding on the go,' he called back.

Doobie stood up from his seated position on the top stair of the landing, taking another swig from the dead couple's brandy bottle. Beyond him drifted the weak protestations of their fallen comrade from the Recovery room. Doubtless he wasn't much caring for the medicine with which Scolex was plying him.

'Oh really?' said Doobie, joining him now in peering through the nets. 'A wedding … taking place right under our noses? Cheeky. That shouldn't go unchallenged.'

He gulped another mouthful of the stuff and looked inside the doors of the fitted wardrobe.

'Comrade Scolex!' he called, sifting through the old bloke's racks of clothes. 'Seems we've got ourselves a marriage to attend! In here, as soon as you're ready please, for a quick costume change. Do you know if the head apparel is close at hand?'

'Yus, Chief,' came Scolex's reply from the quietened Recovery area.

Frenchie was handed the pinstripe suit, the

trousers and the trilby.

Scolex rolled in and was accosted immediately by the sight of Doobie waving at him the beige v-necked sweater, grey flannel trousers and flat cap. He tossed something to Doobie in return.

'Put them on,' said Doobie. 'By the way, what *is* the current status of our wayward friend?'

Scolex regarded him with positive outlook. 'Oh, 'e's doin' alright. The incision points are healin' up good. The oestrogen seems to be yieldin' results. And the patient appears to be lucid enough. He was goin' on about seeing his Ma again, so ... I had to give 'im one of the sedative concoctions. Seems to have done the trick. That, plus a change of the seawater.'

Doobie made the final, positional tweaks to his auburn wig, then inspected the others' attire.

Stifling a smirk at Frenchie's chic undertaker

look and at Scolex's aristocratic golfer's image, he enquired cheerily: 'Shall we tee-orfff then, chaps? I'm game for a spot of marriage crashing if you are.'

Down the stairs they bounded, their combined racket failing to raise the awareness of Pelius, who was drifting obliviously to a deeper sleep stratum, with the foamy bathwater lapping at his earlobes.

'So, what's the plan?' said Frenchie as they assembled in the porch.

Doobie pointed beyond the right pane of frosted glass, then to the left. 'I want you to begin walking down Wilbur Avenue. Scolex, you toddle off up The Chase. I'll dawdle along this 'ere Walford Grove, and I will be expecting to see you both - at sensible separation, mind - in the High Street. No suspicion shall be generated by Shockers Republic.'

With tactics settled, the trio slipped out and carefully closed the door. Doobie knew he really could dawdle it; safe in the knowledge that both comrades had the more pavement to cover.

It didn't take long for him to spot a pair of probable, undercover Securitat officers.

There they were, at the junction of this road

and the High Street: pretending to mingle with the real wedding throng as it proceeded along Church Lane in cheerful technicolour, towards the gates of St. Bertrand's. It was the rigid postures, the blank, staring eyes and their wooden presence which so easily betrayed them.

How wretchedly predictable of this place! thought Doobie as he ambled along. Not even *one* pretty, picturesque wedding could be seen to be ruined here - for it could cast a terminal pall over everyone's summer and beyond. Ahhh! And if it were to be spoilt, then the villagers might be forced, at last, to accept their reality: about what a horrid little microcosm of bad inbreeding they are living in.

He caught sight of Frenchie already on the other side of the High Street, actually looking dead cool in that trilby.

Now crossing over the road, he saw no sign at all of Scolex ... which was more than a bit troubling.

Pushing past the next, obvious, undercover manikin who was taking a quick drag of fake fag at the gates, Doobie was able to filter into the main people traffic, so that he coalesced shoulders with Frenchie's Mysterious Undertaker Man.

'I've decided that now is not quite the right time to risk a direct confrontation with these stiffies,' he mumbled to his comrade. 'At least, not until we find out about the welfare of Scolex.'

'They've got him?'

'Not certain.'

'Ah, yesss,' smiled Frenchie. 'I have an unrelated question for you.'

'Ask it.'

'My question is: just how far do you think we currently are in that quest towards world domination?'

Doobie eyeballed him for a moment, to assess the degree of mocking, since he had got to know by now the sarcastic and waspish turns of Frenchie's mind.

Apparently satisfied that he was being straight this time, he answered with: 'Our progress has been rapid and effective in streamlining the local population to acceptable levels. This policy must continue. I am convinced Shockers Republic will accomplish its objective here by the close of our next Five Month Plan. Every day we -'

His low burble was silenced fully by the

blasts of swirling organ coming from within St. Bertrand's, and by the sound of some crisply enunciated, soaring words from the choristers; those words radiating with sheen.

'What an unholy cacophony,' he hissed, realising they had become too near the dwindling rump of attendees - and were starting to appear a little exposed.

'Indeed,' agreed Frenchie. 'Those melodious upstarts should be polished off, too.'

'Well, my friend ... shall we?' said Doobie, in mock jocularity, taking the great door from the preceding guest. 'Shall we watch how matrimony's done?'

'Simply love to,' grinned his comrade.

Throughout the hushed reverence and the whispers of sibilance, seated near the rear of the musty old building, Doobie was deep in thought *and* in time, pondering further about ... further objectives.

He had temporarily left behind his immediate concerns about Scolex and the possible viability of there being only a trio of Shockers without the Big Man. Instead, he had travelled in future time, to a Lurkham which wore fully their mSR boot imprints.

There, at sunrise. He had overseen the last of the butchering. Standing there he was, under a sky of shifting red, atop the tallest of the frazzled mounds.

'Do you ... take this man to be your ..?'

Looking down at the tangled, twisted shambles beneath him: Lurkham village, in the rawest of architectural styles. Doobie's style.

'I do.'

All bodies, now extinct. Lying there before him in these raised heaps, ready and finalised for his inspection. Classified and segregated, even in death, according to sexual and racial stereotype.

'So, do you ... take this woman to be your ..?'

The last unfortunate was burning on the improvised stake, fashioned from the ceiling beams of fallen houses by Shockers Republic's First Minister for Social Development, a certain Dr Scolex.

'I do.'

The last villager was almost gone to pure carbon. Going … going … gone. And then what?

Presumably, a relocation of the Republic from this scene of utter desolation, to concentrate on new areas.

But … how could the Republic grow larger its loyal ranks? How? It was the same, age-old question which Doobie had been left grappling with.

'Thus I now announce you as the husband and the wife.'

How could Shockers Republic multiply its potential for revolutionary thought and fervour … when all it seemed to do was to keep removing all potential recruits in its orgiastic, slaughter sprees? How to resolve this and to move *forwards* for a change? Grrrrr! How to do it?!

Doobie was still frowning by the time Frenchie's latest words filtered in.

'You're missing all the pomp and procession,' he said. 'And such a colourful couple this is.'

The pair of Shockers sidled out from the pew, almost blending in with the throng outside, once Frenchie's trilby was on again.

Doobie caught a few, interested glances at his barnet and ignored all.

Someone was waving at them from the flint wall on the far side of the churchyard.

Ahhh, it was Comrade Scolex! He was giving Doobie a discreet thumbs-up and a mock wipe of perspiration from his forehead.

So, a quartet of Shockers looked to be the viable option again …

'How do you rate the loving couple?' enquired Frenchie as the wedding party fussed over - and were directed to - their positions before the photographer's lens.

'Not highly,' Doobie sneered. 'The bride looks too pale for its groom.'

'Hey! Isn't she ..? She is! She was Tragic Troy's first victim!'

'Yes. Well observed. The girl in the blue coat. Well, well. She's gone up in the world.'

Now it was time for the more intimate snaps of the newlyweds. They honestly seemed a very happy couple: all cuddles and smiles; wrapped up in one other.

Next, the satisfied photographer started to round up the couple's respective in-laws for a further bout of camera action.

'Now can we have Mrs Anita perched together with all her lovely bridesmaids, please?' they heard him say.

And that was the cue for the girl in the low-cut dress of ultramarine with the tummy bump to come into view of all those gathered.

The girl, on the point of her designation as Prima.

Something occurred to the trio of Shockers, akin to a flash transmission, as that girl in blue with the indeterminate blonde hair settled into position with her fellow bridesmaids.

Something internally connected with Doobie: an assertion, suppressing all his usual thought processes, that an age-old problem might not be a problem anymore.

Radiating briskly from his variant of central cortex, this novel certainty tripped from his lips. '*She!*' croaked his breathy voice.

'You're ... *lovely,*' cooed Scolex over at the jagged wall, his countenance gone all daft and dreamy. Transfixed he was by her shoulder-length, russet locks and by the high pink tones of her cheekbones. 'Jus' as me mum used to appear in all her younger photos,' he whispered tremulously.

Yet Frenchie saw her as brunette: neatly bobbed with big, brown eyes; saucy, sexy gamine. 'Choose me,' he slurred. 'Climb out of that dress and don't you be feeling so blue with *me.*'

Shaking his head with vigour to regain some composure, Doobie forced open his dewy eyes and got a grip on himself.

'Do you not see, comrades?' he stuttered, taking another involuntary glance at the blonde adventure awaiting them. 'Do you not see that She is our collective future? Cripes! By absolute decree of the elected Praesidium, She must be incorporated henceforth and wholly into Shockers Republic!'

And when he glanced again, She seemed to meet it: seeking, perhaps, the origin of that rasping, masculine voice she'd somehow detected through the mêlée.

Then was concluded the protracted, photographic session. Some frothy chit-chat resumed in the churchyard, before the time came for the new family of Mr and Mrs Wesley Bright to lead proceedings by stepping into their festooned landau, en route to the place of reception.

The Shockers Republicans never lowered their gaze - not until the landau was gone from view betwixt the hedges of the single track, with its attendant trail of gleaming cars.

'We can't afford to lose her now - even though I feel She's local,' said Doobie. 'In fact I'm sure She is. Simply, how have we kept missing her all this time?!'

'So what's her name?' asked Frenchie as they began to fan apart for the homeward return.

Doobie looked up with measured deliberation and announced: 'For us in the mSR, She can go by the name of ... Prima. Yes, Prima.

The First One.'

SUNDAY 26 APRIL 381

That night, sleep did not come easily to the residents of 11 Sweet Drive.

Frenchie padded down to the lounge and was totally unsurprised to find that both Doobie and Scolex were flopped in the florid sofa chairs: both wistfully looking out at the street lamp, at the assortment of moths revolving about it in their dizzy orbits.

'So you're findin' it hard, too?' was the comment of Scolex.

'Indeed,' he replied, crashing out into the shapeless pouffe with a bottle of something or other from the drinks' cabinet. 'Sleep's difficult as well.'

'You can't get 'er out of the mind, I'll wager.'

'Indeed. In deep, she is.'

Scolex chuckled as Doobie turned from viewing those hapless moths.

It looked as though he'd been at the bottle himself, going by the wild, ragged look on his face.

'You shouldn't simply speak for yourself,' chided Doobie. 'Prima is to be loved equally by all comrades. Each one of us must show her how much we care.'

'But what if she won't accept our kind of hospitality?' Frenchie's eyebrow was raised.

'Then there'd have to be a degree of coercion involved,' he stated, not looking up. 'For when Prima is in our possession, we shall need all things fulfilled.'

Frenchie took another swig and sat up keenly. 'Such as ..?'

'Such as fings like caterin', cleanin', washin' clothes, general repairs, … 'ugs and cuddles,' interjected Scolex.

'Yes,' smiled Frenchie. 'Good point.'

'No!' said Doobie, in more forbidding tone. 'I'm sure our lazy comrade in the Recovery unit will soon be performing some of those tasks for us.'

He began to speak with more deliberation. 'Let it now be known that there is a Greater Reason for Prima's incorporation.'

'Indeed ..?'

'To continue the flow of Shockers' genes to generations yet unborn,' he said, as though reciting from a prepared script. 'Prima is primed to be our Virgin Lands: the ideal region for us to sow and to cultivate. It is our intrinsic right to permit the perpetuation of ourselves.'

'Well, yes!' grinned Frenchie, relaxing expansively on his pouffe. 'I think I could do my reproductive duties without hint of a problem.'

Doobie suddenly raged, flinging the cushion at him. 'You are not to speak of Prima in such a way - RIGHT?!'

For a tense moment, Frenchie scowled and looked as if he was about to rise up. Then his stance softened. He was man enough to rein in his emotions, when required - unlike certain others in the room. 'Of course, comrade,' he smiled. 'Prima is above that kind of talk.'

The rather charged atmosphere of the living room was moderated at this juncture by the sound of something solid tumbling down the last few stairs.

Then there was the final bump - followed by a groan of accompanying pain. 'Oooooof!' was what they could hear.

Scolex was the first to his feet. He ceased the incessant scratching of the itchy, red patches which had blossomed overnight upon his forearms, and shambled towards the hallway.

Next came a thud and a scuff of boot, contacting the wall mounted mirror out there, and a half-strangled, fearful cry of: 'What am I doing ... dressed like *this*?!'

The voice was more or less of Pelius, they could tell that much. But it had more variation in pitch now and was straying up the register.

Doobie snapped on the light to find Scolex was already helping up their poorly comrade.

Ah! He was still looking pale. And Doobie could see, through the layers of improvised sheeting, there had been some ... positive developments.

Two small mounds were now poking from the region of Pelius' chest. Plus, lower down, gone was the assumed bulge of masculinity. Instead, he wore a smoother, streamlined aspect.

He was looking older, too. Baby-faced no more; lines and furrows creased his forehead and around his eyes. Doobie recognised clearly that pain was a recent visitor to him.

'How are you feeling, old girl?' he enquired.

Pelius seemed to be wincing. One of his slender hands went to the rosy bandage at his throat as he attempted to speak again.

'Don't you worry,' said Doobie. 'You need some more healing time.'

Scolex tidied up the fragments of reflective glass from the carpet, and Doobie realised that the lack of a mirror there might not be such a bad thing. It would not be in Pelius' best interest just yet to catch sight of his appearance. He might grow depressed. And the effects of the general anaesthetic were apt to play havoc with one's state of emotional well-being anyhow.

The patient's red-tinged eyes looked to be welling up, as Frenchie gently escorted him back upstairs towards their room. Evidently he'd now outgrown the basic facilities of the bathroom and was ready for sleeping on the floor again with his comrades.

As Pelius turned the corner of the staircase, Doobie was still debating internally whether or not the enlargement of those hips was as a result of the hormone jabs - or was simply due to the inactivity of laying in the bathwater for too long.

'I guess if fings don't work out with that Prima girl,' rasped Scolex in his ear, 'then we could always hone our romantic skills on our very own Pelius. What say you?'

'I say her name is Pelia,' replied Doobie coolly, moving off in the direction of the kitchen. 'But we won't need to do something as base as that.

'Get some rest. For tomorrow begins our search for the authentic Prima in earnest.'

FRIDAY 1 MAY 381

The girl known as Prima scrubbed at the last saucepan and placed it on the draining board.

Gran was beckoning her out again to the vegetable patch of the small, walled garden. She had the lounger all ready for her.

'Alright,' smiled Prima through the open window. 'I'm on my way.'

Daffodil was indulging in a squawking frenzy in his cage, the flaps of his wings wafting his moulted under-feathers in the elevating spring air.

'Settle, boy!' she told him, before setting foot on the back step. 'Stop acting up so frisky.'

She almost skipped her way down the garden path, feeling good with herself on this lovely, mild day. This past fortnight, the condition of her hair and skin had improved considerably. And, thank goodness, she wasn't feeling nearly so tired and emotional.

Gran straightened up from her gardening, then planted a kiss on Prima's forehead.

'Now you just put your feet up, ducky,' she said, guiding her to the lounger on the lawn. 'Position it where's best - but not so it's in the shade. A good dose of vitamin A from the sunshine is as important for Baby as are all the other extracts and mineral potions they say you need down at surgery.'

'Gran!' laughed Prima, settling in comfortably, 'They're all very good with me. Doctor Burns says I'm doing fine, without problems, and the nurses in Maternity say I'm progressing well. So there we have it, from the lips of the professionals!'

'I know, Dear. I know I'm fussing again.'

'But I mustn't neglect today's exercises for maintaining suppleness of back and tummy muscles,' added Prima. 'It can get so boring, though. All that standing, with feet slightly apart, twisting gently to the right and then to the left. Not forgetting, of course, to keep straight both the spine and feet. Actually, I'll be glad when this whole thing's over ...'

Gran had resumed her trowelling of the vegetable patch, working the earth in small, deft movements. 'This time will pass, child. Almost halfway through your term already - think about it like that. That way of thinking got me through life's little upheavals. Your mum was the easier one, being the second, and a few pounds lighter.'

She broke off for a moment and looked across at Prima. 'That reminds me. Have they not told you of your AST result yet? You might have to chase them for it.'

'Gran!' said Prima in mock chiding tone. 'It was only yesterday that I went to Doctor Burns to give it! Relax, it's early days. In fact, they call it AFP - Alpha Feto … something or other.'

'It's the test for twins, though, is it not?'

'Yes. A raised level indicates if it's twins.'

Gran smiled fondly. 'Twins are what's in our family.'

'But it could also be an indicator of a spina bifida baby.'

'Oh,' said Gran, with something of a fraught look. 'We don't need that.' She started to dig again with the trowel, a little more harshly than before. At length, she said: 'I'll join you in prayers for a low level of AST - and for a bouncing baby boy, come October-time.'

'That's what we're hoping,' smiled Prima as she took a hold of Gran's other gloved hand, squeezing it with some real affection.

She lay back in the sun's rays, her thoughts turning to her best friend, Anita.

Husband Wesley and she were closer still to the sun's warmth than this, in their first week of honeymoon. Fooling around those sun-kissed bays of the Southern Shore they would be.

Good luck to them! she thought. They looked an harmonious couple, and Prima was genuinely happy for them. Genuinely happy. Yes.

The wedding had gone like a dream - all aspects of it.

She'd appreciated Anita's insistence that she join them at the Swarbrigge reception, and that she seek out those eligible bachelors in attendance. Prima had tried to shine that night, but ... the reality had been found wanting.

Most guys, it seemed, would remain bachelors for the indefinite future, judging by the risible contents of their chat-up lines. For instance, the boy she'd danced with at the start - tall, dark and brooding with those Jess-style cheekbones - even *he* hadn't been able to conceal his inherent shallowness; by pointing to her tummy bump and then roughly whispering in her ear: 'You're sure it will be alright to funk you, despite your living cargo ..?'

'Certainly not!' she'd responded, with a vehement slap to those wondrous cheekbones of his.

For the remainder of the evening, he'd worn a look of more than simply practised brooding!

No, there was no man up to it. Prima would be relying on some all-female assistance for this one, then. Despite her *living cargo*, she would sail on and manage this process without indifference or hindrance from the opposite sex. Or … mightn't it be better to start referring to Them as the *opposing* sex? she wondered.

Upon the very completion of this thought, started to ring the telephone in the living room.

Gran was, by this time, facing away from her and merrily weeding the other bed, in advance of the wallflowers she had planned for there.

'Phone's ringing, Gran!' she called, contemplating a mid-morning cup of coffee.

Gran shuffled off towards the kitchen door

with a wave, and Prima settled back for a few minutes longer, returning to her thoughts.

A sensation like a fluttering butterfly in her stomach passed. Prima gave a little cry and her hands gently cradled it. 'It is you,' she whispered. 'Moving for me, you clever one. Just you wait until Aunty Anita comes home next week, and then you can perform this trick to her and to the nurses at Swarbrigge.'

Prima's mouth broke into a grin, her countenance complementing perfectly the day's clemency. The time was indeed right for milky coffee and biscuits.

Gran was back at the kitchen door. She looked to be frowning.

What on earth's happened now to Iris of Ankovi ..? mused Prima.

It seemed things couldn't get much worse for Gran's ill-fated friend: be they health issues, money worries, or blatantly unkind acts of the Good Lord - like the devastating lightning strike upon her thatched roof a year back. Since then, her list of woes had seemed endless and growing.

'Yes?' enquired Prima to her static grandmother. 'Is she okay - Iris, I presume?'

'No, not her,' she said, waving a dismissive hand. 'No news from her. It's your father on the line. Says he'd like to speak with you.'

'Oh, gosh.'

Another sensation ran down her body. Not Baby's this time: it was adrenaline, plummeting her heart. A shaking finger tugged repeatedly at her bottom lip. 'Why ..? Why's he want to speak?' she said through drying mouth. 'What's he want with us?'

Gran half smiled. 'No, ducky, I think it's alright. He is sounding conciliatory.'

Prima lay there, quite rigidly.

She must have returned her a sceptical look, because Gran stepped over to her and held out a helping hand. 'Go on! Speak to him,' she smiled. 'I can hear there's remorse in his voice.'

Prima thought about it for a bit. Mulled over it, she did. Thought about his mounting phone bill the longer she left it, also. Then she groaned and took Gran's hand. 'Oh, if I must.'

'Family will be happier, ducky.'

Sure, sure it will! she thought, entering the relative gloom of indoors. What's his motive?

What's he really after?

She took the phone and Gran stroked her shoulders.

His voice. 'Hello ..? Hello?!'

Sounding tetchy at the imposed wait. And this pleased her a little; fortified her.

'Hello. Look, Darling, I don't know if you're there or not …'

Don't you Darling me!

' … but I want you to know how sorry I am regarding my conduct to you, my general attitude and my total lack of respect for you during your teenage years.

'I want you to know that your mother and I love you to your very foundations. You are very precious to us and we are both missing you like crazy.

'Do please consider coming home, Darling. Hopefully as soon as possible. Come back, baby, with the new life that you are bearing, and I do hereby promise I will create the loving home you've been missing, and make this the ideal place for your child's arrival; our first beautiful grandchild.'

A sob escaped her twitching lips and transmitted itself to her father's ear.

'Darling? That's you?' The sound of rising hope was definitely in his voice.

'Oh, Dad!' she blabbed, stifling her cries.

'Please do … come home!' It sounded as though he was weeping too.

'I will,' she managed. 'Soon.'

Gran placed down the phone for her and Prima flew upstairs to her room, head in a whirl.

At exactly the same time as she pulled on her purple blouse and picked up her purse to go out, two other events of forthcoming significance for the village were taking place, as coincidence … or fate … would have it ...

Mr Turby planted the passing kiss upon his wife's cheek, then put the lead on Larry - who was most eager to get going, judging by his excited yelps and by the salivated accumulations at the corners of his mouth.

'We shall just be on our rounds,' he said in his cheerless way. 'One day we'll come across that scourge of miscreants, I can promise you.'

'Yes, Dear,' replied Jill. 'Keep your eyes open.'

'Well, obviously! Hardly to close them ...'

Then the pair were off, marching and trotting respectively to the front gate.

Crossing Sweet Drive, they headed up Walford Grove on the first leg of their daily, anticlockwise circuit of the village ...

It was just as well that Walford Grove *had* been the choice ... in the interests of the continued peace and stability of Shockers Republic. For the three, existing male members had just stepped outside their borrowed house only some three doors away from Mr Turby and his Larry.

The trio appeared to be persisting with those rather eccentric disguises of before: Frenchie under the inclined trilby, Scolex in the flat cap and grey flannels, and Doobie in that fetching, curly auburn wig.

He knew his blond stubble didn't quite go with it, and neither did the stormy look on his face as they trudged in diffuse file past the last homes of The Chase, on Lurkham's western flank.

'Keep your eyes open,' he snarled back to the rest. 'After this, we'll have to assume She's not a local. Our search area would have to widen …'

Prima kissed her Gran on both cheeks and said: 'I need to sort out my head. I won't be long gone. Just need a change of scene, to run it through my mind again. I've never heard Dad speak in that way. It is quite … unsettling for me.'

'I know it's genuine,' smiled Gran. 'I know the workings of my son-in-law.'

Prima smiled sweetly her way.

And then she was gone, crossing the High Street, then dawdling past the shops.

She wasn't intending to pay much attention to all the produce and wares on show today; her mind instead pondering this unexpected chance of rapprochement with Dad.

Her eyes registered the upright figure of Mr Turby: separating from the main body of pedestrians he was in his sprightly, almost military way; crossing over to Church Lane with loyal doggy. She absently wondered if he might be paying Dad a visit, in connection with the latest LRA issues.

With rising curiosity, Prima decided to observe them further.

Parking herself outside the window of Crichton's Bakery on the corner of Walford Grove, she was able to catch the progress of the bossy little man and his pooch all the way up Mum and Dad's road. Except, they turned off before reaching there, taking the path along the wall of St. Bertrand's towards the allotments.

She did not focus particularly upon some figures on the other side of Walford Grove, who were standing loosely about the greengrocer's displays; fondling now and then the vegetables, as would the real, discerning punters.

Her tummy rumbled. She could tell it wasn't Baby kicking this time. It was her appetite. And the thought of something topped with icing began to greatly appeal.

She followed her nose, crossing the road to the shops opposite, heading straight for Jenny's Cake Shop.

Yet it somehow registered with her that certain visual aspects of her environment were not quite right. She had picked up some coordinated movements in the corner of her eyes.

Looking briefly across, she saw those figures advancing on her from the greengrocer's.

A trio of them.

She took sudden fright, to discover their keenness of stare was fixed solely upon her. She perceived the composite look of lust and malevolence in their faces - especially in the one with the excessively auburn hair who was brandishing the cricket bat.

Marching in step, halfway across the High Street, they were; seeming to reach out for her.

Prima completed her dash to the open door, glad to find that it was Jenny herself at the counter.

Kicking away the stop, she pushed shut the door. The entrance bell clanged protestingly and Jenny got to her feet, nonplussed by Prima's unusual behaviour.

'I'm sorry,' said the girl, her eyes not straying from the ... *empty?!* ... pavement outside. 'Sorry about this, but I'm feeling a little threatened just now.'

She continued to peep beyond the trays of mouthwatering cakes and jam-filled doughnuts, yet saw no trace of encroaching shadows. No trace at all.

'It's probably my tired mind playing tricks again,' she said with a baffled smile.

Jenny removed her glasses and placed a supportive arm round Prima's waist. She peered outside also. 'All I can see beyond here, my dear, is a beautiful spring day. And none of the folk that I do see look out of place. Friends and villagers, just doing their normal rounds.'

'Hmmm, you're quite right. How silly of me!' she laughed, feeling rather the better for it.

Jenny leant towards her and winked: 'Why

not take a cake of your choice? They say a little naughtiness keeps one nice, by raising the sugar levels a tad. Go on, help yourself!' And she gestured for Prima to make her selection.

'Thanks. It's very kind of you.'

'And while you're at it, why not take something tasty for your tiny?'

Prima looked confused momentarily. 'My tiny?' she repeated, before it dawned on her. 'Ah, yes. Better make that two eclairs then, thanks.'

Seeing no sign of those suspicious characters out there, she raised the latch and bade Jenny a warm farewell.

Now Prima *could* have set off down the High Street whence she had come. If she had done so, then things might have turned out so differently for her, for her unborn child, and for the entire village.

Yet the day was set fair and she required locations to meander: to consider at which time she should make her homecoming. Too soon and it would appear desperate. Too late and this rare stone of Dad's benevolence might slip from her hands and splinter asunder; too difficult to restore.

So it was for this reason that Prima chose

the footpath at the end of the parade: the one which would lead her past the dense hedgerows to the open space of Commoners Common.

She began to stroll, allowing her hands to brush the young leaves of the overhanging branches as she chomped on eclair number one. On a day such as this, everything seemed a pleasure.

Observing the dancing progress of a yellow butterfly - maybe a High Clouded Sulphur - beside her, as it tested the nectar of a thousand flower clusters, she cast her mind to the soaring future: to a time when her son or daughter would be receptive to such; able and willing to appreciate all these wonderful aspects of nature.

Her thoughts were interrupted, however, by a present day stimulus: by the snapping sound of that brittle twig she'd remembered side-stepping at the start of the footpath.

Aware there was a walker behind, Prima moved on a couple of strides, to maintain her distance along the path's closing quarter.

From here, the common looked most appealing in which to find that necessary peace of mind.

Bereft now of its cast iron goalposts, and

with its grass cut to a tidy length in readiness for the opening match of the cricket season, Commoners appeared a more extensive area than she had previously imagined.

She thought she might take herself over to the field's top corner, to stretch out for a while in the balmy sunshine.

'Wish I'd brought along a book now,' she grumbled under her breath.

It was at this point that the faint breeze conducted the sound of some heavy feet, cutting clumsy swathes through the fringing vegetation at her rear. And it sounded as though both fringes were being trampled simultaneously!

This got her thinking. Either the person behind was built like a barn, who moved with an unnaturally wide gait, or else … it wasn't just one person behind her.

As she entered the common, Prima checked discreetly over her shoulder - and her heart sank at her findings. 'Oh, God,' she murmured as a pulse of adrenaline prepared her for a subsequent … anything.

It was the weirdos; the three weirdos again.

Standing in a line across the footpath: the

slobbish, man mountain on the left, in a flat cap and
with split, flannel trousers; the keen, dark-eyed one
on the other side, wearing the sober suit with the
muddied legs; and the one in the middle, with the
ludicrous wig planted atop his head.

He had to be the leader of the trio - Prima
could feel the intensity of malice aforethought
blazing through his narrowed eye slits. She sensed
his searing power; molten with all those darkest
emotions of spite, of hate, of rage, of … of rape?

And things were less assured than of ten
minutes earlier: no Jenny and her cake shop here in
which to take refuge. Simply a large area of field,
bounded by its hedgerows, with two distant figures
of a mother and her toddler receding from view in
the northeastern corner.

She took a couple of involuntary steps back
as the leader raised an arm, in what seemed like a
salutation.

The leader of the men cleared his throat by
spitting in a disgusting fashion. His smile was a
grimace which fractured uneasily across his face.

She took another step back, trying not to
make it obvious.

'Prima!' he said, lowering his arm. 'We are

here to officially request your incorporation into the magnanimous state of Shockers Republic. We shall all like to combine with you, so that this great union can be perpetuated through the generations: leading to the persuasion of all cynics and non-believers; for them to succumb to the powers of our revolutionary thought.'

He cleared his throat and was about to continue with some more.

'Excuse me,' she called out with some confidence, 'but I think there appears to be some kind of a misunderstanding.'

The leader tilted his head, glancing quizzically at her. 'How's that?' he said, hands on hips.

'Well, my name is not Prima,' she smiled, 'and it never has been. You must be looking for someone else.' And with that neatly explained, she started to walk on.

'No, no!' called out his voice. 'You are the one we seek. You are our Prima.'

She stopped, to find that the sinister gang had advanced on her the same distance: that the degree of threat remained the same.

'Excuse me!' she said with a wisp of rising

anger. 'Have you got a problem with recognition? You've mistaken me for someone else. Now … Good Afternoon to you all!' And she started to walk on again, this time more determinedly.

She checked back and saw the trio were marching after her. Becoming worried by the situation, her determined walk had segued to a run.

'Oh, but you are the one!' shouted Doobie to the coquettish blonde ahead of him.

'It *is* you!' cried Scolex, chasing the splitting image of his dead mother's heyday.

'Therefore, it's time to be off with those panties!' leered Frenchie to the slinky, bobbed brunette.

She started to sprint, as best she could, in a hopeful diagonal across the common. Over there lay her only possible exit: the way of that mother and toddler, leading towards the allotments.

From there, she would try and make her way to Mum and Dad's; forging a path into one of the neighbouring gardens, where she would hammer on their patio doors for all her worth to be let in. The homecoming a little premature - but at least Babe and herself would be safe from these pressurising monsters.

'Yeah, that's right!' shouted Doobie, sounding not so far off. 'Now that you've raised no objections to our proposed merger, it's only right that you shall next enable us to verify the degree of fertility which exists in your ... productive areas. Stop your soppy running away, Prima, and allow us to properly inspect!'

'Off with those panties!' repeated Frenchie.

'Knicks off now!' puffed Scolex.

'My God!' cried the girl, feeling Babe tumbling about below her diaphragm.

Her right ankle almost buckled in an unseen dip, but her forward motion carried her onward.

She had no idea of what this level of exertion might be doing to her child; yet she knew, above all else, that she was now in a battle to fend off rape - and possible death.

A battle which she dare not lose.

So very much she wanted to be that loving mother to her unborn child. So determined, to protect him or her from any mortal on this earth - or gang of such - who might *dare* to threaten her monumental dream from coming to fruition. She would run until her lungs burst, rather than to accept such.

'Prima, you silly thing!' said Doobie, hovering over to her right. 'Your route is about to be cut off. Submit to our verification procedure.'

And Prima could see, as he was speaking, that his sidekick in the dark garb and trilby was charging over to the strategically vital corner of the field. She heard the fat one's flapping footfalls over to her left and wondered if her game really was up.

Then suddenly, the first signs of her rising fury and indignation welled to the surface.

'YOU'LL HAVE TO FUNKING WELL CATCH ME FIRST!' she yelled in the overheating air of this May day.

To this outburst, a dog responded with a couple of rapid barks.

Not far off, by the sound of it: coming from the other side of the hedge afore them, in Farmer Robson's Northern Field.

Prima felt the last surge of adrenaline as she sped on, to win this race to its uncertain finish.

'HELP!' she cried out with her remaining air. 'HELP ME SOMEONE!'

The dog barked again, sounding closer now.

In the background she could make out its master's voice - a voice which didn't seem to possess the deep, robust qualities of Farmer Robson's.

'HELP ME, HELP ME, HELP ME!' she reaffirmed, as the solid line of hedge reared up to snag her with its dense latticework of thorns.

Doobie made an impatient lunge at the flapping tail of her blouse, but came away with nothing. 'I'll pin apart your lips if I have to!' he hissed, a couple of lengths back.

Then Prima caught sight of the pooch's movement beyond the hedge: a blur of biscuity brown through a small gap, over to her right. Barking insistently, it was loitering - almost offering her encouragement to join with it on the other side.

Impossible that, surely?! she asked herself. Babe and I won't fit through here.

But she had to give it her best shot.

Dropping painfully to her knees at the final moment - and feeling Babe nearly in her chest - she scrambled through the hawthorn. Its wooden barbs tore at her hands, arms and face, opposing her headway.

Despite this flurry of sensory and motor activity, Prima recognised that the authoritative voice now calling to her belonged, of course, to Mr Turby. And yes: Larry, his spaniel, was of biscuity brown. Why, she'd been watching them just half an hour ago!

'You are needing some assistance, young lady, from your feverish attempts to tear asunder Farmer Robson's two hundred year old hedge?!' he barked, in his sardonic style. 'Now, tell me what's going on over there?'

Prima wriggled her ragged, top half through, holding up her scratched hands. 'Please, Mr Turby!' she besought him. 'Pull me out of here quickly!'

He started to oblige - but it was not quick enough.

'Aaaah!' she yelped, feeling Doobie's fingers clamp round both her ankles.

'Not so fast, me fishy one,' came his heated words behind her, as the other weirdos lent their muscular support to the grappling of her tiring calves.

Whilst Larry spent his time barking foul, canine threats at the unholy trinity and by springing up at the hedge, his master dug his feet in the field's furrowed boundary and proceeded to tug Prima, her hands tightly in his.

'Those murderous lot of … bastards … been causing you some grief, eh?' he said, with a puff and a grimace, as both parties gave their all for her on their respective sides of the hedge. 'They'll meet their match soon, I … promise you … that!'

'Oh yeah? You talking 'bout us, frigging Neighbourhood Snoop Man?!' replied Doobie, yanking quite savagely their victim's ankles. 'Your old dog and your doggy wife are going to be in severe trouble with us, once Shockers Republic have obtained what is its rightful state property. Now you let go of our Prima - or both your canine friends will die!'

Mr Turby seemed to turn redder in the face, struggling for an instant to redouble his grip.

'Oww, this is hurting ..!' winced Prima through squeezed-shut eyes. 'Can't you all just leave me alone … let me get on with my life … and behave like civilised human beings? Oww!'

But her words went unheeded.

'How dare you speak of my wife like that!' shouted Mr Turby, with a savage tug of his own, causing Prima yet more pain. 'I'll have all your guts for garters, that is for sure!'

'Really?' came the voice of Doobie. 'I'd like to see that, honestly I would. But I doubt you'd ever find the time to do it. I bet you spend at least half your spare time with your pants round your ankles, getting enjoyment from your pet -'

'What the *hell* are you talki-?!'

'LOOK, PLEASE JUST STOP HURTING ME!' cried Prima, at her wits' end.

'I don't know where you ... inhuman group of ... short-arsed, balding ... SCUM are from,' fumed Mr Turby, with successive yanks of Prima's arms. 'Hades itself, most probably. But I can assure you this: your days of ravaging my village are numbered. I will send back the lot of you miserable parasites of life and of sunny geniality to the deepest, dankest hellhole from where you were vomited. I will ensure this by mine own hands.'

'Whooo-hoooo!' This drew cries of derision from the opposing side ... but there was a slight hollowness to their laughter.

'Right then,' said Doobie, at length. 'That's it. We're going to disembowel your doggy later tonight, we'll boil up your wife's spinal column for tomorrow's lunch, then force-feed you the tasty mix in your kitchen for tomorrow's supper.'

'Oh, I think you're all talk,' said Mr Turby, with another tug of the girl. 'All talk, no hair and … no trousers.'

And with that, the gap between Prima's taut midriff became just wide enough for Larry - who was, by now, sufficiently riled and frustrated by all this tense, human interaction - to push through his muzzle, and to start giving the trio of protagonists a display of proper, canine vexation.

Mr Turby was abler to pull Prima to him, while the Shockers contended with the bloodcurdling snarls and the growing threat of dog bite.

Into the mix came the wailing sound of a Securitat car siren, which didn't sound that far away.

'Are you alright?' Mr Turby asked her, cradling her in a supportive arm. 'You think you can walk?'

She was wincing some more. Her eyes were tear-lined, and one hand was clutching her stomach, as though feeling for something. 'I don't know,' she replied in a whisper. 'I think it has done me some harm.'

Mr Turby pointed behind him to the area of scattered buildings, on the horizon of their green expanse. 'Can you make it to there, do you think? That's Farmer Robson's. You'll be safe.'

'Ohhh, I don't know.' She was wiping her eyes. 'It seems so far away.'

'Nonsense,' he said with a smile. 'Now take my hand and off we go. Each step, it be an increment nearer to sanctuary.

'JUST GIVE US TWO MINUTES, LARRY!' he called back.

Amid the variety of foul shouts and curses emanating from the other side of the hedge, as another Shockers Republican got his knuckles bitten, Prima placed her hand in Thomas Turby's. Off they started, in parallel furrows towards Robson's farm.

'No, no! Let it get a hold on your arm *first*,' came the voice of Frenchie, 'an' then I'll spill its bleedin' brains with this stick ...'

'Wait a minute!' puffed Scolex. 'Its teefs are too sharp for that tactic. Why not entice 'im out with the stick and *then* clobber 'im?'

'No. I've the best idea ..,' said the remaining Shocker's voice.

They were walking quite steadily now. Prima turned momentarily to see the tensed hindquarters of Larry were still protruding from the hedge. Such a stout defender he was! Those barks were coming thick and fast, and his tail wagged vigorously from side to side. He appeared to be relishing whatever it was the weirdos had next devised.

All seemed quiet on the farm, although she did notice several of the upstairs windows looked open. Perhaps Farmer Robson plus wife were both taking their afternoon nap, she thought - hoping they could be roused without difficulty.

'For how long had those evil ones been menacing you?' asked Mr Turby.

'Onwards from the High Street.'

'Bastards ..,' he muttered, more to himself.

Suddenly Prima doubled up in apparent agony. With a scream of pain, her legs crumpled and she fell to the earth. She was starting to break down in tears.

Mr Turby grimaced. 'What is it *now*? You know we do need to get to the farmhouse as quickly as we can.

'THAT'S IT LARRY! COME ALONG

NOW!'

One hand was on her stomach again. Pallor was spreading over her face.

'What is up with you? What is it, girl?!'

Prima grimaced back. 'My Babe,' she moaned. 'Babe's dying.'

'Uh? Your what?!'

She said nothing more. Her crumpled look of certainty about her condition showed all.

' ... baby, huh?' he mumbled, twiddling his lower lip with thumb and forefinger. He was standing there over her, kind of protectively.

Then, with clarity, he announced: 'We need to get you to *our* house. Once there, I'll arrange for Doctor Burns to make a home visit. Yes, a domiciliary one. Come! Grab a hold of me and let us be on our way!

'THAT IS QUITE ENOUGH NOW, LARRY!'

He snatched up her extending arm, almost tugging her along on the revised bearing; towards the sheds and outbuildings, where the sunlight dazzled the windscreen of Farmer Robson's white pick-up.

'Yes, upon second thoughts, there's no need at all to intrude on Robson,' he said, starting to break into a trot with her. 'Doctor Burns will be our man of the hour.'

Just then, at the far fringe of field, the sharp-edged stone hurled by Frenchie hit home.

The sound of Larry's stifled squeal echoed forth as the flint projectile cracked his frontal skull.

A laddish cheer erupted upon Doobie's follow-up drive with his cricket bat, which caused Larry's slump to the hedgerow's verge.

'Funk it!' came the voice of Scolex. 'Securitat's made it to 'ere! Four of 'em … allotments side!'

Larry's owner turned back to witness the Shockers' hurried, yet triumphant, entry through the gap into the Northern Field. Like enraged wasps emerging from the nest, they fanned out in pursuit.

'Forgive me, dearest boy,' said Mr Turby, pulling open the squealing passenger door of Robson's pick-up. 'I pray that your injury is not your end. I'll be back to tend you - once I've taken care of a most pressing matter.' But his tone did not sound hopeful.

Guiding Prima inside with a firm hand, he scooted round to the driver's side.

Envisaging that he might have to hot-wire the darned thing, he was pleasantly surprised to find the ignition key to be sitting on the dashboard's dusty shelf, amongst all the clutter. Obviously Farmer Robson's sense of security towards his possessions did not extend to his mucky pick-up truck.

This will teach the old blunderer a lesson to be more careful in the future, thought Mr Turby to himself, as he turned the key.

'Ready?' he asked Prima, looking beyond her forlorn profile to the field. He saw the distant, advancing figures of the abominable trio: on the chase and on the run at the same time.

The truck made a noisy wheel spin and moved off quickly along the dirt track, passing by the front door of the farmhouse. Its driver smirked up at the bare-chested farmer, who was leaning out of the bedroom window; amused at hearing the dullard's exclamatory cries of disbelief.

'Hang on, girl,' he told his silent passenger as he flung the truck round the first, sharp bend of the single track. 'This could be a fairly rough ride.'

Thomas Turby was not wrong. By the time they had made it to the outskirts of Lurkham - by excessive use of the gas and brake pedals, some loose steering and a dash of good fortune - the near-side wing mirror had been wrenched off, and Prima had hit her head on the dashboard.

'Soon have you home!' he said a little breathlessly, spinning the stolen vehicle hard right and sending it down The Chase.

For discretion's sake, he elected to continue down the single track leading to Ankovi.

Utilising the very lay-by in which Shockers Republic had lain low some two months earlier with their erstwhile associate, name of Troy, Mr Turby brought the truck to a violent stop and snapped off the ignition.

At the same time as Doobie and colleagues were being scattered and assailed in the field by tranquilliser darts, fired by a crack Securitat cohort, Prima was pulled from the passenger seat by Mr Turby and was marched along a diffuse and rambling footpath, behind the gardens of Sweet Drive.

'To where are we going now?' she protested. 'Please take me back to Gran's.'

Her footing was lumpen, there was a gash on her temple, and a discoloured patch was becoming noticeable in the crotch area of her torn and muddy leggings.

'But I've already told you,' he intoned with a first trace of scornful superiority, 'Doctor Burns is waiting for you at my house. He'll doubtless need to check things over.'

'Oh, then let it be soon,' she whispered as the surrounding leaves flapped past her ashen face. 'For I can't take much more of this.'

At last they came to a walled area of garden. Mr Turby removed his hand from her shoulder, delved in his trouser pocket and produced a key, with which he unlocked the arched, metallic door set into the wall. With some caution, he pushed it ajar.

All was quiet. There was no Jill sunbathing in the garden, then.

He led Prima inside and locked the door.

'That's good. Careful up the steps,' he said, guiding her past the greenhouse to the lawn, over its regulation cut stripes.

Here he paused again, checking for signs of Jill moving about in the downstairs windows.

All was quiet.

Moving along the side of the garage, he fished out the back door key and, with a couple of wrist turns, himself and the troubled girl were indoors - and out of public view.

How easy, he mused. How easy this has all been! From the availability of Robson's pick-up (with ignition keys conveniently situated there on the dashboard) to a Jill-free house. It wasn't often that she wandered out.

He mused onwards, considering if he was being at all paranoid in thinking these events were somehow being ... facilitated ... today? He started to recall similarly helpful situations occurring prior to that ... previous occasion. To liken them as jigsaw pieces, being manoeuvred by stealth by someone - or something - into place. For him.

Of course. And there it was - the next facilitation!

The folded note, lying upon the table of polished oak.

Mr Turby snatched it up. Bearing no look of surprise on his face, he learnt that Jill would be out for a good while longer. Until late tonight. Visiting Larisa, her second cousin, in Swarbrigge she was.

An annual event, for one day of the year.

How strange, he thought, that it had to be today.

So ... the free time would allow him plenty of leeway and liberty to achieve his want.

'Along here, Dear,' he said to the Rogers girl, 'and then go up the stairs.'

Prima gulped down the last of her chilled water and swallowed his advice.

She was just preparing to mount the tenth riser when, with a fatalistic cry, she teetered on its edge and began to topple backwards into Mr Turby's arms.

'Don't worry, I've got you,' he said in a strained way. 'There, there.'

His grip around her hips and the brief contact of her leggings with the front of his trousers, initiated for him the stirrings of an erection.

Temporarily, he thought it best to avoid further sight of the girl's shapely rear view, focusing instead his eyes on the lines of wallpaper up the staircase.

'Into the opposite room,' he said, a little

shakily, leading her to the spare bedroom.

Another animalistic impulse came to mind ... and, this time, remained.

A female. With us, in our house. A female, of distracted state, who is not our wife.

But you can't! countered his rational side. This girl we're shunting around in front of us as a piece of furniture, happens to be the daughter of Michael and Jane Rogers. And, as you know, Michael is the one frigging villager who identifies most closely with our conservation ideals for Lurkham - to return it to the happy standards of yesteryear. So why to contemplate indulging in such a sly piece of exploitation with his only child? Do we really want an implacable enemy to be facing us across the table at the next meeting of the LRA? No, we blooming well don't!

I know, I know! his other half protested. *But we need to get closer to her, in order to obtain the second, vital constituent. Stone the crows! This whole scenario is clearly quite a turn-on for us ... and in the line of duty, who knows what might occur here ..?*

'Get on the bed!' he said, in treacle-thick tone, pushing her forward to the mattress.

She began to pull herself up. 'The doctor, you said. Where be Doctor Burns?'

Mr Turby placed his hand at the top of her leggings. 'He's been called. He'll be over soon. So let's prepare you for the visit.' And he made to pull them down, exposing the rear of her cotton panties.

She began to struggle. 'No!' she protested, repeatedly attempting to get a hold of her diminishing coverage.

'Come on now! Let us at least make preparations.'

Mr Turby knelt beside her on the bed and started to openly apply some inexpensive lubricant to himself. 'It is time for you to realise,' he said, clamping suddenly her fair hair and pushing her face into the pillow, 'that I was once a practising doctor myself, and that it is evident to me that you are undergoing a fatal miscarriage.

'If you do not allow me to help you, then you will die a slow, agonising death: poisoned by your unborn child, which your body cannot expel!'

Prima was moaning her muffled protestations into the pillow, mentioning Dr Burns, even her father now.

Mr Turby maintained the pressure on her

neck and, with his other hand, peeled off her panties. With dry mouth and rapid beating heart, he parted her lips. She was thrashing about even more.

'I *am* a doctor!' he insisted. 'And I *will* cure you of your poisoning. Let's get in there.'

His lies didn't seem to be absorbed by her, so he pressed ahead anyway. First went in his forefinger, then his middle digit; sinking into her warm interior. His ring finger was next, followed by the tip of his littlest.

Mr Turby drew some breath at this juncture, urging Michael's daughter to do likewise. 'Bear with me now. This part might cause you to wince a bit.'

That said, he gatecrashed his thumb and remainder of his little finger into her writhing form.

'Good girl,' he whispered as the cuff of his wrist was introduced.

He'd sometimes pondered how this might have felt had Jill been open to it. As masterful as he was feeling right now? Activity like this had been frowned upon in their sexual era.

Today was his time.

Michael's girl went rigid again, and stopped her thrashing around as his search intensified within the passage.

Thumb and forefinger pincered together, finding nothing substantial, until … they brushed past the cooler, smoother thing. Fingers clamping, he felt for more.

'I think I have managed to locate the source of your misfortune,' he announced, relaxing the constriction of her throat by means of compensation.

Gripping the foetus around its soft middle, he began the process of its extraction.

Prima, meanwhile, uttered a constant, low moan; as if mourning the loss of all her dreams.

Four months into the approach … and its substantial threads all undone in an hour's worth of base, male savagery.

Mr Turby withdrew his limb, holding up the aforementioned thing to the light, between thumb and glistening forefinger. He saw that, if things had worked out, this would have become Michael's grandson. Its small, formed fingers of both hands were clenched, but its face looked serene.

Overall, its colouration still seemed to be of oxygenated pink.

Fading, yet Mike's grandson had residual life … if he was not mistaken. The closing window for action would not be long.

Prima's languid attempt at raising her head from the pillow's enveloping confinement was cut brutally short by a hard chop from Mr Turby's dry, left hand.

'Sleep for a bit, child,' he whispered. 'When the Appeal is made to the Watchers' World, you will resurface. Together we shall witness the manner of its approbation.'

And with that, Mr Turby locked her inside the guest room, striding purposefully across the landing to the bathroom with the barely alive foetus cupped in his hand.

He pulled open the door of the cabinet. Impatient fingers pushed aside his shaving effects and took hold of the specimen bottle at its rear.

Then it was down the stairs with his gruesome cargo, two at a time.

In the kitchen, he withdrew the smallest carving knife from the rack and hurried into the living room.

He might have been imagining it, but the thing in his hand seemed colder to the touch already.

Unlocking the glass door cabinet, Mr Turby reached for the leather bound book of the top corner. He ran his index finger down its ribbed spine, feeling that comfort.

This time, the vertical silver lettering running down it had somehow regenerated; its clarity magically restored. 'Book Of Remedeyeth' it spelt.

Grasping it, he hurriedly pulled the curtains for privacy and snapped on the study light. The room was lent a secretive glow.

Mr Turby felt his raised heart rate and the trace of perspiration upon his top lip as he set down the book on the sofa table. Beside it were placed the carving knife, the foetus and the specimen bottle containing his hair strands.

He opened the book, his fingertips warm and tingly. Six and a half years, going on seven, since he had last ventured this far.

The Book Of Remedeyeth: handed down to him by his father, when Thomas had been a strapping twenty-five year old. And, so his father had informed him, handed down through the Turby (Turberville) lineage through many generations; too far back to trace or mention.

'Let this fact be known to you,' had said his father during that stifling July evening, with a sharp glint in his eyes. 'Though this script appears strange and outlandish, part of your intellect will grow the power to translate it - and all will make good sense to you.'

The younger Thomas had leafed through a handful of its pages, feeling only bafflement at their unrelenting lines of Latinate script: as a wall, without seeming footholds.

'All will be understood, before you may have occasion to make such Appeal,' he was told.

'And it is to our advantage that our family seems to have enjoyed a much closer, historic affiliation to it than have the other strands of humanity.

'Prior to our colonisation of Westernlands, our surname was Turbellarius - a name of Latinate origin. Thus we have of ourselves a natural affinity to this most priceless work of antiquity.'

His late father's assertion had, indeed, proven to be correct.

One day, in his fifth year of stewardship, his latent, ancestral eyes had opened and he had become receptive to the reading of those curvy hieroglyphics. A knowledge which he discovered did improve with age.

When that occasion had arisen, he had realised that such literary footholds were no longer required. He had surmounted the relevant chapter with ease.

And here was that earlier Appeal before him now: 'Appeal For The Dearth Of Minor Trespassers'.

It had done the trick: the Watchers had upheld it. Things unseen had been raised to dispel that particular plague on sociability. All cured within eleven weeks.

Mr Turby leafed through the volume's further pages, more quickly now.

The current problem required some badder medicine. Something substantial in order to dislodge it.

Hmmm. Swiftly he flicked past the disturbing folio with the depiction of a man: a man looking in fear at the emergence of a cluster of tentacular growths from a longitudinal slice across his abdomen - which looked to have been carved open by some laughing, pirouetting emaciate.

Next, the pages started to out-turn his fingers, flicking forwards at a rate of knots, as though the wind had a hold of them.

'Shim!' exclaimed Mr Turby with eyebrows raising, withdrawing his digits so as not to impede the progress of this phenomenon.

The billowing continued, until he thought there was a real chance it would take him to the end cover of the book's leathery hide: that it might snap shut and deny him further access.

But not quite. Three page turns before the end cover, did cease this unnatural process ... displaying before him the chapter: 'Appeal For The Dearth Of Invading Armies Of Besiege To The Oppidial Surrounds'.

'Ooof,' remarked Mr Turby, shaking his head. 'It's the big guns, then.'

Clearly the Watchers would only be countenancing such a drastic kind of response to the issue - should his Appeal find approval.

'Okay,' he said, clearing his throat. He shot a quick glance to the clock on the study desk. 'Time for Appeal is nigh.'

The light in this vicinity seemed to be intensifying, contrasting with the room's darker tone. Yes, it was definitely brighter now.

'Catullevenali mirabilis erebus,' he spoke, commencing the recitation in the yawning silence.

All familiar household sounds appeared to be in recession.

Upon reaching the first symbol of punctuation, Mr Turby picked up the carving knife.

Turning the little foetus face-up, he proceeded to slice out a narrow, longitudinal strip; noting as he did so that a proportion of the tissue was still of that healthy, pink colouration - and not yet dead. Encouraging!

He placed the strip upon the book's crisp page in correct, vertical orientation.

Next, he unscrewed the lid of the specimen bottle and tipped out some of the perkiest Turby hair strands.

These, he placed carefully across the sliver of baby's flesh in correct, horizontal orientation.

Following this placement of his offering, Mr Turby spoke into the book; his unfocusing eyes looking beyond those mere pages to somewhere deeper.

'The Organic Cross I set before you. My Dedication is now cast. Your considered decision I humbly await.' He concluded these words with: 'Defixio. Berebescu. Phrix phrox.'

For just a moment, he witnessed the passageway as he had on that previous occasion.

The passageway through the book.

Through the mesh of Latinate text, Mr Turby could make out the swirling mists of electric blue: his submission being the cause of those eddies, as it coursed its path to the unfathomable depths.

The book's translucence quickly dimmed and the glow on the living room ceiling was gone.

The hair strands and the tissue were no longer there.

Mr Turby closed the book, aware of the strange warmth to his fingertips.

He exhaled in relief. That was that done, then. Done and dusted. Now would come the wait.

How long had it taken for things to occur last time? he considered. The conifer-snapping, rabbit-splicing thing seemed to have entered the world the following night - and no later.

He recalled the awful, bloodcurdling scream which had awakened himself and Jill on that sticky, summer's night. How near it had sounded, as though from within the borders of their back garden. And that had been exactly the case!

Early the next morning, before work, he had traipsed outside to investigate - and had come across the heaped pile of earth where his vegetable patch was meant to be, and the splintered screen of conifers at the back fence. Yes ... it had come a-visiting just one night later, so he believed.

Suddenly from upstairs came the combined sound of Michael's girl's panicky cries and of the bedroom door being pummelled repeatedly by her fists.

'Help! Let me out!' she quavered. 'Someone get me out of here!'

Soon the neighbours might detect her - especially if she got open the double glazing.

'In a minute!' called up Mr Turby. 'We'll soon have you out!'

With that, he returned the Book Of Remedeyeth to the top corner of the bookcase, wrapped her miscarried remnants into yesterday's newspaper and plunged the whole sorry thing to the lower reaches of the kitchen's refuse bin.

As he dashed upstairs, Mike's daughter had resumed her frantic hammering.

He unlocked, and as soon as she saw him, Prima recoiled to the middle of the room.

'My babe!' she began to snarl. 'You took away my babe!' Understandably, there was a charged, indignant quality to her tone.

'That's not true - and you know it!' he replied. 'Your baby suffered fatal damage as a result of your earlier entanglement. I merely extracted it to save your life - and this is all the thanks I get, is it?! I really don't know why I bothered.' And he maintained his look of hurt, long enough for her sense of anger and injustice to soften just that little bit.

'Where is it? I want to see.'

'Long gone and impossible. For I have flushed him away.'

She stood there, her shoulders hunched, her troubled face looking beyond the wallpaper's garish design. 'I want to go home now,' she said delicately. 'Please let me go, Mr Turby.'

'I will escort you home in half an hour's

time, I promise,' he said with a half-smile.

'Oh, please NOW!' she insisted.

'But I insist upon this!' he said, beckoning to her. 'Come downstairs and partake of some refreshment.'

He led her aimless form down the stairs. 'You are a most courageous young woman. Here you are, after the most testing of days, ready to take all your accumulated wisdom and experience into the dawn of the next day.'

It looked like she rather enjoyed her chilled orange juice though, gulping it down at a rate.

Mr Turby checked the sky and noted that the sufficient level of shade had developed for their excursion.

With the cocked shotgun inside his jacket, he led her out. Pausing at the top of the driveway for a swift check down both sides of Sweet Drive, he stepped out with her, heading in a northerly direction up Walford Grove. Nothing to him seemed out of place or suspicious.

Yet maybe the Trio of Evil are waiting farther up Church Lane, he thought. Watching us from the churchyard, from the allotments.

Ah, Thomas! Drop this paranoia. Snap out of it, man!

He picked up the pace across the High Street, squeezing tighter her little hand as they broke into a quickening run.

No trace of the marauders up Michael's road either.

Perhaps the good chaps of that Securitat squad had been successful in rounding them up? he wondered. Or maybe it was Farmer Robson with his trusty gun who had managed to mow the bastards down and done something useful for a change? In which case, his Appeal for their dismissal might have been lodged in vain.

Yet his father had told him of the irrevocability of those Appeals, once lodged. They would simply have to be, and to run their course.

'Ah, it looks like your father and mother are in,' he said, glimpsing the orange glow through the living room curtains.

The girl known as Prima was shivering, her teeth lightly chattering despite the clement evening air. 'It looks so, yes.'

Placing his hand lightly upon her shoulder, Mr Turby edged up to her and said: 'I guess that you and your folks will have much to catch up on.

'All I would ask of you is, that if you intend to relate to them any details of what recently occurred, you should not paint my … intervention … my lifesaving intervention as anything other than in the positive light in which I approached and undertook it.'

He stroked her matted strands of hair with his thumb, saying in his most syrupy way: 'Please realise that I saved a beautiful young mother's life this afternoon. I played my part in her survival.' And he planted his kiss on her cheek before she had time to back away or to utter a negative or hurtful response.

Then she properly backed away, stating a casual: 'I'll remember to.'

She appeared to take a deeper breath, then pushed open her parents' front gate, striding towards the door. She pressed the buzzer confidently and waited for the fateful moment, aware that Mr Turby had slipped from view and was lost to the anonymity of the night.

The door was yanked open and her father's imposing shadow spread across her: the father she had last seen some two and a half months ago, before her pregnancy had been the cause of her family's rift. Now, of course, it no longer would be ...

'My Darling?' he called doubtfully at first, trying to discern his daughter from the caller's haggard exterior.

'Daddy! Oh, Daddy, it's me!' she cried, falling over the threshold into the expanding arms of Michael Rogers; both their feelings strong and unstoppable.

Turning from behind the trunk of the wild cherry opposite, Mr Turby could not, for some reason, bring himself to view this joyous reunion of father and daughter. There was the emotion of resentment, almost; that she was now safe in the arms of someone else ... of another male.

'Silly are these human attachments,' he chided himself as he beat his homeward retreat. 'I thought my capacity for feeling such would have atrophied at this stage of life, instead of my experiencing the pangs of a jealous youth.'

Yet what a girl! The visage, the straightforward attitude, the slight tendency to subservience ... all these qualities made Michael's girl a real pleasure to get to know. He could now understand just why that Trio / Quartet of Evil - yes, what *had* happened to the other one? - had been so determined in their pursuance of her. She could completely eclipse the remaining, local womenfolk.

Starting down Wilbur Avenue, Mr Turby glanced up at the alignment of the early summer's constellations. He smiled at the majesty of the astral display. A glorious finale to one of his more interesting days of late.

He tried casting back his mind to the time of the last, upheld Appeal. Specifically, what had been the changes to the local weather pattern? Hmmm. The first manifestation of the Watchers' approbation had been ... That's right!

That summer had hitherto been as a damp squib, with a continuous run of grey days and evening downpours of hard, chilling rain. The next morning, following his incantation, had the humid conditions blanketed all. Against predictions but there it was: enervating himself and his office colleagues come the afternoon; sticking shirts and blouses to backs by home time.

It was within this cloying oppression that the thing unseen had entered the world through his vegetable patch; to perform its destructive acts of depravity. Optimal conditions for that agent of monstrosity to do its worst.

Passing by the copse of trees on the corner

of Wilbur Avenue and that of his home turf of Sweet Drive, Mr Turby's mind turned to Larry, his dear Larry.

Was he still alive, following the events of today? Might he still be trying to wend his homeward way through the fields and the single track? It was too dark to check right now - it would have to be early tomorrow. Or ... had that stifled squeal signified the end to the physical life of his Loyal Larry? In all likelihood ... yes. A final murder, posted to the Evil Ones' bloody ledger.

'Come the Spectacular,' he repeated a few times upon approaching his unlit home. 'Do please account for their tally of death in my village. Do your good work upon them.'

Walking this last stretch without sight of Larry beside him - with his excited tail wagging as their walks always concluded - left him feeling rather flat and empty.

He had just put key into lock, glad to be getting indoors, when the flood of bright car lights forced his shadow up the rendering. The purr of its engine ceased and out stepped Jill.

Turning to greet her, Thomas Turby was distantly concluding: I suppose if dear Larry really has gone, then you'll have to do as my sole long-term companion for the remaining years.

'Hello, Dear!' he called with a cheesy smile. 'Had a good time with Larisa?'

She was starting to reply … but he was already travelling … towards a future liaison elsewhere: enjoying a deeper osculation to the lips of Michael's exquisite little daughter.

Oh, how pleasantly things are turning, he smiled, as he escorted the wife inside. God alone knows if I will find my sleep tonight; for these are, after all, exciting times. Time for licentious kisses and for targeted, bestial slaughter. Please come into my life!

MORNING OF SATURDAY 2 MAY 381

In the candle's flickering, uncertain light, the pair continued to gouge and to chip away at the face of loamy clay. Armed with pick and shovel - the best tools for the job they'd been able to source from the Charming Couple's garden shed - Frenchie and Scolex had done their level best in constructing the underground passageway.

They had commenced the dig last evening, once Shockers Republic had recuperated from the earlier fiasco played out on that knobbly, rutted field.

Good progress had been made. In grunted consensus, they reckoned to have mined their way directly below the garden border demarcating the Charming Couple's from next door's of No. 13.

'Git out of the light, mate,' puffed Scolex, whilst taking a break from his toil and trying to ascertain the compass pointer's lie.

He nodded, apparently happy that their east-northeast bearing was bang on course. 'If Chief's generous and gives us another two days,' he said, picking up the shovel again, 'then I bet we'll be right under the ass of vile Neighbourhood Snoop Man - and of our girl, Prima's.'

'It would help speed things up if His Lordship deigned to get *his* hands a bit grubbier, and to lend us support where it matters … at this rock face,' said Frenchie, with slight echo in the dank surroundings. 'All he seems to be doing is popping down here with a few more wooden boards to shore us up with, then returning to the warm, dry surroundings of the lounge to put feet upon sofa.'

'Yeah, but don't forget that it's an important contribution that Chief is makin'.' Scolex had put down the shovel. 'If the six or so lengths behind us *'adn't* been bolstered with those floorboards from upstairs, I can tell you we'd have known all about it - buried up to our traps in this clumpy crap.'

Frenchie propped himself up against his vertical pick handle. 'Yes, right,' he explained, 'but the thing is: what makes him so sure our Prima's with Mr Nosey at all, three houses away at No. 17?

He does already live there with a wife, you know! Somehow I don't think she'd put up with there being a nubile at home besides her!'

'Yeah, but the Guv'nor must 'ave an inklin' of somethin' to request that we dig this. We know he wouldn't ask this of us if there weren't no ulterior motive.'

Frenchie raised a doubtful eyebrow. 'You seriously believe that ..?'

As if on cue, a moment or so after, came the sound of a splashing thump at the head of the tunnel, as someone just dropped in through the hole of the Charming Couple's kitchen floor.

It was Doobie's muscular, panther-like silhouette, picking its way around the compacted piles of earth they had so far excavated.

'How you both doing, comrades?' he asked in the cramped environment. 'Making the expected progress?'

'We believe so,' said Scolex brightly. 'Should be through in about two days' time.'

Doobie was inspecting the texture at the rock-face. 'Two days? *Two* whole days, you say?'

'Yus.' 'We do say.'

Doobie was shaking his head. 'Oh no. No, no, no - that's too long! She could be lost to us by then. We must strike while the iron is hot!'

It was at this point that Frenchie mentioned about the positive correlation existing between the use of an extra pair of hands and an increased productivity rate.

Doobie narrowed his eyes and appeared to listen. 'Yeah, I get the gist of it. Good point! And I think it's about time that Pelius - oh, I mean Pelia - gets off her expanding backside and becomes our fourth pair of hands. I was nearly forgetting she's still one of us!'

He looked towards Scolex. 'She should be alright for some physical toil by now, right? Eight or nine days' worth of healing is surely long enough. Must be!'

Scolex pondered the question for a while as might a doctor; weighing up the potential risks to the patient's health and well-being. In his private capacity, he imagined the conditions down here might well spell the end for Comrade Pelia. But well he knew that the interests of the State rescinded all others - that, plus the baleful stare he knew would be coming his way from Chief.

'Yus, she'll be fully 'ealed up by now,' was

his reply.

Doobie prepared to make his exit. 'Keep up the good work, comrades. I'll be sending down your clown assistant soon. I want to see a regular rotation of the workforce, so that each comrade comes up for air and enjoys a sit-down refreshment every three or so hours. I shall plan for it now.

'This, my friends, represents the only workable system by which Shockers Republic shall capture its rightful symbiont. Dig onwards! Dig deeper to our collective future!'

And with his left fist clenched ahead of him, Doobie began walking, his boots making squishy progress over the sodden substrate.

The pair watched him disappear from view up the Charming Couple's stepladder, before recommencing their labours.

AFTERNOON OF SATURDAY 2 MAY 381

It was around a quarter past one, just as Mr Turby was chewing the last forkful of macaroni cheese, that the telephone rang.

At once, his heart was pressed into action and his peristaltic process temporarily halted.

As Jill raced from the kitchen to answer it, a delicious vision came knocking: that it could be Michael's daughter on the other end of the line.

Lost and directionless since yesterday's traumatic events, might not she have been yearning to hear the familiar voice of calm, controlled reason from the man who knew her better than most - perhaps more intimately than all her previous lovers? Could she indeed be seeking an illicit meeting with him, to further expose her inner self: to confide in him all her dreams, hopes and fears? How exquisite these thoughts!

Mr Turby nearly choked on his sip of water, however, when that sublime image was supplanted by another: of Michael Rogers himself; purple faced, ready to spit venom and vengeance at him, and to threaten the continued existence of his genitalia. Had that silly little daughter broken down under last night's questioning and disclosed all events?

His cardiovascular tension was certainly increasing when Jill turned towards him with a puzzled look and signalled that he should take the call off her.

He was quickly on the balls of his feet. 'Yes?' he said down the whispering line. 'This is the Turby residence. Speak up and tell me of your business.'

A vaguely male voice started to be heard. 'You are the lodger of recent Appeal?' it enquired, in a sparse, clipped manner.

Taking a moment to get his mind into gear, with heart rate still elevated, Mr Turby confirmed that it was he.

'Then I take pleasure in conveying our provisional approval of such.'

'Oh, good,' said Mr Turby, a little short of breath. 'That sounds like good news. So ... when to begin it?'

'Good news indeed,' intoned the emotionless voice. 'Yet firstly your verbal instruction is required for its activation.'

'Oh, I am willing, Ready and willing.'

The line seemed to be developing a background sound of alternating disturbance.

'I wish for things to proceed as soon as possible!' said Mr Turby in louder tone, to compensate for it.

The sounds of interference were starting to dominate. Then, imperceptibly, the mushy tones evolved to something else.

The furrow deepened on Mr Turby's brow, and his eyes widened with the dawning realisation that he might be hearing the fevered whispers and mutterings of an unknown intelligence.

Voices, yes! That is what they were. Discussing between themselves the outstanding aspects in simmering tongue through the ether.

Uncertain if the orthodox voice would reappear, he was preparing to replace the handset ... when the whisperings receded to mere background noise.

'It is confirmed that the grounds for your Appeal are valid,' came the announcement. 'Prepare for all necessary change.'

'I shall do,' nodded Mr Turby, before some curiosity got the better of him. 'And who might you be, if you don't mind my asking?'

Judging by the prolonged silence, it seemed as if he was not to know. To be kept in the dark.

But then ...

'You are to know that the Gatekeeper to your wishes has spoken,' came its final utterance, before the restoration of the dialling tone.

Mr Turby was left still frowning.

How strange, he thought, that there hadn't been a telephone 'interview' the last time I had invoked things. Hmmm. Perhaps it was for one of two reasons? First, the problem to be solved on this occasion might well require a heavier outlay of supernatural force than previously. And second, perhaps the Watchers had made great strides in the Customer Service department since then.

Either way, he knew one thing: there could be no going back now.

He was aware of his wife's footfalls over the hall carpet.

'Everything alright, Dear?' she enquired. 'I couldn't understand the caller. Sounded as a wretched foreigner.'

He moistened the roof of his mouth with his tongue. Right now he could do with a coffee or something. Two sugars, with cream on top, together with a plateful of chocolate biscuits would round off the afternoon in pleasant enough fashion.

'Just one of my contacts,' he sniffed on his way to the kitchen. 'He can be a strange fellow, that one - given the line of work he's in.'

'Oh, I see,' smiled his wife, in her meek way.

He silently imitated her as he prepared for himself the coffee. *Oh ... I seeee.*

He heard the first drops of rain striking the back patio, his thoughts turning once more to yesterday: to the tear-rimmed eyes of Mikey's daughter.

He hoped she was over it, healing nicely in there and smiling again. Genuinely, he did. But he sure was missing her company.

Does she miss mine? he asked himself as he poured in the cream. Does she not view me as filling her role of fatherly figure and more? For I could give her so much more.

These were the thoughts borne by Mr Turby as he sank back into the other sofa chair, at sufficient distance from his wife as the rain lashed down.

SUNDAY 3 MAY 381

Rain which would not stop.

All night it had persisted, hammering down on the tiled roofs, keeping most of the villagers from their sleep.

By morning, heavy runoff from Farmer Robson's fields, which lay mostly to the north and west of Lurkham, had caused the River Sebus to breach its banks; turning the lake to the west of The Chase into a sizeable area of water, as it made steady inroads into the neglected, lower reaches of those gardens.

From this heady source, the river became engorged, cutting deeper in its course and rolling tumultuously onwards to the inundated fields of Farmer Jarvis, from where it released all.

The roads were becoming impassible. The single track route to Ankovi contained, in places, standing troughs of runoff. Even the High Street was being swept by rippling tides of floodwater, which mounted the kerbs and threatened the front doors.

Most of the villagers stayed indoors, regarding with astonishment the intensity of the relentlessly pounding rain; which appeared to drop in sheer vertical from the glowering, leaden sky.

It was Angela Perks, the veteran newsagent lady, who was the first to learn of some unexpected info from the outside world.

Conversing with Maria, her friend of longstanding from the well-to-do East Side of Swarbrigge, she was astonished to hear that weather conditions of a most pleasant nature were still being enjoyed by Maria and her fellow residents. Glorious, unbroken sunshine there, apparently, for the past two days!

'That really is most baffling,' sighed Mrs Perks, raising her eyes. 'I know our climatic pattern is apt to be fickle, but how can it be that your clement weather has not been able to encroach upon Lurkham's airspace? Cannot it even provide us with an hour's respite from this awful deluge? Ooh, I do find that weird ...' She didn't half sound peeved about it! The nagging feeling persisted in Mrs Perks that summer was being stolen away from here.

Meanwhile, several properties away to her south, someone was staring skywards at the monstrous offloading: drumming his fingers in imitation; wondering if, at last, bigger things were happening.

7:05PM, SUNDAY 3 MAY 381

A tremor … for just one millionth of a second.

A seismic tremble from the subterranean depths: a subtle readjustment, perhaps, of a continental plate's leading edge.

Imperceptible to most living things, it was however detected via the scaly feet of Daffodil, perching in his usual area of cage on the sideboard at Prima's gran's.

Shockers Republic might have felt it too, had Doobie and Co. not been so preoccupied just then, in trying to extract Pelia from the earthen pile of the latest tunnel collapse to befall them.

At last they had her free, at a location of

roughly six feet beneath the saturated lawn of No. 15 - the immediate neighbours of their intended target.

Doobie glanced at the rivulets of water trickling through the horizontal planks of the tunnel's roof from the soil above, and stated: 'We'll be needing diving apparatus to proceed at this rate. It can't *still* be raining cats and dogs, surely?!'

'I expect it's dear Turby,' explained Frenchie, as he assisted the moaning Pelia to her stockinged feet. 'It's him: sprinkling us continuously with his garden hose; trying to put us off.'

Doobie cupped some of the dripping tunnel water and flicked it at him. 'Don't be so daft and defeatist,' he said. 'Clear up this mess and redouble your paltry digging efforts!'

So ... the Shockers had missed the evidence.

Not so the Geological Survey Station in the town of Dobra, one hundred and ten miles away to the southeast.

The technician monitoring the seismometer could not fail to notice the singular spike. He was quickly on the phone to his supervisor, his voice sounding enthusiastic and bright.

'Alexand'r, I have for you some interesting

news. A transient point of instability has just appeared, of magnitude eight-decimal-eight. Of small estimated slippage area, perhaps of only a couple of square miles. Its epicentre, as far as I'm able to calculate, is beneath the small Westernlands village going by the name of ... hmmm ... yes, Lurkham.'

The tech listened avidly to the words of his colleague, nodding his head. 'Will do,' he said. 'Yes, tomorrow we'll be there with our buckets and spades and our sonar equipment!'

He replaced the receiver with a satisfied smile, wondering which discoveries he and his field team might glean from this exceedingly rare geological event.

MIDDAY, MONDAY 4 MAY 381

Yet the technician and his fellows from the Geological Survey never made it that close - only to the outskirts of the village.

Leaving Dobra at sunrise, they had enjoyed a pleasant run in their van across the agricultural belt of the upper Southern Heartlands: passing through the afforested border region, until they came to the true heartland of the West, with its picturesque hamlets and timeless villages of cultivated orderliness and attention to detail.

Approaching the village of Lurkham along the Eastern Track, a couple of the geologists started to remark about the surprising abundance of standing water in these parts, and just how excessive was this flooding of the surrounding fields. The rainclouds responsible for this drenching seemed to have long since dissipated. The unbroken sunshine was almost too hot through the glass, for those on the van's exposed side.

They rounded the last muddy bend - and found themselves confronted by a huddle of Securitat patrol cars and officers. The driver slammed on his brakes and the sky-blue van skidded to a halt in time. One of those officers had begun his stilted walk towards them, holding up a cautionary hand.

'You cannot progress any further,' he said. 'The route ahead is inviable.'

Glancing behind him, the geologists caught sight of a milk-float's rear end, some way beyond the group of patrol cars. Beyond that, the view of Lurkham was indistinct; somehow blurred by a high summer's haziness.

'The route ahead is inviable,' repeated the officer with a grimace. 'Kindly retrace your route.'

Yesterday's seismograph technician leant out of the passenger window and tried to explain the situation, holding up part of the hand-held equipment to add weight to their story. 'We need access to the village,' he told him. 'Access, so we can assess the current seismic situation. Something unusual has happened here.'

The officer scratched his forehead and muttered something akin to: ' … you can say that again …' - before striding back to his colleagues, maybe for further consultation.

Presently, he beckoned them forth, instructing them to alight on foot with some of their gear. 'You may take your necessary readings at a safe distance from the energy field.'

'Energy field?' asked the chief technician.

The officer beckoned him closer. 'Come and see this, please.'

Leading them between the patrol cars, he approached the rear of the milk-float. And drawing closer, it became evident to them that something really quite strange was going on.

They realised their eyes had not been deceiving them.

Just past the float, the surrounding air shimmered and wavered in perpetual agitation, with shifting bands of opacity. The continuation of the road could be glimpsed through it, plus the row of cottages to the right as it widened to form Lurkham's main high street.

Through watchful eyes, the chief tech could make out the unsteady figures of some of the villagers on the other side of the haze.

A group of three or four of them: crouching, kneeling beside something, just out of sight.

Approximately in the position where the milk-float's cab might be.

'Tell me,' said the Securitat officer, 'what is it that could do ... this?' And then he moved away from the concealed side of the float.

The chief tech cried out an involuntary: 'Good God ..!' and crumpled to his knees, feeling his mid-morning snack rising within him.

The remains he espied were those of a Securitat officer: a pair of navy, trousered legs and polished boots - and that was all. As though some unseen guillotine had spliced him through at the midriff in one clean and bloodless action.

Then he realised that the float itself was not of intact structure either: that same, invisible cutting implement had effectively severed its compartment area. Those crates situated by the haze's leading edge had been melted to amorphous, blue tongues of plastic.

Through there, the distorted group of

villagers were gesticulating. Signalling urgently for some outside help.

It was when the shifting bands of opacity moderated for an instant in his line of vision, did the chief technician finally glean the source of their concerns; of what it was they were surrounding.

The milkman's head and shoulders were being cradled by the distraught pair of female villagers. But the worst part of it was, that the milkie ... *still seemed alive.*

Propped up in a pinky pool of his own setting tissues, his agonised eyes were rolled permanently skywards; his mouth a yawning rictus.

'Too much!' blurted the tech suddenly, wheeling around and having to relieve himself of that troubled, mid-morning snack after all, in the shade of the truncated milk-float.

The Securitat officer gave him time to compose himself, then asked of him the question again: 'So what natural phenomenon are you and your group aware of, which can cause this level of damage to humans: which can seal off an entire village from its surrounds, knocking out all lines of communication?'

The technician's brow furrowed over his

blanched face as he struggled for any past comparisons. 'I've never seen the likes of this before,' he admitted, as one of the shifting figures on the other side drew nearer. 'It seems as a beam of thermal energy, maybe of wave-like form, transmitted from unknown origin. We really can't speculate on anything, just yet.'

They could discern the approaching figure to be that of a brawny, hirsute villager - perhaps he might be one of their farmers, or the publican, or the butcher. He was waving his arms about in exaggerated fashion, mouthing something like 'RESCUE!' - although he was probably shouting it - and indicating that, if possible, it should be undertaken by air, to circumvent the scorching barrier.

The officer gestured back to the villager, indicating that a similar plan was already afoot. 'Heli-copter ... half an hour ... away!' he shouted towards him.

'And you're certain the beam encircles the whole village?' asked the chief technician. 'With no gaps being detected anywhere?'

'Yes and no, respectively. The beam's extent was one of the first things we checked. The investigation was going well and to instruction,' he sighed, glancing to the pair of legs with their polished boots, ' ... until Lieutnant Grachev went in for a closer look.'

The technician caught a final glimpse of Brian Sparks, landlord of The Dashin' Rodent.

Through the gauzy air, the shoulders of the big man seemed to slump in disappointment and despondency, as he receded into the muzzy, middle distance.

'Then let's hope,' remarked the technician to all those who could hear, 'that the good people of this village maintain the qualities of hope and perseverance; whilst we, in their outside world, can set to work about devising them a means of escape from this most lethal of barriers.

'Gentlemen! Let us begin things ...'

AFTERNOON OF MONDAY 4 MAY 381

It was Farmer Robson who observed the development of the first earth crack. Its location was in his Northern Field, about two hundred lengths from the house where he'd been standing for the past twenty minutes.

It had been the sound of the explosion which had pulled him from the milking of his herd.

He had bolted from the murky cowshed at the booms of apparent gunfire, fearful that the farm itself was under attack.

'Watch yourself, Harald!' had cried Mrs Robson in his wake.

But it was no such attack.

Instinctively, he'd raised his arms to shield

himself from the effects of the airborne metallic flash. Instantaneously it had been, but his brain had clocked the spiralling descent of twisted rotor blades, the shearing of the helicopter's cabin and the fatal rupture of its fuel tanks.

As the wreckage plummeted behind the hazy gauze, Farmer Robson quickly guessed what the 'copter had ran into: that weird weather front, which had somehow materialised in these parts a little after sunrise.

He had watched it growing in definition at breakfast, until it had curtained the near horizons. Though his eyesight was not so keen as previously, by coffee time he thought he could see the shimmering envelope straddling further down the valley's contours and along the village's western fringe.

Never before, in his lifetime of land custody, had Farmer Robson encountered such a meteorological phenomenon. Neither had he ever witnessed a helicopter crash - aircraft, as a rule, passing over seldom here. Until now.

It hadn't taken long for the Securitat boys and the rescue services to get on the scene.

He had caught sight of their vehicles' glinting windscreens as the convoy snaked its way along the Swarbrigge Road, to join the rest in attendance there, t'other side of the shimmer screen.

He could see there was a right commotion going on, as the miniature figures of navy blue broke through the boundary hedge and commenced their charge towards the smouldering crash site, thirty or forty lengths into his southwestern cornfield.

'Oy!' he cried out, commencing his rather lumbering run down the grassy ridges and furrows of the Northern Field, over the same patch of turf where, three days earlier, young Prima and Thomas Turby had taken flight. 'Can I be helping you boys in any way?!'

He thought he might have grabbed enough of their attention - a few of the distant men appeared to be looking his way and pointing - but it was so hard to see anything substantial for long through that unnatural veil.

But Farmer Robson never made it to them.

From seeming nowhere came a deep and low rumble, which graduated to a rising, tearing crescendo.

The ground appeared to tremble for a second or two: of enough duration, anyhow, to unsettle his solid stance and to rock him back to the earth with a bump.

'What the ..?' was his response to the growing disturbance a long way over to his left shoulder.

Something was happening to his land! He could tell that much by the creaking, wrenching sound.

He forced himself up and began a tentative march to the east of the field.

At about the same time, his wife came dashing out of the cowshed in a justified state of concern about these seismic events.

'Steady!' he barked, raising his hand. 'Just watch the ground you're on!'

And, as he spoke, there was the sound of a steady ripping, as if the subterranean forces had overcome the tenacious grip of the field's binding roots, and were rendering apart the earth.

'Watch yourself!' he shouted to his distressed wife, who was by now a chasm away from him: this area of Northern Field having undergone some kind of a lateral cleavage, two lengths across and one in depth.

'Oh, what the hell is happening to this place?' yelled his wife, casting her eyes to the inscrutable trench.

Farmer Robson tapped both his chops, frantically mulling things over, as a section of his boundary hedge was displaced by the restive ground.

The fissure was enlarging - no question about that. More surface vegetation was torn asunder and cast aside. Enlarging in an approximate southeastern line, it was now cutting a swathe of damage through the village allotments.

'Get back to the house, Darlin',' he called over to his wife. 'Keep tryin' with the phone. In the meantime, I'm going to try and make my way down to Brian's and The Rodent, to warn them of this. Who'd have thought we'd be havin' a ruddy earthquake in this godforsaken region? Whatever next, I ask?'

'Oh, do be careful!' she besought him, as he strode off downfield, chuntering under his breath … and mindful to keep a discrete distance from the zone of disturbed earth.

DUSK, MONDAY 4 MAY 381

Most of the village was out and about by the time the shifting, orange disc of sun had apparently set.

With seemingly no chance of egress from Lurkham, all the good people could do was to follow the fracture's creeping progress: from its jagged bisection of Church Lane and across the High Street, just missing the cornerstones of Crichton's Bakery; to its clinical incision through the back gardens of Walford Grove and the road surface of Sweet Drive (just two doors away from where an altogether different kind of topographical redistribution was nearing its conclusion).

And then its progress faltered, some several lengths into the Southern Field of Farmer Jarvis.

Half a mile on from its rude appearance the crack stopped, not far from the edge of the heat barrier. With raised torches, the villagers observed its last twitch.

Young Dougie Sparks lowered his lantern and said: 'Well, this looks to be the extent of it.'

'I wouldn't be so sure just yet,' said his father, puffing out his cheeks. 'These things can run and run - at least they do in the documentaries.'

At this point, they noticed the flashlight of Dr Burns, swinging its way towards the fissure between the parted boundary hedge.

'Be everything alright, Doc?' bellowed the senior publican. 'Happened to find us a way out of here, or summat'?'

But instead of his issuing them a retort, Dr Burns appeared to be engrossed by something else.

Extending his hand to acknowledge the landlord, his head was craned to the fissure at an inquisitive angle.

And it was in this position that he remained, until the party of villagers had called it a day and returned to their unheated and unlit homes.

EARLY, TUESDAY 5 MAY 381

Thomas Turby and his wife were awoken by the sound of their front door being pounded by someone's heavy fist.

Mr Turby rose from his sofa chair immediately. 'What is it now?!' he remarked to his wife, somewhat theatrically.

Following a moment of careful scrutiny through the spyhole, he opened up - and was confronted by the bizarre sight of Dr Burns ... wearing some kind of a *protective suit and face mask with air filter!*

'Yes, Doctor?' he said, as the caller wasted no further time in pleasantries and simply barged past him. 'Doctor Burns! What is the cause of this impoliteness?!' he said in bruising outrage.

'Shut the door!' came the muffled response. 'Shut the frigging door, Tom - AND MAKE IT QUICK!'

Mr Turby seemed in no hurry to, gently prodding it. 'But why? What's the matter?'

Dr Burns had to slam it for him. 'Because … there's something going on in the air here!'

Mr Turby's tone changed considerably as he led his guest towards the kitchen. 'Something bad? In the air?!' He looked quite wide-eyed. 'Then tell me more over coffee.'

Dr Burns put down his briefcase. 'Are you and Jill feeling okay this morning? Nothing out of the ordinary?'

Mr Turby shook his head. 'Fine. Why should we not be so?'

Dr Burns removed his face mask. 'That's good. Because our confined atmosphere here appears rife with an unknown organism, maybe of pathogenic nature.'

'An organism?' said Mr Turby, bemused. 'Are you sure, Doctor?'

'Oh, yes,' he replied, grabbing hold of his cup. 'Last night it was when I first glimpsed it. I became aware of some kind of a steady emission from the crack that's split Lurkham in two.

'Upon closer inspection, I saw the venting to be of a particulate nature and - though the quality of light at that time was diminishing - these mysterious particles appeared to be of a reflective hue of powder blue, the way they were dancing around in my flashlight.

'Anyhow, being a man of science, I resolved to take a sample of the silent emanation. Holding my breath, I drew the sterilised capsule through their stream and navigated my way back with it to the surgery.

'Given that we've no power due to this change in our local environment, I popped the prepared sample on the tray of our surgery's battery-powered microscope.'

'And what was there? What did you glimpse?' asked Mr Turby, his forehead frowning as he downed his coffee to the dregs.

'Nothing,' said the doctor, eyeing him keenly, ' … that I haven't seen before. Well, at least nothing that hasn't been documented in the medical texts over these past hundred years.'

'Yes, so then it must be a *something* -

animal, vegetable or mineral!' commented Mr
Turby.

'Oh, it is,' he replied, pushing his empty cup
beside his host's. 'Something akin to those
organisms classified as belonging to Class
Thallophyta.'

'And who in the hell are those?!' exclaimed
an impatient Mr Turby. 'Do kindly put me out of my
ignorant misery and cease talking in riddles.'

'As I was about to say … the shape of those
spores in the microscope's field of view gave me a
clue as to their probable identity.

'The sight of those cylindrical, mature spores
with the serrated ridges twisting down their length,
took me back to my days at medical school: back
specifically, I think, to the period when my
contemporaries and I were introduced to the life
cycles of those plants without need of either leaves,
stems or roots. The ones which reproduce by way of
spores: namely the algae, the lichens, the fungi.

'I recognised them as belonging to … the
multifarious family of moulds.'

'Is that so?' said Mr Turby. 'And pray tell
what's so bad about a mould? Seems commonplace
enough.'

'Yes, I'm aware of that!' snapped the doctor. 'But it's the sheer concentration of these buggers - roughly a million spores per square inch by my estimates - which will pose the biggest threat to public health.

'I cannot explain their appearance here, nor justify their abnormal density, but I *do* know that human populations have never before had to contend with such a level of fungal infestation.

'We are entering something new here. And I would recommend that both you and Jill stay indoors until further notice - as I shall be advising to all those who will listen. This could be serious.'

'I see,' said Mr Turby, slowly wringing his hands. 'Serious situation.'

Both men were too deep in their thoughts to notice the slight movement of hallway carpet, just beyond the kitchen. Its surface rose a fraction over a small area, before the protuberance stealthily subsided.

'Are we the first you have come to warn, Doctor?' asked Mr Turby, standing now at the window to see for himself the curious milkiness of the morning air.

'Indeed so. I tried to shout the same advice

across the fissure to Mr Rogers - but it was clear he was distracted by something else - perhaps on the search for his daughter, who I didn't see there.'

'Oh?' Mr Turby's ears pricked up slightly.

'Maybe she had given them the runaround again or something.'

'That so?' said Mr Turby, maintaining his poker face. 'The wayward filly.'

Not long after, the doctor realigned his face mask. 'Well, I really should be on my way, my friend,' he said, gathering up his briefcase containing today's samples. 'And please remember to keep that door shut once I've gone - or you'll be breathing in more than just air!'

Mr Turby nodded as Dr Burns made his swift egress. 'Thank you for coming along.'

Already contemplating whether or not to disregard the good doctor's advice and to conduct his own, preliminary search for his sorely missed Prima, he was unaware of the glint of a crafty eye, looking up at him through the newly created hole in that same area of hallway carpet.

With an eventual sigh, he elected to soon return upstairs to the wife and to mull over those reported events. Besides, it was now time for her bedside cuppa.

He began filling up the kettle and set to work ... as that watchful eye slipped from sight.

The Shocker formerly known as Pelius slipped down from the sweaty back of Scolex, almost onto the earthen pile with its shards of jagged floorboard - nearly causing herself a nasty injury.

'Careful, careful!' chided Doobie, easing her to the squelchy earth floor. 'You've just healed up - don't ruin so soon my surgical artistry!' And he gave her a warning slap below the curve of her chest swelling, then demanded: 'Now tell us in detail what you saw.'

'Our man - Neighbourhood Snoop Man,' she said. 'He's definitely up there - but I didn't see our Prima with him.'

At that very moment they could hear his footsteps directly overhead, on his way to mounting the stairs.

When all relevant sounds had receded, did Doobie order Frenchie to commence the final tearing of the Turby's hallway carpet: to ruthlessly hack at it with his flick-knife - and to enjoy it.

'I want to congratulate you all,' said Doobie in low, confidential tone, 'for the considerable amount of work and labour hours you have expended in getting us to this position. Three days and four nights on ... and here we are! Now let us meet the old war criminal who has abducted the living, breathing property that is rightfully ours.'

And with that said, he fisted right through the jagged square of carpet, grabbing hold of the floorboard surrounds, and pushed himself onwards and upwards.

When it was his turn to exit the passage, however, Scolex appeared to lose his footing and started to slip back inside with a groan.

Doobie just about held on to him, slapping his cheeks repeatedly until he came to.

'Comrade, what troubles you? Is this just chronic fatigue through too many late nights - or a more concerning lack of match fitness?'

'I ... I'm alright, Chief,' he replied, quite

breathlessly. 'Guess I've been feelin' somewhat lightheaded since we began this excavations mission. I'll prob'ly be alright when I get some natural sun on me, an' some real fresh air in me system.'

'Let us hope so.' But Doobie was still eyeing him sceptically. 'Standards cannot slip at this critical phase. In addition, remember that Shockers Republic is under no obligation whatsoever to carry passengers.'

'Yus,' puffed Scolex, trying to stand up again. 'I always remember that.'

Frenchie was the first of them to assemble at the foot of the stairs, in rapt concentration: attempting to elicit the lightly conversational voices of Snoop Man and his missus in the master bedroom.

When all were in operational position, Doobie motioned for their stealthy advance to begin.

MORNING OF TUESDAY 5 MAY 381

Farmer Robson had risen early, following a fitful night of sleep. Now he was on his way back from an hour's solitary milking in the cowshed, after Mrs R had cried off tired.

Unusual, but it hadn't surprised him greatly. He had the impression she'd spent the night tossing and turning in her sleep also.

Opening the kitchen door, he was accosted straightaway by the sound of the breakfast tray clattering over the floor tiles. He saw his wife there, face down, her head appearing to twitch.

'Petal?' he enquired, dashing over to her amongst the scattered sausages and broken eggs of their ruined brekkie. 'You're not sickening for something, are ye?'

He turned her head, wincing upon noticing
just how ashen had grown her complexion - and by
the way her nostril seemed to drip a steady stream
of greyish fluid. Her eyes remained half closed and
her head was still sporadically twitching.

'Petal, are you hearing me alright? You wish
for me to fetch Doc Burnsie?'

His wife's sole response was to allow a
fluid-filled bubble to build in that left nostril, which
promptly popped all over his hand.

Farmer Robson raised himself up, both his
knee joints clicking in the process. 'Right, that's
quite enough for me,' he muttered, reaching for his
jacket. 'The good Doc Burnsie it shall be.'

He propped up his wife's head using one of
the cushions from the living room couch, noting the
peculiar, mushy quality at the back of her neck. He
told himself it must be a case of her increased
perspiration due to her running a temperature, as he
dabbed dry her nose.

That was when, with her eyes still closed,
Mrs Robson spoke thickly: 'Hold me, Harald, for
just a little longer.' There was a seductive quality
about it, which was quite unexpected.

At the pull of her request, he did such and

cradled her damp neck again.

He detected the first whiff of something not too pleasant. Sniffing clear his nasal cavities, Farmer Robson attempted to catch another trace of the odour.

There! It hit him once more - a smell laden with moisture: as the cloying earth; like dampened bread when left to fester. Wafting, apparently, from his wife's slightly parted lips.

He pulled back, faintly nauseated; faintly troubled that he seemed unable to withdraw his hand from the back of her head. All felt hot and sticky round there.

Farmer Robson was just attempting, for the second time, to wrest free his glued-up appendage ... when Mrs Robson's eyes flicked open, blazing at him with intensity.

Her lips appeared fuller, infused somehow with rose-pink vivacity, as she whispered: 'Just one last kiss for us, Harald. Make it one to remember.' Her irises looked to be dancing brightly.

It seemed at first that Harald might oblige her.

Then he caught a blast of that fetid breath again - and remembered about the necessity of fetching Dr Burns.

If only he could get this damn paw free of her neck! It just wasn't right: all this tackiness; this adhesion!

Not that he had any say in the events which quickly followed.

Grabbing hold of him with a strength that belied her supposed infirmity, Mrs Robson pulled him onto her; twisting his trapped arm ... which he didn't seem to be feeling any more.

'What in God's name do you think you ar-'

His wide-eyed cry of exasperation was snuffed out by a combination of her foul exhalations and by the ferocity of her bear hug, which pulled his mouth on to hers. His eyes remained wide as he kicked with his legs to become free. But trapped he was, in her most passionate of embraces.

Gamely trying to avoid making oral contact with his wife's cold, liquid tongue, Farmer Robson's fevered mind began to consider the word Invasion.

Yes! He felt as though he was being invaded by her.

This intensity of hers: from where - or from whom - had she mastered these lingual skills so suddenly? His 'usual' Mrs R would have baulked immediately at the idea of such erotic tongue insertion / interaction; declaring it as being way too lewd and too messy for them to be indulging in.

Then her tongue somehow flicked its way past his gritted teeth, squirming along to his pharynx with its chilling undulations: and threatening to continue deeper down his gullet.

Still she held him - though how tightly, he was no longer sure. Things seemed to be changing in relation to how he was receiving his sensory information.

Though he was trying his darnedest to break free from this constrictive grip, he felt he was steadily losing the ability to know whether his efforts were working. The feeling in his extremities was deserting him by the second.

And another thing became apparent to him as her tongue slipped inexorably down his anterior gut: he sensed a growing layer of moistness forming across his chest and abdomen; as though her copious secretions had bridged his clothing barriers - and were adhering him to her.

With dawning horror, Farmer Robson watched his wife's facial features recede into a rippling, grey backdrop; all the while her rapacious tongue lapping him internally.

He started to feel himself sinking into her, in thorough absorption. He could feel his skin commencing to ripple and buckle, too - but still there was no associated pain, thank goodness.

No getting out of it, he knew this much. Losing his identity, was he. Independence dwindling. Yet he could live with such. After all ... he was uniting with his wife - not a bad fate to befall anyone, all things considered.

Upon the tiled floor, their co-joined shape slowly completed its process of coalescence; the smooth sphere of grey matrix undergoing its trembly pulsations.

Following a further, short period of internal and external acclimatisation, the organism initiated its roll ... in amoebic fashion towards the outside door.

Extending pseudopodia to assess its next options, the sphere was able to flatten itself sufficiently for its constituent material to simply ooze through the gap between door and floor.

Fattening itself once more on the porch step, the fungal fiend could now follow its instincts without bounds.

It started rolling - faster now - towards the barn, from where it had already detected some faunal traces via its rudimentary receptors.

For an urge, of something akin to hunger, was forming within.

AFTERNOON OF TUESDAY 5 MAY 381

Thomas Turby crashed thrice his fist upon the front door. 'Quickly, Jill, open up!' he puffed through his improvised face mask. 'Open up, it's me!'

When his wife obliged, he pushed past her in much the same way as had Dr Burns, around seven and a half hours earlier.

'Thank God for that!' he said, taking a jumpy look behind him before slamming the door. 'You would *not* credit the time I've just had!'

Jill shuffled over to him in her bare feet. 'And neither would you,' she sobbed. 'With me.'

Pulling off his mask to get a better look at things, Mr Turby saw for the first time the bruising on her face and the bloodstains down her nightshirt. Her hair was all over the place: most unkempt, as though she'd *pulled herself through a hedge backwards*. She was starting to whimper.

'What the hell have you gone and done now?!' he said, cradling her gently, whilst being careful not to get any of the blood on him. 'Tell me what's happened during my absence.'

He suspected it could be upsetting to hear, but he had to know, whatever the content. Surely it couldn't be any more shocking to process than any of the outdoors stuff ...

And in halting sobs, his dutiful wife began to relate to him the ghastly details of her unsolicited visitation.

She supposed that the four of them had been waiting for her in the bedroom all along.

Waiting, that is, until her husband could no longer contain his secret yearning, and had set out, swathed in his old trench coat; his face mask a series of dampened cloths.

His pretext had seemed plausible enough - about assisting the good doctor in notifying the rest of the village about the threat to public health.

When he had slipped out, and just as Jill

Turby was replacing her empty teacup in its saucer, did the intruders charge the room.

It was the quartet! The Quartet of Evil ... about which her husband knew well: their leader, the spiky blond skinhead with the commanding stare; the fat and flabby pale one; the tall, swarthier one with the film star's looks; and the other, of apparently indeterminate sex - in short PVC skirt, with a pair of young girl's swellings poking from its chest.

They had quickly surrounded her, the uncouth leader demanding to know where someone called 'Our Prima' had been secreted by Thomas and herself. He started shaking her to obtain a response, while the others instinctively gripped her wrists and ankles. 'You tell us of her location,' he had yammered. 'And we're not going anywhere until you do!'

And despite Jill's protestations of genuine ignorance in all this, the foul gang had next stripped her of the silk nightshirt and had proceeded to wreak upon her their inimical frustrations.

All dignity had been stripped asunder, whilst turns were taken to cruelly humble and humiliate the wife of Mr Turby, upon the very sheets she had been enjoying her slumber an hour before.

In the traumatic scenario, she'd had a fleeting impression that it was only the fat and flabby one who had not somehow invaded her. She sensed his harbouring an unwillingness to - perhaps due to his carrying of an undisclosed injury or something.

'So *this* ... is what you *get* ... for being *married* ... to the most ... *irksome bastard* ... of Lurk'em,' panted the lead skinhead as he completed his procedure. 'Evidently he has gone to secrete our beloved Prima girl to a safer place.'

He had stared into her eyes, then contemptuously stated: 'You do know already that your Neighbourhood Snoop Man hubby holds Prima much higher above you in his heart ..?'

And with that the violators were off her back and gone: whooping down the stairs, elbowing over deliberately her prized ornaments as they'd bounded past.

'That, my Dear ..,' she moaned in her husband's dampened chest, 'is what happened here while you have been away.' She was crying again.

Mr Turby hugged her for a while longer. He was trying to remain steady and constant for her, to be protective ... but his arms were beginning to tremble with somatic rage.

The Evil Ones - here in this house! Looking for him and looking for 'Prima', as they termed her! And now poor Jill had been caught in the crossfire - in her right place but at quite the wrong time.

'I'm sorry, Dearest,' he whispered, placing a passing kiss above her bruised brow. 'How dare they have done this to you. If there was any way I could get through to Securitat, then rest assured I wou-'

His stopped ... because his eyes had just discovered the ripped flap of hallway carpet and the earth clumps lying around it.

He followed his gaze up the first risers, to the muddy foot signatures planted upon them.

Slowly shaking his head, Mr Turby broke away from his overly clingy partner and walked over to the offending area. 'Why ... the devious little buggers ..!'

He lifted up the flap and saw the yawning darkness through his missing floorboards. 'Why ... the burrowing little buggers! How dare they ..?!'

He was in half a mind to grab his sawn-off shotgun and venture down the hole right that moment, to bring all matters to their just conclusion - to wherever that scourge had dug on to. But there were more pertinent things in his life right now: like Jill's welfare and the latest, alarming findings he had to impart to her concerning the state of village life. She might still be sobbing after hearing all of that ...

'Now settle down, Dear,' he said as kindly as possible, escorting her over to the sofa. 'Allow me to fetch your dressing gown and make you a nice, afternoon cup of tea. You may think *you've* been through the wars lately. Now it's time for me to tell you about *my* day.'

Jill looked up, nonplussed, through her blotchy face.

In the kitchen, Mr Turby was unsurprised to find that their supplies of even the most basic items were now running low. Two remaining teabags - and the sugar was down to a matter of teaspoonfuls. Until the outside world could penetrate the blasted heat barrier, there was no way for such supplies to reach them.

And what would be the point? he asked himself. How many Lurkhamites are still living, judging by what I've seen out there? And who would be around to reliably distribute those imports, assuming they got through?

He'd found not a trace of Mrs Perks at her

newsagents, neither Frank the fruiterer, nor Jumbo Jim at Crichton's Bakery; and neither Brian Sparks nor son Dougie on t'other side of the dividing chasm at The Rodent. It was all very mind disturbing. Or had they made it and somehow got out ..?

Unless ... there exists another way for the outside world to contact us, he pondered, slamming his hand on the kitchen shelf as he stirred the cuppas. Like ... underground? Of course!

Clearly the Quartet of Evil had already arrived at such an option. It probably hadn't taken them long to cotton on to things, what with their undoubted, rich experience in the dark arts of self-preservation.

Mr Turby mused on the notion as he nipped upstairs, stepping over the encrusted carpets and into their tainted bedroom to fetch Jill's dressing gown.

He stopped off briefly in the bathroom, to extract a couple of sedative tablets from the cabinet with which to spike her tea.

Before sitting down to impart her his news, he checked on the outside world: peeping through the curtains slit - looking for sightings of any further horror.

Thankfully, there was nothing evident at this time.

Sure, the sky still had its bruised, purplish tinge where the heat barrier sat; yet the houses opposite remained upright and his garden gate remained unopened, just the way he'd left it.

Too quiet out there though, he told himself, taking his first sip. Not a sign of human activity. Not right at all. It must be … Their … siesta time, he thought with a shudder. That might be the only thing keeping Them off the streets.

He turned to Jill, switched on a smile and actually sat down beside her.

She was not looking up from her cuppa, as though in traumatised shock. But she appeared sufficiently receptive to his preliminary openings of chat, so he began to tell her about the day; his last day.

'As you may remember, Jill, I set out from here around a quarter of an hour after Doctor Burns had left. I hope you're able to recall that the gist of his unscheduled visit was that, as a concerned scientist, he was believing the villagers to be in toxic peril from a vastly abnormal concentration of fungal spores he'd been sampling from our confined air.

'Hence, it was my duty as Chairman of the LRA to pace the pavements and to ring the doorbells - to at least inform all about this supposed threat. Well, that was the theory …

'I started down our side of Sweet Drive. Dashing next door, I received a successful answer from both Jo and Dave, and then from Edie and Walter. All seemed fine. I told them to stay indoors till further notice, and to keep their windows fastened shut.

'By the way, you ought to have seen just how close is the edge of that fissure to Joanna and David's living room wall - shocking! About a foot of garden remains before the ground opens up. The bloody thing's made complete rubble of their side garage! I wouldn't want to be in their position, that's for sure.

'Whilst I was at it, I peered into the crack in the tarmac of Sweet Drive, to see if I could locate for myself any of the particles emanating from its interior, as had apparently witnessed the good doctor. But there were none detected.

'All I did observe was this kind of glassy blue deposit lining its length, as though something had solidified or crystallised to a mineral ultramarine. Yet I had no intention of lowering myself down there for a closer look - none at all!

For I had an important errand to carry out, given that telecommunications no longer function here.

'Along Sweet Drive I continued. The only house from which I received no answer was Deidre and Doug's at Eleven. Weird that they should be gone like that. Two weeks on, with not a sight of them. If I'd had more time at my disposal, I would have tried for them round the back.

'Just crossing the bridge into The Chase I was, when I saw something very odd: a kind of liquid, which was flowing onto the road surface from one of the semi-detached houses to the right.

'And as I approached this fluid, I saw that a definite hand was flailing from within it.

'Prostrate, with head twisted away from me, the man-shape looked to be dripping wet: saturated it was from tip to toe.

"Hello there,' I ventured, rather inanely to the mystery villager within. 'Is everything going alright with you?'

'The man in the semi-solid state tried rotating his head to me, attempting to prop himself up on his melting elbows. Seeing that he didn't look quite the ticket, I stepped around to spare him all the effort.

'Well, the sight which greeted me was appalling: the man's contorted face was seemingly buried within a thick mucoid layer, like he was drowning in there. His hands - and his limbs in general - appeared smaller than they should have been. As they clutched at the loose chippings on the road, I noticed their marked loss in definition and function.

"Hello?! Can you hear me okay in there?' I enquired loudly, looking round for something with which to begin scraping some air holes through his copious secretion.

'Maybe this was the awful symptom, I told myself, of whatever it was the good doctor had proposed. Nevertheless, in my opinion this chap was still alive and was still worth saving.

'From the gutter I obtained part of a tree branch. I was just about to urge the poor fellow to hold still, and to put his trust in me to fashion him some blowholes - when there was a piercing, war-like shriek in my left ear ... and I was sent tumbling sideways.

'Bowled over to the road surface with a bump, was I.

'Quickly adjusting my slipped face cloths and finding my bearings once more, I saw the violent dislike - hatred, even - in the eyes of a flame-haired woman who was standing over me.

'Presumably this was his wife or girlfriend or whatever - she was not a local, anyhow.

'She was pointing a shaking finger at me, hoarsely whispering: "We don't need any help. No outside help's needed!'

'In reasonable tone, I begged to differ with her. "Oh, but I think he does, madam, by the looks of him. He's dying on his feet - or what's left of them. We need to open up his airways and get some oxygen flowing through there. *Oxygen?! ... In?!* Surely it's obvious!'

"NO!' she shouted, with a quick look back to the opened doorway of their shabby semi. "Bri's doing fine,' she said, waving her finger at me again. "He's on the mend - on the proper course - an' needs no outside interference from YOU!'

"On the *proper course* to where, exactly?' I said, picking myself up and dusting myself down.

'I had the bit between my teeth and wasn't going to go lightly on this. I might have met her hubby - Brian Hooper (I presume it was?) - just the once during a previous Summer Fete, but I was *not* prepared to leave him in this sorry state in the middle of the road. "On the proper course to where, madam - can you enlighten me?' I hectored.

'And in the silence, as I backed up to her garden wall, I received my biggest shock of the day ... up until then.

'For there, behind Hooper's shoulder-high privet hedge, reared up an unfolding shape. Clad in black, the insectile figure kept on growing, onward and upward.

'It was the sheer height of the stick-like apparition which caused me to ejaculate some colourful expletives, and to take a couple of involuntary steps back into the road.

'Two and a half usual lengths in height, the thing was technically a giant. Just why it was lurking behind Hooper's and this rude bitch's hedge was a total mystery. And how well I could feel its emanation of oppressive evil - the air around me reeked of it.

'The figure was motionless: its strangely domed head tilted my way at a peculiar angle; its beady eyes all silvery and reflective as they stared at / through me from their dark recesses. Its thin, rangy arms remained as static extensions from its pole of a trunk.

'While the flame-haired woman stepped slowly backwards up her garden path - dragging the fluid remnants of her beloved Mr Hooper with her - I found myself almost transfixed to the spot; held there amidst a bewildering cocktail of emotions.

'Determined I was, to stand my ground in the face of this surreal intrusion a hedge width away from me. And determined also to discover what on earth was to come next. I, as sure as hell, wasn't going to run away.

'Well, three minutes of mutual observation must have elapsed before the first communication occurred. And even I got a shock from it.

'That domed head tilted slightly towards the normal and the gaunt thing's papery lips parted just a fraction. I seemed to hear its words slightly before those lips articulated them, as though watching a poorly-dubbed screenplay.

"You may join us now or join us later - the choice is yours,' it said. But … it wasn't *its* voice - no! Incredibly, it was the *voice of the flame-haired loon*, transmitting somehow through its parchment slit. "Move away from the threshold of this homestead,' it told me, 'and await your turn. Await your irreversible process.'

'I was flummoxed. I tried to formulate an

appropriate response to its nonsense. "Now what process might that be, hmmm? Do kindly elaborate.'

'But the enigmatical figure replied nought, sidling stealthily towards the start of the hedge with its shining eyes always fixed on me. The crazed woman was back at Hooper's front door, staring at me too as she wiped dry her hands on a floral teacloth.

'Clearly, the atmosphere was very wrong here. I sensed the insectile thing to be attempting an imminent entrapment of me; or at least to inflict some kind of a grievous assault on my person.

'So I began to back off, stepping back on the road (avoiding, as best I could, the liquid effusion deposited earlier by the messy Mr Hooper). At all times, I kept my eyes trained upon the lanky freak, observing its slinking progress round the privet's edge to the pavement.

'Its lip slit was taut in a perpetual smirk. "Your choice is to run,' it called, in the same, badly-dubbed woman's voice. And it said some more. "Soon we shall assemble for you. Then you will show us better your ... gratitude ...'

'Well! I'd had my fill of that ... guff,' continued Mr Turby, encouraged to find that Jill now appeared to be listening fully to his most shocking of accounts: nodding from time to time, as she swigged the last mouthfuls of her tepid tea.

'The sound of that god-awful, dislocated voice spooked me, and I was off up the street: up The Chase at a gallop towards the High Street, to put as much distance as I could from the stick-shaped monstrosity and its utterances. I had wasted enough time with that triad of weirdness.

'Maybe, I told myself, I would find the remainder of normal villagers in the High Street and beyond.

'But, as you may have already guessed, that was not to be the case.

'Up the High Street I went, banging hard on all the closed shop fronts, drumming up a merry hell - but to no avail.

'Passing Crichton's Bakery, the thought struck me that I might have started the day in anomalous mood and been factually incorrect in assuming it was a sleepy, public holiday or something ... but my mind countered that this was definitely a Tuesday: one which should have been a run-of-the-mill, common or garden Tuesday.

'Buoyed by the thought of a welcome pint at The Dashin' Rodent - if anyone was at home - I negotiated my way across the valley sides of the High Street fissure. I took it nice and gentle down the earthen drop of five or so feet. After all, I didn't want to find myself getting too intimate with that glassy blue deposit now, did I?

'Hauling myself up the final shard of tarmac, the unnatural silence around me was punctured by a high, resonating scream. I almost lost my footing at the distraction and teetered backwards.

'Shrill and jarring, the continuous sound coursed through me. I tried excluding it by pressing both fingers to my ears - but there was no reduction in its intensity. There appeared to me an irrational suggestion that it was emanating through the tarmac below.

'On I strode, sincerely hoping that a second fissure wasn't about to break surface and swallow up the longest serving - and most successful - Chairman of the LRA.

'Still the sound persisted: louder still whenever I half turned my head. So ... I turned around ... and received yet another huge shock to my system.

'For there, slowly approaching me at the crossroads area was that thin, black-clad entity: slowly drawing nearer to me with each shuffle; both its hands clasped around its mouth slit in amplifying mode - confirming it to be the instigator of that appalling sound.

'And with my eyes squinting as best they could through the shimmering haze and the spliced road surface, I could discern there to be others accompanying it. Other shapes ... of like nothing I had seen before ...'

Mr Turby checked his attentive, if glassy-eyed, wife at the other end of the sofa, took a deep breath and continued with his extraordinary account.

'Other shapes, yes, as I was saying. But not one being remotely humanoid. No. For, on either flank of the skin and bone thing, were what appeared to be a number of spherical, grey blobs. To about one third of its abnormally high stature they were - though to shoulder length with you and I - they trundled beside it in steady revolutions.

'The weirdo had ceased its baffling scream and, would you believe, this resulted in the arrival of another detachment of those jelly spheres: rolling in from the direction of Church Lane.

'Merging into the right flank with fluid smoothness, they helped swell their number to around a score or more.

'Then I saw the multitude beyond them - back as far, perhaps, as Frank's deathly quiet greengrocery. It was like an army out there; wending its fluid way towards me and the High Street fissure. Indeed, straining my ear to them, I could hear the concerted, tarmac licks of their squelchy leading edges as the distance closed.

'Unsurprisingly I resumed my quickstep, not far now from the saloon doors of The Dashin' Rodent. With lady luck and a pair of tightly crossed fingers, might I find Brian and young Dougie inside? Strongly barricaded with beams and bar stools, with gutfuls of the most fortifying ale having sustained them, perhaps they would be overjoyed to see me: eager to hear my telling contributions about how to obviate our collective entrapment ...

'But that is not what happened.

'I didn't like the look of things as soon as I'd raised the letter flap.

'Bottles smashed and bar stools overturned. And from the bar top dripped something viscous onto the drenched area of carpet.

"Brian! Dougie!' I hissed, with the sound of those squelchy licks growing louder in my ear. "Do open up if you're in there!'

'No response from within. I knew I had to leave it at that. The thin creature and its rolling multitude had bridged the earth crack, and were advancing past Angela Perks' closed up newsagents.

'From this disturbing proximity, I could even make out that taut, fixed smile of the domed head bastard.

'Round the corner of Wilbur Avenue I scarpered, getting quite warm as you can imagine, in my face mask and trenchcoat.

'Halfway down, I eased off the pace. Looked back … and, sure enough, there was the stick-like thing, quick marching round the corner hedge with its glutinous pals beside it. Its smile was widening, I could see that much.

'And here we are, bang up to date. I scarpered back without encountering any more varieties of life form, thanks be to God.

'Oh, Jill!' he said, briefly focusing on her again. 'What a most terrible time we are having: those horrors lurking outside; and inside, these muddy footprints and shocking accounts of rape and of buggerphuck from within the very walls of our home, our *sanctuary*.'

He was peeping from the side of the curtains

again, waiting for visible signs of strangeness.

Detecting none so far, he turned to her and said: 'Come! You must rest upstairs in the spare room. Doubtless you are suffering from delayed shock and trauma. I'll rustle you up some supper for later.'

Then he realised about the absence of gas supply. Gone it had, at the same time as the electrics. Taking her limp arm all the same, he escorted her up the stairs, glancing once more at the damaged hallway carpet.

Some way beyond his threshold of hearing progressed the steady drip of liquid in the fireplace's darkest recess.

Alone again, Mr Turby returned to the sofa; his forehead a route map of frowns as he tried to mull over the reason - or reasons - for the current, disastrous path of his Appeal.

To cause all of this … madness and mayhem … something big must have gone awry.

No, he told himself, every last procedure had been executed according to the word, to the instruction. Every last phucking procedure. Unless … He began to rasp his chin. Ahhh, possibly.

Unless his Prima's foetal tissue had been …

too far gone at the time of his Submission? Certainly, that situation would mean the two polar lengths of the Cross would come to represent ... death.

Yes, possibly this was the case. For the Organic Cross could only, of course, be enabled by the successful alignment of dying tissue with that of dead - the dead component here being the strands of his hair. O, shimmm! Who knew just *what* might happen if those wretched foetal cells were not alive at the critical time? The Book Of Remedeyeth made no mention of such outcome.

Perhaps it did not dare to.

The frazzled mind of Thomas Turby was just displacing itself to a more pleasant scenario: in the shape of the dead foetus' mother, the errant Prima ... when a feeling of creeping cold passed up his right trouser leg.

Just recounting those extraordinary events he was, which culminated in her unwilling bondage in that very room where his Jill was sleeping off her woes, as the frigid arm of fluid clamped around his shin. Further tendrils snaked higher past his knee.

He cried out at the sight of the jelly trail, leading from the hearth to the nearby carpet.

Trying to stand up and repel the tentacular thing from his leg, he found that he could not: too tightly was it gripping the skin.

He attempted instead to dislodge the palpal protuberances from around his waist, but was again horrified to discover how deeply they were embedded in him - he could only see their shiny, top surfaces. Yet no pain he felt: anaesthetised, it seemed, from any such sensation by its unnaturally low temperature.

'Geroff! Geroff of me!' he managed, flapping his still functioning arms at the growth as it continued its encirclement of his chest area. 'Leave off of me, you jelly fiend!' he wheezed. 'Realise that I am Chairman of the Lurkham Residents Association - and you will bog off from my person, forthwithal!'

But the organism ignored all dissent or disapproval; simply engulfing half of his face with its next pulsation.

The protests continued but were effectively smothered.

His part of the sofa was growing awash with a new kind of being. A being whose previous, humanoid outline was rounding to that of a glutinous sphere.

Once its scattered puddles had been reabsorbed and restored to its greater mass, did the quivering lump - which now constituted the elementary structures of Thomas Turby plus several of his erstwhile, village contemporaries - roll off the sodden furniture in the direction of the hallway, towards the foot of the stairs.

For the scent of a sleeping, troubled human was enticing it that way.

EVENING OF TUESDAY 5 MAY 381

It was the Reverend Okumbwe who at last broke the intense silence in the west transept of St. Bertrand's.

Unclasping his hands from in front of his mouth, he gathered up the spilt crumbs of fruit cake from the table and said to his distraught guest: 'Young lady, I can honestly say I am unable to explain these happ'nings in the context of the Good Lord and Its living and loving world of creation.

'Not having witnessed the like of such before, the sole thing I *can* offer to you with any confidence is that the natural incidence of such things happ'ning here is extremely unlikely: more that they have been set in motion by a process of ... unnaturalness. They be surely not the handiwork of our Good Lord.'

Prima regarded him for a moment longer through strained eyes, contemplated his words, then stared through her half-drained cup of tea. She was looking despondent again, her lower lip quivering.

'I know I'll never see them again. I just know it ...'

'Now let us pray,' whispered quickly Reverend Okumbwe, taking her hand. 'Let us pray for the grace of our Good Lord, so that all our circumstances be restored to their natural path.

'Let us pray that you will successfully locate your parents and grandma again; and that I shall be returned my entire flock unharmed; their village to be unscathed; their land to be unsullied.

'In addition, I would also wish for the safe return of my missing organist. I have to admit I quite miss not hearing his overblown hymn recitals now.'

The reverend looked a little wistful before concluding his prayer.

When all was said and done, he whispered: 'I'll cook you supper again, if you like - providing, of course, we still have enough gas in the canisters.'

'Thank you, Reverend,' she replied somewhat awkwardly. 'I really ought to be helping out more.'

'No, no!' he smiled as he lit the table candles. 'Your task is to simply repose here and to try to recover your spirits.'

Then he walked towards the door at the altar's side, where the living quarters were situated. He was starting to whistle a hymn; beginning to enjoy the company of the girl known as Prima - as everyone seemed to.

It was at the moment of the reverend's disappearance, did sound the short, sharp tapping on the stained glass window behind her.

Prima started in her chair, her eyes growing large as she whirled around.

The unmistakable face of her grandmother was squinting in!

'Gran!' cried out Prima. 'Where on earth have you been?' she called, proceeding to unfasten that same, stained glass window.

'No, my dear,' said Gran a tad uncertainly. 'I'm feeling too old and infirm to ever get in that way. Would it not be easier to unbolt the main doors for me?'

She was speaking in that strange, detached way, as though her denture might have come unstuck, resulting in the over-enunciation of her words.

Prima took stock of the situation for a moment: equally aware of Reverend Okumbwe's stipulation that the main doors were to remain stoutly bolted At All Times.

But Gran was calling to her again.

'I'm hurting,' her lips now seemed to be mouthing.

A flow of compassion overran her granddaughter, causing her to dash along the nearest pew and down the nave to the great oak doors.

Reverend Okumbwe had just got the supper going and was exiting the side door, preparing to converse a little more with the girl on some lighter themes - when he caught sight of her about to slip the highest bolt.

'Oh, no!' he cried, dashing forwards in his flapping cassock. 'Please refrain from that action, as things aren't yet well enough in the outside world!'

But by then, Prima had the latch in her hand and was raising it.

For Gran's latest account of things simply *had* to be heard by her. Only *she* might know as to the fates of Mum and Dad. This morning, they and Prima had set out separately on different routes to try and locate Gran! And now *she* was here ... so where on earth had *they* got to?!

'Gran! Come in!' she called, filling with emotions as she pulled open the door, drawing in the milky air.

No one there for her to greet, though.

Gingerly she stepped out, with Reverend Okumbwe gripping her by the waist and urging caution and vigilance as, together, they breathed in the haze.

The situation of apparent calm was changed, however, once she stepped over the threshold of tiled porch on to the gravel path.

Torn suddenly from the reverend's grip, Prima was shunted around the side by limbs of considerable power.

Thin, sinewy appendages manipulated her collapse into swathes of velvety black; cushioning her screams to muffled silence.

Simultaneously, the gelatinous shape - which had barely been able to contain its weeping form upon the sloping porch gable - found its opportune moment to drip down on the head of the curly-haired human and to secure all his vital breathing holes.

It was from the shadow of the proximal yew tree that Prima was forced to endure the sight of Reverend Okumbwe's dwindling, human moments.

Held fast in the ratchet grip of the skeletal, stick-like entity, the poor girl was made to witness his transition from dying life form to one anew.

On his knees, the preacher manfully tried to extract the glutinous mass from his airways - yet the adhesion continued to enjoy its tenacious absorption of his face.

His waning sensation was the detection of familiar chemicals within the matrix. Discerned by him already was the organist's trace: of dusty cassock with a degree of unwashed mustiness and imbued perspiration from all those years of chord-crunching. He knew it well that the organist was all about him, adulterating his cells and his tissues; turning all things homogenous ... and that fact was somehow comforting for him.

And just before the bony entity carried off Prima, swaddled tightly as a roll of carpet, did she espy from the corner of her eyes a translucent image of Gran: sliding to the ground outside the window at which she'd first appeared.

Prima could only whimper as Gran next transmuted to a squishy sphere and started to trundle along the gravel path, leaving a slime trail in its wake.

There, it came to the quivering mass of ex-Reverend Okumbwe and drew to a stop, as though welcoming the latest transformation to its likeness.

Prima was bundled away in the hideous dark, not sorry to miss it.

WEDNESDAY 6 MAY 381

'So, what's the next, super idea to get her here with us?' said Frenchie, having just wrenched off the last cupboard door from its hinges, leaving the kitchen of the Charming Couple's looking decidedly bare and minimalist.

The door was tossed over to Doobie, who positioned it on the lino floor against the other wooden and chipboard materials so that its midpoint was clear. Then he leapt up and proceeded to snap it in two.

Its splintering sound caused Scolex to stir again on the sofa, where he'd lain since being excused from such duty of destruction on the grounds of his having a 'thumpin' 'eadache'.

At length, Doobie conceded eye contact to

the primary kitchen wrecker and smiled: 'What was it you were saying?'

Frenchie lowered the hammer. 'I said, how to get our Prima back here so we can all start to seduce her and get squirming?'

'Isn't it clear?' sneered Doobie. 'We try, try and try some more! But only, comrade, when you will have successfully collected enough stuff for our winter fuel stockpile; and when Pelia will have finished constructing our face masks from her spare pairs of tights. And also when this weird style of weather will decide to improve itself.'

He lurched towards the kitchen window, rasped his chin and said: 'I still don't like the look of it. Hell, even this mist don't look right. If you're as observant as me, you can see particles in the mix. See? Particles what 'ave a life of their own and what zing around … bouncing off things and each other, like they're seriously energised. Boy, just look at 'em go!' And he stood there, transfixed by the balletic, molecular display, while his empty stomach rumbled.

'Yes, that reminds me,' he said, turning to the others. 'Where's our next square meal arising from? Any thoughts?'

'Whenever we next find a larder from where

we can replenish,' countered Frenchie, smiling.

'So ... what are you waiting for, Smartypants? Get searching! Get retrieving!'

Frenchie turned the hammer around in his hands as the first trickles of ... something ... welled up from the half-covered hole in the kitchen floor. 'Oh, sure I will - once, that is, I've satisfied myself we have sufficient winter fuel.'

Doobie glared at him for a full half-minute, with Frenchie revolving the hammer's shaft in his palm until the deadlock passed.

'You've got yourself a busy day then,' he spat finally, slinking off towards the hallway. 'Better keep your head down and graft.'

There was the sound of footfalls down the stairs.

It was Pelia in her blouse and long skirt, carrying a pair of scissors and those snipped-up tights as promised.

'Here you are,' she said in her crackly, indeterminate voice. 'I've done the best job I can with them.'

Doobie grabbed one, inspected it, then said: 'What is the matter with your face today? It's gone all blotchy!'

Pelia looked aghast, her hand going self-consciously to the area in question, around the jawline. Her fingers traced the recent spots and blemishes. 'Really I don't know what these can be,' she said, almost apologetically.

Doobie stood there with hand on chin again. 'Either we need to review the level of hormones you're taking ... or else this kinky weather's got into your system, turning you into a plague victim or such like.' He continued his assessment, staring at her in his disquieting way.

'Plague? What on earth can you mean by that?'

'I'm not quite sure - yet. But this warrants a closer look ...'

Pelia was starting to step back, teetering in her platform heels as he advanced - before the sound of Frenchie's urgent voice did infringe upon the room's deteriorating ambience.

'Oo-er!' came his cry from the kitchen. 'We seem to have ourselves a strange kind of liquid for company!'

The two piled in the living room, to discover Frenchie kicking vigorously at a stream of flowing liquid - which appeared to be emanating from the hole half-covered by the debris.

A stream of flowing liquid which seemed to be devising its own course: diverging into transient tributaries once Frenchie's boot had made contact with it; moving towards the shadows cast by the cupboards, seeking the numerous gaps of safety between the furniture.

Even Doobie's mouth gawped open at the weird science on display here, as its leading finger began flowing up and over the assorted rubbish blocking its progress, to the haven of darkness below the oven.

Frenchie's boot ruptured its course once more - but, just as before, the two tendrils appeared to be following some survival instinct, pursuing converse directions across the floor … yet attempting reunion at the earliest juncture.

'Take this, you fluid weirdness!' said Doobie, pouring out the rancid remains of the milk carton, taken from the Charming Couple's silent fridge, onto the foremost rivulet's leading edge.

After a second, the compounds blended and the stream displayed a promising, adverse reaction: moving erratically, agitatedly and sometimes back on itself!

Doobie chuckled at this and opted to pour out the rest of the carton, before scattering the sugar along the remaining gaps of floor. 'Try getting around that lot, my drippy friend!' he shouted.

And to his delight, the adulterated body of water began to circulate in frantic eddies and whorls, clockwise, then the other way.

'Stay out of its reach!' he barked to the others. 'Don't let it out of yer sight!'

Next, the fluid body began to speed its rotation over the rubble field, establishing a growing, circumferential wall of the stuff.

Higher and higher it rose, as though its centre sat astride a potter's wheel, being dizzily moulded by hands unseen.

'What the ..?' mouthed Pelia as the fluid wave continued its unabated ascent, beginning to rotate now at differential rates.

Approaching the heights of its startled audience, the column started to cascade onto itself at its spinning apex: nipping inwards at neck level and receding to its base along a proto-trouser line.

'Well, well, well ..,' remarked Doobie, beginning to recognise something within it. 'What have we here? An apparition of someone before our very eyes ..?'

He was not proven wrong: for in the midst of its maddening spin, the column was developing solidity to its structure. A general milkiness was now clouding the thing's previous transparency - but a definite head, trunk and two limb sets were becoming apparent.

The Shockers made ready for it.

Frenchie's flick-knife clicked open. Pelia took a cautious step back from the whirling entity, whilst Doobie made a grab for something sharp from the work surface. Scolex, meanwhile, contributed just a sickly cough and readjusted his position on the sofa, uncharacteristically turning his back on it all.

For tenuous moments in the gloom of the kitchen, the figure of Thomas Turby materialised before them.

Naked and unsteady, with his acorn-like appendage on full view, he was staring straight ahead, wearing no expression.

Then his image was shimmering again, receding into the milky translucency. Its general outline fragmenting.

Turby looked to be undergoing reabsorption

into the fluid sphere.

In moments, the Shockers found themselves facing a greyish, unicellular blob, which quivered on its vaguely shaped foot.

Frenchie was the first to attack it, slashing diagonally across from top right to lower left. 'Enjoy that, Fatty?!' he laughed, slashing again at the hulking thing from the other direction.

Fatty Turby appeared *not* to have appreciated this.

It gave an almighty rumble and began rolling towards the antagonist, veering at him with an acceleration which was quite alarming.

Scrambling over the toppled washing machine with a startled cry, Frenchie entered the living room area; the blob hot on his boot heels, leaving its trail of slime over the carpet - which had already been splattered and encrusted with more than its fair share of comestibles and household products.

Doobie tutted and calmly lit his penultimate match, while Scolex rejected Pelia's insistent attempts to lead him from sofa to hallway - and to relative security.

That left just the fittest pair of Shockers to

battle the blob in fateful combat.

At the back of the sofa, Frenchie feigned to the left, then to the right, goading his adversary.

In response, the blob slowed its sticky rotation to a canter, perhaps considering its next stratagem.

As he capered there, Frenchie caught sight of its optical structures fixed blandly upon him: about three pairs of lens-shaped masses within the grey matrix.

Perhaps they see only crude movements, he mused, as do the simpler organisms - with little in the way of resolution or refinement?

So he began to taunt it, in order to test this theory.

Skipping from one end of the sofa to the other with a gleeful grin, he taunted with: 'Seen me yet, you jellified tit?!'

Turned out that the blob *had* been keeping close tabs on him, after all.

A wiggle to the left, a wobble to the right, followed by a late millisecond quiver of its pseudopodium ... and the blob burst forth: up and over the sheer face of sofa towards the surprised

Shocker.

Frenchie's surprise caused him to lose his footing ... and the blob bore over him.

'OH NO YOU DON'T!' roared Doobie, appearing round the party-wall with the burning chair leg in his hand. 'Why not suck on this instead?' And he thrust the flame-licked curtain strip at the thing's blubbery surface.

The flame's application induced its hasty retreat, as it snaked round the sofa's edge. Doobie kept up the pressure and Frenchie was able to recover his poise.

Next, Doobie placed the burning object on its rolling hindquarters, as if to brand it.

'Try it some more, you Turby bastard!' he smiled, as the blob squealed internally - as might a stressed piggy when swathed in blankets.

Pleasantly encouraged, Doobie poked it again to elicit the same response.

The thing was kept in constant retreat for the next minute or so, whilst Pelia peered through the lounge doors' frosted glass at these extraordinary proceedings.

The sole moment of alarm for Shockers

Republic came when the last of the curtain material had been consumed by the flame: when Frenchie had to start tearing up the remaining one with his knife - allowing the blob to regain fully its hostile intent.

Rounding the corner of the armchair it was, preparing for a power roll towards the legs of Doobie.

Yet before this could happen, the strip was transferred between comrades, and the beacon was relit with the very last match.

Doobie pounced before it could launch its bid, feeding it the fire with a cry of: 'Piss orfff back to where you came, you fungal fiend!'

And to his welcome surprise, the lick of flame caused the blob's adjacent matrix to scorch and to wither: to resemble the look, the texture and aroma of something like barbecued pork.

It squealed, more loudly this time. Doobie flashed his beacon over a wider area of the wounded thing's hide. Crackling up and drying out, the blob collapsed over the carpet. Melted areas were dripping down now, as would candle wax.

'Well, well. I *always* thought our favourite Neighbourhood Snooper was all bluster with no backbone ..,' he said to Frenchie, whilst casually rolling the torch over the back of the sofa - causing new, noxious smoulderings to begin.

Frenchie was frowning. 'What's with the arson? This is supposed to be our accommodation base ..!'

'Was!' smiled Doobie by way of correction. 'Perfect is the situation to transfer our centre of operations to the house of our erstwhile friend here,' he laughed, kicking part of the blob's congealing remains with his boot tip.

'Just ponder the resources available to us at the other end of that tunnel. We've gobbled up all the available food here, I do believe. Plus, I've grown tired of staring at this florid wallpaper - and have grown tired of the unsavoury atmos about us.

'Besides, BlobbyTurby's wifey might still be there … that is if BlobbyTurby and his fungal phuckers haven't got to her first. You ponder such too?'

Frenchie coughed in the enveloping pall of fumes. 'I guess I now do, given that you're destroying the accommodation options as we speak.'

'Then that's swell.'

Doobie began walking towards the tunnel's

entrance in the kitchen floor, kicking away the lightest rubble from it.

He turned back to Frenchie. 'Now if you would be so good as to fetch our comrades and to inform them of our improved domestic facilities, then we'll be off.'

With that said, Doobie lowered himself into the pit: a freshly wrapped curtain strip aloft his burning torch as he readied to make the uncomfortable trip.

Before departing the smoky scene, he gave a quick reminder to Frenchie about the perils of neglecting Pelia's face masks - and of the weak condition of Comrade Scolex.

'Do drag him gently,' he urged. 'Yet, having said that, a few bumps and bangs along the way might give him the impetus he so requires for the begetting of some ruder health. I'll be seeing ya!'

And then he was gone, removing his presence from the growing furnace of the Charming Couple's home.

THURSDAY 7 MAY 381

That is the manner in which the magnanimous Shockers Republic found itself holed up in the ex-household of the extinct Neighbourhood Snoop Man, his wifey and his doggy.

Naturally enough, the first action that Doobie had performed upon exiting the hole at the foot of their stairs, was to urinate around the front door area in the customary 'warding off' gesture; to establish correctly those property rights.

However, he had been less than right about the level of plentiful food reserves existing here.

The pair of mean and swingeingly selfish Neighbourhood Snoops had seemed to let things run pretty thin.

Thus he hoped it wasn't going to take too long for the mSR to obtain their Prima, then to depart for good this wretched environment.

Doobie had been partly correct about Mrs Neighbourhood Snoop.

Ready and waiting for them she had been, not long after he'd poked up his head from the tunnel and deposited that musk.

The only setback was: Turby and his glutinous pals clearly *had* got to her first.

Quivering behind the shower curtain she was, when Doobie called on her with his flame of purification.

Again, the blob beat its retreat from his initial strafing without significant detriment; slurping over the bath's enamel face in the direction of the landing.

There he pressed home his advantage, uttering his 'Piss off back wherefrom you came, you fungal fiend!' line as he torched her: the final incarnation of Mrs Jill Turby frazzling, then rupturing.

Doobie afforded himself a smile, extinguishing for a wee bit his proven weapon of dispatch. 'Now we are at home. All we last require is our girl, name of Prima ...

'Prepare yourselves for Extraordinary Meeting of the Praesidium of Shockers Republic,' he informed the others, once they were assembled. 'Dining room. Ten minutes. Be there!'

'And if you fail to come back this time with our Beloved, I will be forced to make you even less of a man. Of this you can be ruddy certain.'

Pelia seemed to cower in the doorway, fidgeting with her mud-encrusted skirt and nervously scratching at the patch of scar tissue under her blouse. She looked to Frenchie beside her for some moral support - who was already fixing their tormentor with a challenging stare.

'Now get out of my sight, you two!' snarled Doobie.

Shuffling his sheets of doodled paper at the head of the dining table, he stated: 'The Extraordinary Meeting of the Praesidium of

Shockers Republic is hereby concluded. We'll reconvene once we have her.'

'But Doobie ... it's raining!' piped up Pelia. 'We've looked everywhere in this sodding village. It's a hopeless situation!'

'HOPELESS?! DON'T YOU EVER SAY THAT!'

He spun behind to the hunched, hulking figure in the corner of the room. 'Inform these two wasters to get a grip and to follow their orders. And ensure they've got their masks on!'

Unfolding his arms, Scolex began to lumber round the table towards them. 'Git moving,' he wheezed. 'Git moving now.'

The two slowly backtracked into the hallway, with Frenchie preparing to open the door; clearly unimpressed by Doobie's latest, motivational tactic.

'Alright,' he told him, as he pulled on his stocking mask. 'So we shall. But we're not promising anything. The Fungal Fiends have likely got her by now.'

'OUT!' shouted Doobie, denying them both eye contact. 'And Pelia! *Do* try to start acting more feminine. Two weeks on and you're still tottering around the place in a highly unsexy way.'

He waited until they were gone from the scene, before heading for the living room.

There, he joined his lightly wheezing pal at the window, both now peering through the slanting rain towards those semi-detached houses of Sweet Drive.

He sighed, and his comrade picked up on it.

'I'm sure they'll find 'er,' mumbled Scolex by way of reassurance.

Doobie grabbed at the nearest available ornament on the window ledge - a blue and white floral paperweight.

Seemed like dear Mr Turby really had enjoyed building his collection of paperweights. Was a *real* turn-on for him, judging by the variety on display.

He clasped its cool sphere.

'Of course they will!' he replied. 'For that is their instruction: to get her here by any means, in order for her to tend us all. To tend us all our foibles and male insecurities.'

'Yus.' Scolex dabbed at the next blood drop

which had been slowly trickling from a nostril.

Again Doobie sighed, and then looked across the road to the empty houses, where normality was no longer residing. 'Wretched Frenchie's most likely right,' he conceded, clenching the paperweight more tightly. 'The jellified freaks probably *have* glooped her. It's a … highly likely outcome.'

He shook his head in disbelief. 'Blimey, Scolex. What *is* this all about? These blobs with their blooming slime trails. And someone … *somethin'* else beyond them that I can't quite visualise. Somethin' else, just out of sight.'

'Yus,' replied Scolex, looking a trifle confused. 'Jus' outta sight.'

Doobie suddenly whirled round and, with a cry of frustration, hurled dear Mister Turby's blue and white floral paperweight at the doors of the glass cabinet.

Shattering one of the panes, the projectile further decapitated a couple of china ornaments within.

All in all a pleasing result, he told himself.

Rather a pity that Mister Neighbourhood Snoop Man wouldn't ever be coming back home to inspect this mess. For all that remained of his good, fungal self was splattered about in the charred wreckage of the Charming Couple's habitation, at t'other end of the tunnel. How nicely the devastating inferno of three doors away had taken care of him!

Doobie regarded the broken shards on the carpet. Now, stepping over to the nearest chair, he picked it up and advanced towards the damaged cabinet, as though to finish the job.

Scolex reached him at the last moment and gently restrained him, teasing the chair leg from his grip. 'Chief, stay calm!' he puffed. 'No need to git all steamed up.'

'THERE'S EVERY NEED TO GET STEAMED UP!' yelled Doobie, kicking the wainscoting, then storming back to the window. 'DON'T YOU COMPREHEND?! WE'RE NOT BOSSIN' IT ANY MORE! FOR THE FIRST TIME IN OUR ILLUSTRIOUS CAREER, WE'RE NOT RUNNIN' THE SHOW!'

Then, in somewhat calmer fashion, he stated: 'It's been a long time since the formation of the proto-Shockers Republic to now. From our first day at Infants' school, to adulthood: to our recent unification with Pelia and to the arrogant - and mostly overbearing - Frenchie. When you pause to consider it, we've come a long way.'

'Yus.'

'Recall how you and I acknowledged one another from the depths of our duffel-coats at the playground's fringe, while the other brats around us made hoarse their little larynges and hared around the grounds in their first pairs of lace-ups, grazing open their grubby knees?'

'Yus, I do.'

'O, from happy origins we've come,' said Doobie, yawning widely. 'Right, that's enough for a bit. I'm goin' for some shuteye. Just be sure to wake us as soon as those misfits return with our Prima.'

'Nite, Chief.' Scolex again tasted the copper smell of blood at the back of his mouth … and wondered if he was dying.

Upstairs, Doobie found some relief upon collapsing onto the duvet of Turby's double bed.

Pushing aside some initial, revolting images of historic lovemaking scenarios that baldy-blobs and his wife might or might not have performed upon this very structure, his mind turned itself to considering those things of greater pertinence to the situation of the mSR.

Events of Shockers Republic's traumatic modern history were coming now to the fore, in a blur of ghastly collage: of predatory slime moulds ... the deterioration of village humanity ... heat barrier ... communal fun with cobalt-60 ... Troy the simpleton ... gender reassignment therapy ... football scuffle in The Dashin' Rodent ... and, of course, their Prima ...

A little over seven hours later, it is the constant hammering of the rain that wakes him from his slumber upon Turby's double bed.

'The sods!' he spits, upon realising the lateness of the day and the quietness of his comrades' activities. Nothing appears to be going on downstairs!

'Are they not back yet?! SCOLEX! Attend me immediately!'

At length, there *is* a sound from downstairs. A thudding sound.

Doobie tries to discern its location. From the living room, he seems to think as he gets to his feet.

He grabs his extinguished torch and heads for the stairs.

Sounds of Scolex, groaning and rubbing his head.

'You okay?' calls Doobie, looking through the crack of the door.

Scolex is lying crumpled at the foot of the sofa, face to the carpet. 'I ... think so, yus,' comes his tardy reply. 'I guess I must of tumbled off 'ere whilst asleep ...' He is sounding quite groggy.

'ASLEEP?!' Doobie storms in, kicking out at his leg. 'I thought I told you to wake me when our intrepid heroes were back!'

Scolex tries clearing his throat. 'I've bin trying - really I 'ave,' he says, bringing up a splatter of warm blood from his lungs, which blends readily into the scarlet pattern already staining his t-shirt. His t-shirt which looks baggier than before.

'God, Schofield! What the jizz is up with your health recently?' says Doobie with a look of startlement. 'Your decline in condition makes you a shadow of your former, obese and massive self.'

'I know, Chief, I know,' he replies, scratching again his sore head. 'I dunno what it is I've got in me. It's like a spreadin' poison, that gives me the world's worst ever gut rot an' makes me bring up bits of my airbags. Chief, I dunno where all this is gonna end ...' And with that said, his hacking coughs resume.

Doobie stands there, glaring at him with hands on hips. 'Now look. As you well know, Comrade Scolex, the magnanimous Shockers Republic can ill afford to carry passengers. We must all be prepared to contribute to its greater good. So, if your basic condition is to remain as similar rubbish, then this General Secretary will have no compunction but to seek your permanent expulsion and deportation from mSR.'

Scolex appears to be growing more ashen ... and that's when the front door is rapped hard a couple of times.

Doobie breaks his glare and goes to answer it, gripping hold of his torch and lighting it by means of one from a new Turby matchbox.

Standing there outside, like a pair of drenched rodents, are Frenchie and Pelia.

Their stocking masks cling to their faces and both seem more than eager to obtain access inside.

Frenchie and Pelia alone out there ... very much on their ownsome.

'Oy, oy, oy!' says Doobie, with other ideas. 'Ain't you heard of quarantine, my dear comrades?'

He begins to wave the burgeoning flame about their upper midgut regions, causing them to totter backwards in the unrelenting rain with their arms flailing. 'Such a pity,' he says humourlessly. 'This cleansing procedure would have been so much shorter, had you done as I bid and returned home with our beloved Prima.'

He extinguishes the flame to glower at them himself. 'So where is she? Whereabouts have you secreted her? Do you perhaps attempt to tease me, by concealing her behind your backs?'

Frenchie advances to the doormat. 'Alas, she could not be found.'

In response, Doobie stamps cruelly on his boot. 'She could not be found, eh? Tell me this then: just how hard have you two been looking?!'

Frenchie, it seems, has a ready answer for this - but it is spoken instead by Pelia.

'We've looked extensively round this funkin' village,' she says, brushing back her flopping, sodden fringe with a hand. 'Really we have. All the way from the festerin' allotments, right the way to the friggin' heat barrier down the Southern Field.

Not a trace of her was found. Just the numerous slime trails we encountered, criss-crossing one another in every conceivable direction.'

'Really?' says Doobie, full of sarcasm, still glaring at her. 'And you expect me to swallow all this hogwash, right?'

Pelia raises her brow quickly to Frenchie, then back again.

'So, you are telling me you both failed to cross the fissure to search the entire eastern side of the village? Am I hearing this correctly? Hello?!'

Yet before Pelia has time to refute it, does the trill of a ringing telephone fill the house.

'What the ..?' manages Doobie, before tearing back to the hallway. 'This sound can no longer be physically possible!'

Indeed, it should not be: for the adverse changes to the environment over the past three days completely and permanently affected Lurkham's telecommunications, rendering them useless. And it had been in commemoration of that very fact that Doobie had ... wrenched off the handset following his ceremony of urination!

But here sits the telephone with its brutally severed connections, somehow restored and gaily ringing.

Doobie snatches it up. 'What ... you ... want ..?!'

On the other end of the line: a hint of high, panicky breathing.

Girl's breathing ... or a child's, by the sound of it.

Doobie's ear pricks up. Never having *received* a dirty call before, he swallows in anticipation at what could follow.

More breaths, exhaled under stress.

A physical struggle, as if the caller is not alone.

Doobie starts to lose a little of his patience, muttering: 'Whatever it is you've got to tell me, get on with it. I'm a right busy one currently.'

Then, through the crackle, speaks a voice of significant sibilance: a voice which would invite the disquiet of any listener.

A voice which begins to interest Doobie.

'Ohhh ... we have ... forever if it is required,' it seems to say, laconically.

There follows another series of stressed breaths, before a second voice speaks.

It is the voice of a girl.

The moment prior to hearing her fateful words, does Doobie's mind compute the captive's likely identity. His eyes enlarge, his mouth begins to drop.

'Look out for me!' *She* manages to say, clearly being held against her will. 'Soon! In the castle I be!'

The sound of distant scuffling and that sibilant tone again, which might now be congratulating her on her correct delivery of message ... and then the connection is severed.

Doobie stands there amidst the other two, still clutching the phone. 'Chaps, I suspect I've just been hearing the words of Prima at the other end. The words of our beloved Prima.'

Frenchie smiles. 'And how does she sound - sexed up and ready for us?'

Doobie absently shakes his head. 'Not exactly. She sounds in trouble and strife.'

And as the bedraggled rump of Shockers slope off to the drier interior of the house, there

Doobie remains: struggling to recollect any previous sightings of a castle, or of any like structure in the local vicinity.

Without success, he lifts the handset in sudden, rising hope of hearing her again. But finds the line is long since dead.

MORNING SESSION OF FIRST LUMEN

So loudly this time, that he thinks it must be a thunderstorm. But when Doobie is physically thrown from the bed of the dead Turbys and onto the carpet, he accepts that something of greater magnitude must be at work.

The rumbling goes on, tossing the remainder of the Turby wife's undamaged possessions off the dressing table and promptly shattering the majority.

He fights to right himself but remains grounded as the shaking continues. He hears the concerted yelps of outrage coming from his stricken comrades in the next room, knowing he is not alone in this.

All of a sudden, there opens up a crack in the plasterwork of the bedroom's far wall, sending up a plume of dust. He coughs, blinking furiously to expel the wretched motes from vision.

'COMRADES!' he shouts. 'IT APPEARS WE ARE IN THE MIDST OF A FRIGGIN' SEISMIC SHIFT! STAY CALM AND TRY TO AVOID ANY INTIMACY WITH FALLING MASONRY!'

It is only Frenchie's searing comment which reaches him. 'What a good idea! We hadn't thought of that ..!'

The rumbling reaches its crescendo, and a deep wrenching sound begins to emanate through the structure. A sound which suggests that subterranean layers are violently buckling, and being forced upwards to form a novel kind of anticline.

At this stage, even Doobie is starting to wonder how much more this stupid Turby homestead can withstand of this crude variant of rattle 'n' roll.

Then the sense of uproarious motion gradually subsides, allowing the billowing dust to settle about them.

As he gets to his feet, Doobie is of the certainty that the light passing through the missing bedroom window has a different quality to that of earlier.

He finds his colleagues in various poses of disarray, picking themselves up off the dismembered floor. Some of the boards have snapped, their jagged edges piercing the carpets.

'What the bloody hell's this all about?' exclaims Pelia, nursing her bruised arm.

Doobie is on the point of admonishing her for such unladylike language, when Frenchie utters a cry of surprise from his position at the skewed window frame.

'The landscape!' he declares, pointing excitedly towards the clearing scene outdoors. 'That terrain is different, for sure!'

The others weave their way round the obstacles to him - excepting Scolex, who lies propped up against the broken bed ... and looks more than a little broken himself.

And through disbelieving eyes, those remaining, alert Shockers begin to take in their new environment. Here is what their senses now report ...

The bleak and dreary outlook of earlier has simply ... gone! The row of semi-detached housing opposite is no longer there. Even the season looks to be a different one!

Replacing all that went before it is a densely forested terrain of undulating hills, leading all the way to the pink-tinged horizon.

In the intermediate distance is a steeper hill, clad in similar, lush vegetation.

Higher up, its sides grow sheer, and atop its rocky promontory perches the stark silhouette of a towered construction. It mushrooms there in its brooding solitude against the backdrop of a cool, autumnal sky. Its shape suggests that, over time, its ebon gables and turrets have been grafted on to existing ones, giving the tower a defiantly overreached, burdened look.

Doobie slowly turns to face his wide-eyed comrades. 'Gentlemen,' he says, pointing in the approximate direction of where the allotments of Lurkham village had been situated. 'I do believe we have located that aforementioned, castellated building as personally described to me.'

He regards them individually, his eyes burning with some charged intensity.

'Shockers Republic now knows where resides our unhappy, distraught Prima. Let us make her smile again. And let no one forget that it is our collective responsibility to ensure her safe incorporation within our great state.

'Soon we shall venture outside, where there will surely be unpleasant dangers to face. And please remember that the climatic conditions out there will likely prove harmful for us.'

He starts to pick his way down the fractured stairwell. 'Five minutes ... in the living room!' he calls back. 'Strategy Meeting of the Praesidium of Shockers Republic: to discuss these latest implications and to plan ... Operation Salvation Smile.'

Doobie bounds down the last of the stairs, a definite kick in his step.

AFTERNOON SESSION OF FIRST LUMEN

With Pelia's masks pulled over their faces, Shockers Republic set off on their quest along the ex-Turby residence's front path.

The ailing Scolex is left to shamble and stumble within the orderly triangle formation of his comrades. Marching at its apex is Doobie, carrying his trusty cricket bat; with Frenchie and Pelia on the flanks, each bearing an unlit torch of torn curtain material.

Their eyes do constantly roam, on the lookout for anything gelatinous, spherical ... and which rolls in a hostile manner.

The garden path upon which they tread is all that seems to remain of Lurkham's past existence.

Thick, frondose vegetation now fringes the place where the kerbstones of Sweet Drive used to sit.

Occasionally the flanking members of the pack observe a curious breeze afar, which cuts temporary swathes through the slopes of forest.

Not caring to contact this dense plant life with his hands in any way - and seeing no ready paths through it - Doobie raises his trusty bat to commence his assault on it. He reassures himself with the fact that never again will this virgin land encounter such violence as is about to be meted out by this most determined of Shockers Republics.

As the flimsy, organic matter snaps at the mercy of his whistling bat, he notes just how sharp are their stems of bottle green - each one amassed with lethal looking spines - and just how readily the battered fronds surrender their spores, in copious coughs to the breeze.

'It's just as well we resort to our masks,' he tells his comrades beside him. 'Potential harm is all about us.'

It becomes apparent to him that there is no birdsong to be heard in the head-high canopy, as he forges the start of a path and commences to perspire from his labours.

Once he begins to feel the sweat soaking into his mask, Doobie opts to hand over the tenure of the green-streaked willow to Frenchie, telling him to: 'Cut loose with it and make hay.'

The fungal shoots tend not to resist the resultant, savage lofts and off-drives; parting easily before them so that progress is steadily made.

Before long, the view to the ex-Turby's front door recedes. In the dimming dusk, the slant of the house's twin gables seem as a pair of downcast eyebrows, fearing for the future of things.

Well, whatever *it* might be fearing - at least Doobie knows he's feeling reasonably optimistic about it all.

As the sheer terrain of the crag begins to affront them and the castle's improbable geometry attempts to daunt, does Doobie detect the first stealthy crack of twig being snapped in the undergrowth ahead.

Some way over to the right, by the sound of it, over to the east.

He motions to Pelia to cease her 'go' of the slashing operations as they scan for movement.

But there follows nothing more … as something perhaps holds its position and bides its time.

On the turn of evening, with their torches now illuminating the extent of their significant passage spliced through this strange, mycelial jungle, Doobie calls time on proceedings.

'Comrades, we have made satisfactory headway. You can see how close we are to nearing the foot of the rocky stump. After a good night's rest, we shall be prepared for its successful scaling.'

Yet he looks disparagingly over to Scolex, who sits there with his face mask actually *off.* Wheezing he is, too; utilising the cricket bat, would you credit it, as a *crutch of support!*

'My friend,' he speaks with genuine concern, kicking away the bat from him. 'If your physical condition does not return within the next, say, six to eight hours, then we may have to accelerate your demise, and to think of you more as some kind of a tainted source of nutrition for us - unless, of course, we happen to chance upon some other example of hapless creature in this environment that's fine for dining upon.'

Scolex doesn't remonstrate to this taunting or even look up. He just waves away the unwelcome attention and turns away from the light of the torches.

Doobie assesses the castle as the others turn tail and begin their trudge back.

Silhouetted against the stars of unrecognisable constellations, he sees that any light which might burn from within is denied access through either window, outlet or porthole.

The structure looks to be a monument to opacity and secrecy: seeming to offer no tangible signs of light, life or hope to the surrounding world. It merely perches there upon its rocky haunches, in baleful negativity.

The thought of Prima being holed up there somewhere - perhaps naked and in bondage - provides Doobie the first stirrings of a stiffy. A stiffy which is quickly dissipated by the sound of another crackle in the fungal undergrowth.

To his right again, by the sound of it. Yes indeed. Sounding more like the clump of a clumsy footstep, than a sly gloop by one of those charming, jellied spheres.

'No time to deal with you tonight,' he mutters under his breath. 'Time for mSR's rest and recuperation. To save our forces for you tomorrow.'

MORNING SESSION OF SECOND LUMEN

The double binary of yellow suns is rising above the line of hills, by the time the refreshed Shockers Republic begins its climb of the crag's lower reaches.

The vegetation grows more sparsely here, and the Shockers' two main operatives, Doobie and Frenchie, are soon able to clamber up the exposed crop of rocks. Pushing their way through the scarp's finer shrubbery, their proximity to the oppressive edifice quickly increases.

'Look!' says Pelia at their resting place, some halfway up the slope. 'You can still see the line of yesterday's quake - the one that shook us up something rotten.' She is pointing to the south. 'The trees have almost concealed it … but not quite. And another thing: there's no sign of the heat barrier now, is there? The distance seems clear and fresh.'

Doobie's eyes linger on the cracked shell of their residence's rendering in the same direction. 'Don't be so sure of that,' he replies through his mask. 'This air is not to be trusted.'

Then he breaks his gaze and remarks virulently: 'Anyway, who are you to be telling us such things? Unless you're a secretly qualified geologist or meteorologist, just shut the funk up and resume your climb!'

He turns his attention to the slope behind them. 'Scolex!' he shouts. 'Of you I nearly forgot! What's your news of today?'

His haggard comrade is *still* crawling slowly up. Fresh blood looks to be trickling from his mouth, and the veins are standing out from his sallow hands and forearms.

'Friend, it appears your condition has not improved one whit, but has deteriorated still further. This is an … unfortunate development,' he says, clearing his throat.

Scolex looks up at last to find Doobie is standing directly over him. He raises a thin, unsteady hand to block out the glare of the alien suns.

Doobie briefly raises his face mask to him. 'Most unfortunate,' he smiles. 'A trusted confidant to me you have been. But you, my friend, have become a burdensome passenger whose journey must end here.'

Raising his muddied boot towards the head of Scolex, Doobie takes some pity at the final moment and quickly alters his aim to that of the shoulder area ... and topples his oldest friend off his painful, bony knees. 'Goodbye to one of mSR's liabilities!'

The eyes of Scolex widen considerably as he tips past the vertical, realising his fate in numb horror. 'Chief, what're you doing this for ..?!' he cries in a betrayed, injured squawk, as he begins his irreversible roll, head over scrawny heels.

Fortunately missing the nearest rocky outcrop, he bounces from view, still wailing his protestations of innocence.

Then his sound is gone.

Frenchie scarpers across to the edge, peers down, then spins round to Doobie. 'What the hell's got into you?!' he shouts. 'You've funking well killed him!'

And, from a distance, Pelia interjects:
'Please tell us exactly how three Shockers are meant
to win the day here ..?'

Doobie glares at them indignantly. 'Now that
we are a streamlined outfit, we shall manage even
better than before! Why, didn't either of you get it?
Scolex got hisself sick, as simple as that. Worsening
by the day he was - surely you could see it! Got
hisself too familiar with that hazardous wave
emitter, I do believe. The one that got buried in
Commoners Common ... wherever that location
went to.'

'But there was no need to *murder* him,'
shouts Frenchie, advancing. 'No need to cull the
population of Shockers Republic by twenty-five
percent, just for the frigging pleasure of it!'

Quick as a flash, Doobie whips out his knife
and declares: 'You do realise that I've just reached
the limits of your sardonic wit and your general
insubordination?!'

Then, diving below Frenchie's no holds
barred kick, he jabs the blade forward and imparts a
nasty slash to his opponent's calf area.

'Comrades, please refrain from following

this path!' beseeches Pelia, her face in contorted disarray, as Frenchie limps back into the fray and scoops up a rocky lump, ready to pulverise his opponent with. 'Infighting will ruin us!'

But neither appear to be listening; with Doobie now leaping on the back of his antagonist, and commencing to pummel Frenchie's neck with his fist.

Despite the pain, Frenchie is able to tip him off, and to cause him to land unceremoniously upon his shoulder blade upon a jutting slab of stone.

Doobie lies there winded, clutching himself, and Frenchie makes for the loose flick-knife ... with which to conclude his unrehearsed bid for glory.

It is the degree of piercing scream which captures the attention of both warring parties.

They see Pelia is just standing there and pointing: pointing up to the black castle beyond them. They extrapolate the line her finger makes: to the insectile-limbed figure ... that's leaning from a first floor opening which has grown suddenly apparent.

Again comes the piercing scream from the domed head thing in the dark robes, as it allows its outsize arms to dangle below the ledge.

At once the Shockers' pointless tussling ceases.

Doobie takes a sure step forward and shouts up: 'That scream I recognise, comrades, don't you?' To a blank silence, he explains further. 'It is the same scream as Neighbourhood Snoop Wifey's, yeah?! *She* uttered the same, horrid noise when we burst inside her room and started to jostle and shake her, remember?'

The scream erupts once more, then coalesces to form sounds like words.

'The one whom you seek can be found within,' it calls.

'AND WHO IS THAT, THEN?!' yells back Doobie. 'PRAY TELL US, WE'VE ALREADY FORGOTTEN! PROVIDE US MORE DETAILS!'

Flexing its pair of stupendous forearms, the gangling creature appears to titter.

Now in the voice of a jocular Neighbourhood Snoop Man, it answers. 'What disappointingly short memories you have. Why, it is the very one who has infiltrated your dreams and waking thoughts for the past fortnight! Come now … and pay her a long overdue visit.'

Doobie stands there stiffly. He eyes his

remaining comrades, then grips harder the shaft of his knife. 'Alright, StickMan!' he says, at length. 'If you say she's there, then let's all spend some quality time with her!'

Those arms of StickMan swing loosely again, then are retracted.

Shortly, its form is gone from the opening completely.

The time now seems right for the trio of Shockers to commence their walk along the gravel footpath - which, until minutes before, had not even existed.

This inclined path leads them directly to the front of the ominous building, from where they can observe the first signs of a doorway. Made, apparently, of the same material as the castle walls, the central hatch opens inwards, to reveal a faintly lit interior.

'Are you sure this is the correct tactic to follow?' asks Pelia, ensuring that she approaches the yawning gap sandwiched quite tightly between her comrades.

'Yes,' replies Doobie, not looking back. 'Of course. Mister Skin and Bone might find it a trifle insulting if we were to reject his invitation. On this occasion, Shockers' diplomacy must come to the fore if we are to obtain what we've come here for.'

There is the suggestion of shifting light inside.

Doobie kicks open the ebony hatch to its greatest extent, recoiling somewhat when he comprehends what awaits them in the hallway of the silent castle.

On either side are lines of glutinous, spherical blobs.

Flanking the great hall to the distant silhouette of StickMan, each sphere judders in apparent synchrony; their vibrations propagating along the lines and back again in a longitudinal wave.

'Oh, bloody hell,' mutters Pelia, taking a nervous step back. 'If we've got to get past a frigging phalanx of fungal fiends in the pursuit of love, then let's forget it. That jellified Neighbourhood Snoop Man caused enough of a problem for us.'

'Shut it - and cease your swearing!' hisses Doobie, grabbing her hand tightly - just as the elastic shape of StickMan appears to unfold once more at the far end of the hallway.

Dim, blue light flickers behind it, as the voice of the dead, departed Mrs Turby wafts across the intervening distance.

'Come in,' it says. 'The villagers will not absorb you - that is a promise. Instead, they are on their best behaviour: they form before you your guard of honour ...'

'I'm a tad dubious of *that!*' whispers Frenchie.

Doobie steps inside, his eyes not deviating from the contorting, convoluting shape of StickMan. 'This ain't no time to be a Doubting Thomas,' he snarls. 'In we go, comrades - as one.'

As they pass through, there is the sensation of loftiness to the great entrance hall. Doobie catches briefly a sight of the ceiling beams, reckoning them to be constructed of some unearthly material, on account of their curious, spangled luminosity.

Yet he concentrates more on ensuring his safe passage through the parted rows of blobs: acutely aware of the need to detect that first, sudden, slurping roll towards him and his comrades, should it come.

As he nears the last of them, he presumes

that each sphere corresponds to at least one of the missing villagers. He notes the centrally defined neural medulla of each blob, sometimes observing a pair of them inside one; wondering if such represent the coalescence of two ex-inhabitants, or … perhaps the mitotic creation of a new one?

Up ahead the blue light still flickers - but StickMan, it seems, has slunk further on, round the corner of the glittering passageway. Its tip-tap footsteps can be heard echoing in the warped atmosphere.

The Shockers discover other passageways are now starting to lead off at regular intervals. Some to the left, some to the right, even some upwards and down-sloped - all bathed in the same flickering light; a light cast as though by the incessant movement of things.

'Now where to?' asks Pelia at one such junction. 'This place gets ever more like a blooming rabbit warren.'

'Yes, how do you *know* that?' Doobie snaps. 'Ever *been* in a rabbit warren?!'

'No, of course not!'

'Well shut up, then. And stop swearing all the time - it's getting on my nerves!'

Pelia protests silently, and the trio push onwards along the main pathway.

'Pri-ma!' calls Frenchie, as they reach a major crossroad. 'We are here to have a good chat with you, that is all! Don't be a shy one now!'

His sentiment appears optimistic, yet his voice has an edge of doubt to it; unsure of eventual outcomes here.

And as Shockers Republic migrate deeper in the depths of the structure, someone outside it all continues to creep amongst the alien undergrowth, well below the reaches of the castle's southern face.

Now and then that person steps upon a twig unseen, which emits an unhelpful, reverberatory crackle.

Regarding the tower with a look of intelligence, the person awaits for a sign of detection.

Seeing none, the person recommences his

trek, pushing through the canopy with his remaining good arm - the one which avoided exposure to the heat barrier.

He takes another assessment of the implausible edifice: his eyes scanning the featureless surfaces for signs of imperfection; for a vulnerability or two ... which might be good enough for the first toe-holds.

EVENING SESSION OF SECOND LUMEN

By the time they catch up again with those snaky footsteps, they have little idea that dusk is calling on the outside world. Much to their chagrin, the Shockers realise they have been going around in circles. After a time, the tunnels appear to look and feel the same in the shifting blue light.

Those lively footsteps up ahead of them are not too many lengths away, so the Shockers Republicans increase their rate of climb up the narrowing passageway.

Its floor grows ever more slippery and its walls offer them little in the way of grip - although its exterior layer imprints when the pressure of a hand is applied, as might a rubber surface.

Doobie still cannot dismiss from mind his lingering suspicion that they are all somehow worming their blind way along the tendrils of a vast, mycelial lattice.

The footsteps of StickMan now possess more of an echoing quality, indicating that a loftier chamber may lie ahead.

Rounding the final corner, the Shockers discover their deduction is correct.

They find themselves entering a long, narrow room with a raised ceiling of the same material as recently observed. Here there's the suggestion of faint light diffusing in through the walls. To one side is what seems to be a stout, wooden table ... and, standing at the far end of it, recognisable by its pair of twinkling, glittering eyes and the gangling area of darkness, is their stick-like host.

There is the sound of its gown unfurling, then its arms extend in arcs of an apparent, welcoming gesture. 'My *dear* gentlemen friends,' sounds its scratchy voice, in the approximate tones of ex-Neighbourhood Man. 'Now that we are all gathered, let us discuss the future terms and conditions.'

'T&C's?' says Frenchie. 'Of what?'

Doobie elbows past him and states, in a no-nonsense fashion: 'We're putting all terms and conditions aside for a while, Mister Skin'n'Bone. We are only here for a gander of our Prima. Shockers Republic now demands the official proof that she is still extant!'

An amused guffaw booms from StickMan, though the tone is no longer in the manner of Mr Turby's.

'"Demands the proof", you say? In time, o in time!'

There follows a swish of its arm, as if to defuse the Shockers' impatience. Instead, the intensity of its own eyes develops in prominence.

'The one known to you as your beloved Prima shall be handed over to you once your so-called Shockers Republic agrees to its improved working arrangements. Namely, these shall be -'

'Hang onnnn! You mean to tell us you are actually daring to *interfere* in our future operations and in our ultimate destiny?' spits Doobie, nearly choking on his words. 'You are inferring that *you* are of a higher power than the magnanimous Shockers Republic?!'

'Why, we don't even know what the funk

you are!' says Frenchie, pointing imperiously. 'Be you man or … tree?!'

'Yes,' adds Pelia, 'you're the strangest thing *I've* ever set my eyes upon.'

Doobie exposes his flick-knife, pointing it in StickMan's direction. 'There! Seems like you've got some explaining to do, Stick&Bones! So why not to make a start, eh?'

StickMan stands there motionlessly at the foot of the long table, then communicates.

'A request for assistance was referred to me by the one known as Neighbourhood Snoop Man. The Appeal was upheld by our Masters - and this is how we find ourselves here: now in seeming opposition to yourselves, the so-called Shockers Republic.'

'A request, you say?' frowns Doobie through his face mask. 'That Turby sprat made such?'

'An appeal for help in what?' asks Frenchie.

'Why, to eradicate your burgeoning little organisation! It would seem that Neighbourhood Snoop Man took great exception to your activities in his village.'

'Wanting our very destruction was he?!'

shrieks Doobie, spitting freely on the porous floor. 'The bald headed bastard that he was!' He is looking livid.

'That is about so,' replies StickMan. 'The man had a previous connection, it would seem, to some of those in the Watchers' World.'

'The *what* world?' enquires Pelia, finding herself quite disconcerted to be hearing the voice of the late Snoop Man emanating from this weirdest of beings afore them.

'Our Masters simply … watch all events here. All is seen by them and cannot be hidden.

'And it seems that your man grew desperate enough to invoke their powers. Except … the unfortunate … got things a little wrong.'

'Explain!' says Doobie, looking relatively wide-eyed. 'What did that amazing man next cock up?!'

'The constitution of the Organic Cross was not faultless …'

StickMan expands its arms in the semi-darkness. 'Nevertheless! A foothold into this world we were granted. An irreversible happening which could not be revoked. And now we do shape it.

'For beyond here is our approximation of a world: our provision of a new landscape for subsequent generations.'

'Generations of what?' says Frenchie, brimming with sardonicism. 'Spherical blobs?'

At this, StickMan chuckles.

'You mean to say it was *your* arrival in this world which created the heat barrier and the god-awful quake?' enquires Pelia. 'And that our playground of a village has gone for ever more?'

At this, StickMan laughs.

'Well, thank you ever so much for screwing up our plans around here!' shouts Doobie. 'We had so much lurking still to do in Lurkham and its inhabitants. And I think I'm growing tired of talking to our chief spoiler …'

StickMan raises a skeletal hand. 'Your wide world contains many more villages than this, my friends. Do not allow the abandonment of one village process to open up a rift between my world and yours. An era of coexistence and cooperation does beckon.'

'Not funkin' likely, mate!' says Doobie bitterly. 'No such compromises!'

'Then,' StickMan hisses, with ruthless certainty in its voice, 'you shall never locate your female prize - it's as simple as that.'

The trio of Shockers struggle to formulate a response.

In the queer light, StickMan appears to grow taller. Its eyes dance as exuberant fireflies.

'So-called Shockers Republic ought not to reject any proposal for a working partnership. There is nothing to be feared by either party: instead, there are splendid advantages to be gained.'

It continues.

'So-called Shockers Republic would act as our vanguard: a scouting menace, which would identify each viable cluster of human habitation, select and then despoil them with atrocities of unimaginable intensity.

'Once filtered of extraneous detritus and worthlessness, our world would next descend on them - to inflict upon the survivors the full … challenge … of malady and mutation we hold at our disposal.

'With the forging of such a partnership, the human breed would be significantly better managed and contained than ever before.'

Doobie clears his throat, coughing up some mucus onto the table's surface, halfway towards StickMan. 'I guess, with the stuff you've sibilated so far on the subject, it sounds like there *might* be already a kind of ... resonance ... existing between the organisations.'

'This is so.'

'Yet, pray inform us how it would be possible for Shockers Republic to travel the globe on your behalf. We don't work in a rushed way - and, with the size of this place, we could get ourselves lost oh-so easily ..!'

'And where does our Prima fit into all this?' comments Frenchie at the rear.

Within its floor-length gown, StickMan treads a half step nearer without them even noticing.

'My friends: in response to the second, necessary question, it is only right that your beloved Prima shall become your immediate property. Once positive agreement is met here, I shall personally guide you to her.

'By the hours of tonight, so-called Shockers Republic could be free to lose itself in sticky frenzy with the poor, frightened girl of human condition.

'I can attest she would surrender herself

unequivocally to any of your suppressed wishes and desires. And, believe me, I know the ones you are concealing; for they are almost palpable at these rarefied heights.'

Not for the first time, the Shockers find themselves lost for words as StickMan continues.

'And in response to your first concern - how you might cover those vast distances on the proposed scouting missions. I know. This world is a daunting proposition, particularly so on foot.

'Of course, I could suggest that the mode by which yourself and your absent, fatter colleague arrived at the village would be sufficient: the petrol fuelled metal box.

'But I and others are prepared to offer you all a greater gift of transportation.'

'What on earth could be better than a top-of-the-range stolen car?' says Doobie.

'Allow me to divulge.' The figure shuffles another half step nearer.

'Perhaps two top-of-the-range stolen cars ..?' proposes Frenchie, unsmiling.

And, though none of the surviving trio detect it, there comes the faintest sound along the passage behind them ... of a great many things in motion. Approaching them through a stealth of inching creeps and slithering slurps.

'The gift which we are prepared to bestow upon you all is the gift of ... flight. Yes! Flight, in the avian guise.'

'*Flight*, you say?' asks Frenchie incredulously.

'*Which* guys?' asks Pelia warily.

Doobie merely stares.

'No other humans involved! Correct indeed! Flight, as how the birdies do it.'

StickMan catches the first signs of advancing fluidity beyond them and continues.

'You shall become a flock of Shapechangers. When you will it, your constitution shall modify to that of a flying life form - a bird.'

'Shapechanger ..?' repeats Doobie slowly. 'Never heard of it ...'

'And which bird variety could present such a devastating deception to the masses ... but a dove? The symbol of peace and harmony ... to become your second skin! Over the interminable distances, your arms shall convey you from one habitation to the next. Your dark, beady eyes shall enhance your powers of observational acuity.

'But we shall require you in greater numbers than this, if we are to embark on our way of lifetimes. There shall have to be a restoration to your original number - and a return to original condition.'

'Meaning what, exactly?' says Doobie, hands on his hips.

'Meaning that you,' replies StickMan, pointing towards Pelia, 'the half-girl, shall become wholly male again; your body untampered with. And that -'

'Impossible!' says Doobie. 'I grow used to her.'

'And that, in addition, your absent, fatter colleague - yes, the one whom you pushed to his death merely two hours ago - be resurrected from his early slumber.'

'To bring him back?!' smiles Frenchie.

'Indeed. As you might know, he harboured a worsening sickness that would have killed him anyhow within the fortnight. Too intimately did he become involved with some molecules of intense excitability. After that, he stood little in the way of chance.'

'He *what*, with molecules?' says Pelia, nonplussed.

'Look, it's simple!' Doobie snarls, turning to her. 'Told it you already! The arse got hisself a fatal dose of radioisotope from that device we embedded in the Common.'

With that he jabs his knife tip against the grain of the table. To his surprise, the notch he has created is quickly infilled by replacement liquid welling forth. He registers no surprise, then stabs curiously at it again. More infilling is observed.

'A ... restoration to the original complement,' continues StickMan, noting his guest's disrespect to the surroundings. 'What say you to the proposal? Pray tell.'

'I say ..,' replies Doobie with growing irascibility, ' ... what the *hell* are you all about? Who the *phuck* do you think you are, you bony bugger, talking about *resurrection* and *molecules of intense excitability* - a bleedin' medicine man?!'

StickMan laughs, whilst taking another discreet half step nearer. 'That is possibly not so far from the truth. And I can always respond to this flash of impudence by demanding, "What the *hell* do you think *you* are all about?"'

'What?!'

'That whilst it is obvious to us your colleagues are of fallible and blundering human construction … you are representative of something really quite different.'

'How d'you mean?' sneered Doobie. 'Just what are you insinuating here?'

'O, I am stating, not insinuating. Your origins were anomalous to say the least: your so-called *mother* being of virtually another species; your absent *father* being of spurious existence at all.'

'You leave the issue of my parentage out of this rubbish debate, right?!'

'So your true hybridity proves difficult to establish.'

'I said LEAVE IT!'

And it is at this point that the first of the mucous balls comes rolling around the corner of the passageway into the chamber. Others glide in behind it, sliding on their slime trails until the vestibule is filled by them.

StickMan reaches the trio. 'You now agree to the proposal,' it coldly states.

Doobie raises his knife, pointing at the bobbling, jostling multitude of gelatinous matter. 'Methinks you are giving us no alternatives here.'

StickMan tilts its bulky cranium again. 'That's quite correct. Besides, as you can see, it's not entirely up to me. The enlightened village population seems to want so-called Shockers Republic on board, too. Feel the levels of their jittery excitement.'

Doobie looks to Pelia and then to Frenchie.

In their eyes he recognises the extent of their unresolved ambivalence - and considers his own.

He looks across to Mister TwinklyEyes … and flashbacks to his brightest vision of the Girl: the one of him grappling with her ankles as they tried to yank her through the hedge.

Yes … His fingers pressing into her flesh, aiming for a higher delight … until that bastard Snoop Dog had pushed through its gnashing snout and interfered with their progress.

And perhaps now their progress with Prima was to be assured. To become … Guaranteed.

He retracts his blade and prepares to address his host on a once and for all basis: knowing that his next words will provide the casting vote of the magnanimous Shockers Republic.

'I can now declare that a strategic partnership will be agreed between ourselves and Mister Stick&Bone plus its Fungal Fiends - once we see some proof that our quarry still breathes.'

StickMan proffers them a deep bow. 'Your acceptance delights us. Now let us keep to our promise: to exhibit to our ... Republican Wing ... its newest acquisition.'

Beckoning them behind, along the passage of flickering blue light, it whispers: 'Girl of human condition lies just through here.'

The trio follow in StickMan's wake; a half smile forming on Doobie's face.

It is not much further before the passage walls start to convey the reflection of light from some artificial source. Its strength continues to increase, so that for the first time, they can see exactly where it is they are placing their feet.

'Girl is here!' exclaims StickMan presently, as they encounter the chamber from where the light is emanating.

Stepping in, they discover the source of luminosity is coming from the floor itself: a brash glare of electric blue.

Central to the chamber is a reclining structure; and there at repose, within moulded contours of her own making, lies their Prima.

O, Prima ... up so close now!

With her head to one side, she appears to sleep soundly. The only feature which could hint at some underlying disharmony is the frown line, etched above the bridge of her nose.

'Ohhh, isn't She lovely?' coos Doobie, eyeing his girl with the locks of dishwater blonde.

'She surely is,' agrees StickMan.

'How did you come by her?'

'Rescued she was from the clutches of that fanatical shaman with dog-collar.'

'Urgh. Uganda,' says Doobie, his eyes busily scrutinising the prize.

'Prima, you see, is destined for bigger things with us.'

'Uh-huh,' smiles Doobie, quite dreamily. 'I see that She is.'

His fingers start to slip inside the top of her black vest, feeling for more of her.

He refers momentarily to StickMan. 'It's not problematic to check the asset in this way ..?'

To which StickMan expresses in the affirmative.

It is not long at all before Prima tosses and turns at Doobie's rough manipulation of her, finally awaking. She screams at the ungodly sight of the male, female and stick-like types in her midst.

'O, no! O, my Lord!' she yells with huge, dark eyes.

'Yes, hello Prima Beloved,' grins Doobie, twisting on her nipple as she tries to dislodge him. 'Welcome to your baptism of love!'

From the rear, Frenchie is approaching for *his* look of her. And, as he readies to delve, there is a sharp, booming sound, followed by a dramatic influx of light from behind her couch's headboard …

To the shock of all those gathered, the silhouette of a man rears up.

A man with a burning torch in his hand.

Its flicker illuminates the compressed features of Doctor Rickmansworth Burns: his mouth and nostrils swathed by a protective, surgical mask.

'Away! Scatter!' he shouts to the marauders in muffled tone, jabbing the torch at them, forcing them back from Prima's vicinity.

'Whoaaa!' cries Doobie, almost receiving a singed forearm as he pulls away from the region of her chest. 'WHO THE FUNK ARE YOU - GATECRASHING OUR SPECIAL PARTY?!'

'I am,' puffs Dr Burns, swinging the torch around in continual, sweeping arcs, 'the General Practitioner of the patient afore me. And it's of my firm belief that her state of health would radically improve with an immediate departure from this hellhole of extreme unholiness!'

With that, he puts Prima's pale hand in his, having briefly transferred the torch to the crook of his damaged left arm, which hangs there limply.

'Come on, my dear,' he insists, as she works herself free of the couch's clingy, epidermal surface. 'It's now or never!'

'THEN IT'S NEVER!' screams Doobie, hurling his flick-knife at the have-a-go hero.

Its blade rips into the doctor's shoulder,

raising some blood from it ... and nearly causing him to drop the torch.

Transferring it again to his good arm, the doctor executes another lunge, this time at StickMan - which causes it to retreat and to raise protectively its multi-jointed arms.

Seeming long moments later, Dr Burns has Prima's hand in his.

Pulling her from the last of the couch's resistance, she totters unsteadily; then he is able to lead her back a couple of steps to the impromptu opening.

He enlarges the hole with a firm kick of his foot and exposes the outside's silvery moonbeams. Urgently he leads her over to the castle's jagged edge, pointing to the knotted swathes of vegetation which climb this building's northern face.

'Hurry, please!' he begs of her. 'The foliage looks weak but is remarkably durable.'

'Doctor, I can't!' she whimpers. 'I'm no good with heights!'

'There's no longer a choice!' He swings his faltering flame again in spiralling arcs at his frothing, festering enemies. 'Don't think about remaining here with *this* lot - spawned from Hell itself, the lot of them!'

'PRIMA, THAT'S TOSH AND YOU KNOW IT!' whines Doobie, as he attempts to kick the torch from the doctor's hand. 'Vile, melodramatic tosh from a vile, melodramatic quack!' he snarls.

A breath or two later, Prima makes her decisive move: gripping the coiled strand of vegetation which the doctor has artfully fixed - using some bizarre medical dissecting instruments - to the castle's corklike substratum. And she begins to take her first, vertical steps down.

'That's it! Good girl!' says the doctor, adroitly withdrawing another length of precut fabric from his shirt pocket with which to feed the fire. 'Just look around - and not down!'

'PRIMA, YOU COME BACK!' hollers Doobie, welling up with the darkest emotions. 'WE'LL NOT LAY ANOTHER HAND UPON YOU! THIS MUCH WE PROMISE!'

Unsurprisingly, there is no positive response from her.

All that's to be heard wafting up is the sound of her exertion, and the flexing of the strand as it twists with her movements.

For the remaining half-minute, whilst trading hatreds with Shockers Republic, the doctor remains steadfast in his alertness; having grown too adept now in the art of torch swirling to be at risk of losing possession of it.

'It's time for me to take my leave of this dump,' he says in tiring breaths. 'How much you lot deserve to languish here in this corrupted landscape, you destroyers of all things quaint and parochial. This is Doctor Rickmansworth Burns, General Practitioner to the departed village of Lurkham, signing off ...'

At this, he pulls out the last of his flammable material, drapes it across the headboard, then steps back to the makeshift window ledge.

'Farewell, you freaks,' he declares, igniting the strip, before tossing his torch behind him for the pull of the moonlit world to claim.

He grabs hold of the strand of coarse fibres and begins to lower himself, utilising his weakened arm more in the style of a clamping pincer.

Doobie has torn over to the chamber's corner where StickMan is hunching, as the masked face of their adversary slips from view. 'DO SOMETHING, STICK&BONE!' he shouts to the cowering thing. 'DON'T LET OUR PRIMA BE SNATCHED!'

StickMan still shields its face. 'The flame! Put out the flame!' it says in a cracked voice. 'Tongue of fire be a dangerous threat to the viability of this construct about us!'

Comrades Doobie and Frenchie take seriously its words, and confront the emboldened inferno of couch; preparing to literally stamp their authority on it, as the herd of gelatinous spheres start to roll upon StickMan's visual cue.

Dr Burns takes a glance down at Prima's crown and the surrounding scene. She is around four lengths from him and doing very well. Yet, there are many more lengths to descend before they can reach the comparative safety of the sloping terrain.

'Impressive work!' he calls, noting her steady gain in confidence of her rope-shinning efforts.

Now it's the time for him to make a similar rate of progress, before the collective … inhumanity … above him extinguish his blaze of deterrence and begin their furious pursuit.

Just as this thought is dissipating, comes the sound of gleeful relief from up above. A round of cheers follow, then do the chants: turning violent, ready for murder.

Dr Burns, looking up at exactly the right instant, sees the aflame, melting headboard coming right for them both.

He tenses, compressing himself on the liana somewhat, hoping to parry some of its impact.

'Whey-heyyyy!' radiates the jeer, as the board's leading edge strikes his other shoulder, causing him to cry aloud with the pain - and for the rope to dangerously gyrate ... as Prima below him wails in fear of an imminent and fatal detachment.

'SOON TAKE YOU OUT OF THE EQUATION, BURNSIE BABY!' comes the unsavoury commentary from the leading skinhead. 'FUNGAL FIENDS ARE ON THEIR WAY, ON THEIR WAY, ON THEIR WAY ..!'

Coming quickly on the heels of this, the next sensation to beset the pair in perilous, aerial suspension is an upward tug of savage proportions, followed by another; as the thin, sinewy hands of the stick-limbed freak haul back a length of the rope.

'FASTER, MISS ROGERS!' the doctor calls down, realising their time is not long. 'PLEASE REDOUBLE YOUR EFFORTS OF DESCENT!'

'I'M TRYING!' she yells back.

But the net result is the same: they are rising, such is the dynamic pull and reach of the ghoul's wrists.

Now with considerable difficulty, Dr Burns extracts the scalpel from his frayed breast pocket, and prepares for the ultimate option: to cut across the organic stem which he is just about managing to clamp between his knees.

'Miss Rogers, I want you to know ..,' he shouts, rather wearily, as he makes the necessary deep slashes and striations. 'I want you to know that, whatever happens to either of us, I have tried my best to steer your life from becoming any darker.'

'I know, Doctor,' comes her weakening response.

'Important to keep you … in the … light. In the light of the living world!'

Their upward surge gathers momentum; whilst that same, snarling voice continues to bellow down at them filth, fury and bile.

'LYING QUACK! LYING BURNSIE! YOU ONLY CAME HERE TO DO DIRTY THINGS TO HER - JUST AS DID BLOBBY SNOOP MAN! UP YOU COME NOW, PERVY,

FOR A DECENT EVISCERATION! COME,
BOY! COMRADES, PREPARE YOURSELVES
FOR AN INTERESTING DISSECTION!'

With a final flourish, Dr Burns completes
his work. Looking up into the ugly mug of the
lippiest skinhead, he utters his simple valedictory
of: 'Screw you, Baldie!' - just as the taut, remaining
fibre of liana yields ... and his and Prima's
downward plunge commences.

There follows a brief, cheated gasp by
Doobie as he sees the prey fall away to the silvery
landscape. At the same time, the sound of an
exasperated moan issues from StickMan's pursed,
facial labia.

How widely Prima's and the doctor's
gravitational fates differ.

Prima finds herself conveyed to a dappled
flank of hillside, full of tussocky grass. Her thighs
and rear cushion the risky fall of ten lengths as she
is rolled, head over heels, into a hollow of the
terrain.

Meanwhile, the doctor becomes caught in a
slight angular spin, which commits him to an upside
down free fall. He heads, without trace of good
fortune, for the region of rocky outcrop lying
further afield.

'LOOK OUT, DOCTOR!' comes Prima's last cry to him, as she witnesses the tragedy of his blighted trajectory: the columnar rocks seeming to rise to meet him, as they twist, deform and tear his body structure to their outrageous design. 'Ohhhh, Doctor ...'

Up above in the confinement chamber, the others inspect the frayed remains of rope. Doobie stands there, glaring at StickMan. 'Now what's your plan ..? Now what to try?!'

But StickMan isn't listening. Clearly distracted, its glittering eyes scan the room's corners with a growing uncertainty.

Doobie is just checking over the edge of the approximated window, to hopefully espy the villagers' fluid army on the move down there, spilling out over the slopes to assist them - when there is the sound of the couch shifting its position ... and the shuffle of something moving out from beneath.

StickMan begins to moan, this time backing away to where the connecting passageway used to be ... until a few moments ago. Now, with a shocked cry, StickMan discovers that the walls of this chamber are uniformly continuous - and that there's no way out.

'WHAT THE FUNK IS GOING ON HERE?!' cries Doobie, as the last section of wall is infilled by its surrounding material.

From what seems an inky puddle at the foot of the couch, arises rapidly some expanding vertical feature.

'What have we here?!' Doobie resumes, priming his blade in readiness of another Mr Turby-like confrontation. 'What kind of freaky physics is *this*?!'

Developing from its narrow base, the dark-clad thing rears taller than the hunched and cowering StickMan. And, once the extent of its fullest vertical prowess is attained, the organism whips back its obscuring forearms to expose its domed cranium of powder blue - larger than StickMan's by half again.

With its face consisting of a pair of wide nostrils where eyes ought to be, the thing lurches towards StickMan.

Too quickly to allow its target the means to unfold from its tightly bunched position, the blue faced thing is upon it: grabbing both arms in its snaky grip and then snapping them off near the sockets.

'OY, OY, OY!' shouts Doobie with knife raised … unsure of quite which action to follow: wondering if a measly blade could ever be sufficient against *this* kind of a thing. 'What 'arm's he ever done you?!'

To StickMan's silent death cries and Doobie's protests, the dismemberment gathers pace.

Both separated arms are snapped at the elbows. Next go the legs; snapped at their knees.

Finally, with both its claws gripping the neck, the appropriate force is applied to lift StickMan's head clean and bloodlessly away, as were the limbs.

The blue faced one stands there, clutching the head until the eyes have lost their lustre and faded. Then it accords it the same fate as the other parts, tossing it disdainfully to the pile of shards in the chamber's bleakest corner.

'Why to deserve that fate ..?' says Doobie.

The menacing thing just scowls, then appears to wilt and wither at the foot of the bed. Reducing rapidly in size, it recedes into the uncertain floor.

Yet it grows clearer to Shockers Republic that weak light now emanates from the gap around the couch.

There is the sound of footfalls disappearing down - what sound like - stone steps.

Frenchie is the first to reach the gap, squinting in at the shaft of powder blue light.

'Well, would you credit it?' he exclaims to the other two. 'We appear to have a phunking spiral staircase, or such like, down there.'

'Are you messin' with us, comrade?' growls Doobie, peering in for himself.

But he can see it's the truth. There, with his own eyes: a spiral staircase, winding below to a level which sparkles. And there, perching at the first turn, is the blue faced, stick-snapping thing.

It slowly beckons their way; looking increasingly to Doobie as being like the biggest, baddest spore of them all.

'King … Spore,' mutters Doobie to himself. 'Yes. That's King Spore, that is.'

'Or whoever,' says Frenchie, upon overhearing. 'And by the look of things, I think it awaits our company.'

'Down … there,' whispers Pelia, awed by the

sea of sparkling, shimmering ultramarine.

Frenchie is back pacing the room, tapping his fingers at regular intervals along the walls; hoping for aural signatures of where the earlier, connecting passageway might still be.

Meanwhile, Doobie has taken his first steps downwards, squatting lower to fit inside the shaft.

The step is uneven but he maintains his balance, locked into the impassioned stare of King Spore.

And by holding this contact, does he find his consciousness shifting also to a different level ...

New sights, new sounds, new textures infiltrate his mind. Novel topography and contours of lands he never knew existed, over which he now traverses.

Others ... like brothers, alongside him: flying secure in the knowledge that failure can no longer be a part of their lives.

Looking down, their frenetic objects of desire have been detected.

Beyond the woodland's fringe and the undulating patchwork of fields, the life forms in question are traced.

There they go, on their busy routines: from ramshackle hut to ostentatious manor house, those thriving specks remain in ignorant bliss of the collared grey formation which glides above them … this formation utilising the very thermals enhanced by the exertions of those everyday folk below.

Although too tainted has become the blood of town and suburb, the seekers have come to realise.

The lifestyles of those urban dwellers: saturated nowadays by their humdrum tensions and desensitised by overexposure to their daily depravities, appear to have denuded themselves of much capability to experience the emotion of *true* fear whenever it might draw near to them. They cannot feel much anymore!

It has been a pleasure to discover that it is instead the taste of life in the rural context which has the greater appeal; providing that necessary sweetness to the seekers' palate.

The lure and taste of those inhabitants of the countryside: haler and heartier are they, whilst being honed by the natural elements about them; the lifeblood of its folk the riper for draining.

For a good blood always needs its purity.

Noiselessly, the brotherly quartet allows gravity to convey it towards that fertile earth ...

Doobie takes another step down the spiral staircase, closer and closer to King Spore.

At length, he turns to the surviving Shockers. Just the whites of his eyes are showing now, his irises having risen towards their orbits.

'Are you sure you know what you're doing?' calls out Pelia, seeming a long, long way from the centre of Doobie's revised universe.

'Brothers,' he says in a deep and slurred monotone, which is not of him. 'Brothers, I see our glorious, future existence. Descend with me and let us begin our reformation. That girl called Prima can wait ...'

Frenchie looks to Pelia, and Pelia looks to Frenchie - surprised at their leader's new-found indifference to the fate of their beloved.

'Through my mind travels I have seen each face and have sampled the intrinsic perfume of a thousand Primas,' he continues, as if reading their mutual thought. 'Come, let me show you ...'

And, little by little, they find themselves being drawn towards taking that first, stone step: to take a glimpse of those promising visions to which he refers. To see if their beloved can indeed be equalled - or surpassed - in terms of allure and sheer infallibility.

Frenchie and Pelia reach the stairwell.

They see Doobie at the second turn.

They see King Spore at the turn below his, beckoning them down with unreformed claw.

'Let us check,' says Frenchie to Pelia. 'At least to dip a toe into the water.'

And he is the final Shocker to probe his way down, his foot appearing to detect the first, tremulous ripple of the staircase's frame.

On they continue with their descent, until Shockers Republic has been engulfed by the swirling haze at the base of the spiral staircase.

THIRD LUMEN

There is but one remaining human able to witness the fateful, topographic convulsions taking place.

The vast fissure across the land is rent open to its widest extent as the growing series of seismic events approaches culmination.

Away from the worst of it, the last viscous activity of chase is concluding a little way past the next spur to the north: where the girl, of recent name Prima, successfully outwits the pursuing detachment of Fungal Fiends for the final time.

With guile, she has kept to the densely forested hollows; but mostly, by keen eye and ear, she has been gaining direction and inspiration from a chatty, green birdie in the treetops.

Shortly after her bumpy landing, she had heard the distant squawks.

Upon realising the hopeless state of the heroic Dr Burns, she'd turned her dizzy head to locate the source of those fruity, tropical flourishes of sound ... and had sworn she could discern the shape of Gran's Daffodil, high up in the twisted boughs of the proximal vegetation! Yes, the compact, tubular shape of a budgie - too small to be that of parrot or parakeet.

She felt sure the regularity of the birdie's insistence was for the purpose of beseeching.

As she curiously approached, and as he flew on to the next floral growth, she gained in herself ever more certainty that its beseeching was intended only for her.

And so the pattern of to flit-and-to follow quickly gained ground.

By the time she could make out the shiny exudation of slime balls from the castle's lower reaches, the girl and her unlikely saviour were already well on the move.

Now she observes their humiliating disarray from afar, as they mill around in confused convergence and frustrated fervour.

Mucous blobs, it would seem, have their limitations when it comes to seeking the wood from the trees.

The deep rumble of the earth returns to dominance; and this time its intentions are too powerful for the land to ignore.

The mutant vegetation is peeled back along the fissure's spine.

The vast promontory shudders, as would a molar in a shrinking gum.

One whole side of the incumbent castle cracks and subsides. An overhanging tower plummets down the hillside. And then, as the crescendo of subterranean assertion decays, the entire, unnatural extrusion implodes; creating a thunderous roar of collapsing rock and captured air.

The structure is reabsorbed, the debris infilling its rotten core.

At exactly the same moment, the encircling heat barrier becomes energised by the unleashing of such forces.

The members of the Geological Survey, who have mounted their six days' vigil aside its western envelope, observe this peak of luminosity, and know not what it heralds.

Exceeding its combustible enthalpy, the thermal barrier spontaneously ignites. The resultant, incendiary wave devours the vegetation and scorches the land in great swathes of devastation.

All terrain is razed: from the north, where Farmer Robson's great barn once stood; to the most southerly aspect, where Farmer Jarvis used to tend his land; from the serpentine twists and turns of the Eastern Track; to the west of the village, where the lake gathered its fill from the Sebus.

When the firestorm has exhausted all available material to burn, the scientists begin to contemplate the carbonised terrain before them.

'Nothing will have escaped it,' says one of the technicians as they cautiously step betwixt the steaming stumps and petrified trunks.

In protective gear they tread around the unrecognised shard which had been the apex of St. Bertrand's steeple.

'God, what destruction ..,' they mutter. 'There used to be a village here ...'

And then comes the miracle, several hours later.

The first, weak cry of a voice buried within the rubble field.

Narrowing the area of search with their dogs and their infrared equipment, they spot the flailing forearm.

' … help me ..,' cries the dry voice, coming from the dust-blasted visage. 'Please take me out of this.'

With all due care, the rescue team is able to do just that; as might they be extracting the imago from its confining cocoon.

The girl, once named Prima, collapses in their dependable arms.

Cocooned again briefly, she is swaddled in their insulating blankets and led away from the zone of smoulder.

'And what was your part in this tragedy?' asks one of the Securitat investigative officers during her transportation.

She coughs the collected grit from her throat and whispers: 'A pretty central one, I think …'

Upon seeing his quizzical look, she hoarsely enquires: 'Don't you know of any more survivors?'

'No, ma'am,' replies one of the rescue boys who is lifting her from the stretcher to the opened doors of the vehicle. 'There's no one else but you.'

Just before she departs the disaster scene, does the girl hear once more that familiar squawk - she thinks it could be coming from atop one of the Survey vans. Not far away from her at all.

A smile splices her cracked lips at the exhilarating realisation. 'Fly long, fly safe my lovely Daffodil.'

The Securitat man remains there motionlessly, wearing a brief frown. Silently mouthing her last word a couple of times, he struggles for an interpretation of it.

Another part of the land still smoulders ... but for a very different reason.

Many lengths south of the beloved's location, in a slight recess where once stood the home of Thomas Turby, a new fire is aglow.

For there, crouching amidst this terrible ruination, is a naked figure who feeds leaves of paper to eager, licking flames. And when they have consumed the current ones, the muscled figure tears out the next batch from the scorched, leather bound book with the ribbed spine.

He watches the flames tasting the next page of hieroglyphs, marvelling at their growing appetite. 'Good children,' he says, feeding them their next.

'Remedies have arrived too late, now that Hell squats its arse here.'

He cackles as the flames demand the book's remainder.

All ... save for one folio, which he starts to fold. 'Could come in useful for another day ..,' he tells himself. 'Or not.'

Presently the figure turns and regards the three grey birds, perching at an unnatural proximity to him.

Each appears to have keenly followed his words and actions with their gimlet eyes.

Rasping his chin in apparent contemplation, he says: 'I lose track of our time, forgive me. I have found myself distracted.

'For I feel now that the one whose salvation we so vigorously attempted has just completed her part in our story. It matters not. All paths do converge ... eventually.

'I feel we shall be meeting her again in several hundred years, indirectly through a male descendant of her bloodline. And how tantalising is that prospect!'

He looks to the trio of sentient doves and states: 'Here is the dawn of our new existence. Let us not blemish it.'

The birds chortle in seeming consensus as the figure extends his arms backwards.

'The search begins for fields anew,' he hisses through a tight, pursing mouth - which now contains that folded folio. 'Land of opportunities, remember ...'

In the blink of an eye, the change occurs: his chest flexing outwards; his arms sprouting to feathered wings. The transformation to avian form completes.

Rising higher to the embers of the lilac sky, the columbine quartet flies with purpose and vigour: toward those lands where the sunbeams will fear to linger; to where the shadows will caper without constraint.

SOLNTSE'S THOUGHTS REGARDING
SHOCKERS IN LURKHAM ...

Now we have more understanding about the formation and chronology of the magnanimous Shockers Republic, and about how it entered its classical phase.

We know not of how far its General Secretary plans to take the organisation - and along which kind of path. We know nothing of those intentions: not until we dig deeper and try to fathom the workings of Comrade Doobie's soul - and of those mysterious origins. This is unlikely, for not even the Watchers could properly elicit them!

We can but hope that the mSR will not turn the skies too dark. But if it does, then only an entity of counterbalance *might* be enough to keep things in check and in correct equilibrium.

Let us hope it will not come to that ...

SHOCKERS IN LURKHAM

Printed in Great Britain
by Amazon